I0597594

Family Forever—Book Two

just another Dream

KIMBERLY BANET

Scrivenings PRESS
Quench your thirst for story.
www.ScriveningsPress.com

Copyright © 2025 by Kimberly Banet

Published by Scrivenings Press LLC
15 Lucky Lane
Morrilton, Arkansas 72110
https://ScriveningsPress.com

Printed in the United States of America

All rights reserved. No part of this publication may be reproduced, stored in a retrieval system, or transmitted in any form or by any means—for example, electronic, photocopy, or recording—without the prior written permission of the publisher. The only exception is brief quotations in printed reviews.

Paperback ISBN 978-1-64917-464-2
eBook ISBN 978-1-64917-465-9

Editors: Ann Harrison and Heidi Glick

Cover by Linda Fulkerson, www.bookmarketinggraphics.com

Scripture quotations are taken from the Holy Bible, New Living Translation, copyright © 1996, 2004, 2007 by Tyndale House Foundation. Used by permission of Tyndale House Publishers, Inc., Carol Stream, Illinois 60188. All rights reserved.

All characters are fictional, and any resemblance to real people, either factual or historical, is purely coincidental.

NO AI TRAINING: Without in any way limiting the author's [and publisher's] exclusive rights under copyright, any use of this publication to "train" generative artificial intelligence (AI) technologies to generate text is expressly prohibited. The author reserves all rights to license uses of this work for generative AI training and development of machine learning language models.

This book is dedicated to our Heavenly Father, from Whom every good thing comes.
And to Jeffrey David Banet, my husband of thirty-six years, seven months, and nine days. You were my greatest gift from God. Thank you for everything. I pray we are reunited in eternity.

Here on earth you will have many trials and sorrows. But take heart, because I have overcome the world. (John 16:33 NLT)

S am Grayson crossed his arms. *I shouldn't be this cold in June.* The rising nausea didn't help either. He pulled himself together to focus on the doctor's words.

"I'm sorry." The emergency room doctor had bags beneath his eyes. He placed a hand on Sam's shoulder. "There's nothing more we can do. We can keep him comfortable, but he won't last through the morning."

Sam swallowed hard. "Will he wake up? Can he hear me?"

"I doubt he'll wake up. I don't know for certain if he can hear you but talk to him just in case."

He nodded. There was nothing else to say.

The doctor left the room.

Sam turned toward the bed where his father lay. The antiseptic smell of the hospital room mixed with the sight of his father connected to tubes and machines made his nausea worse by the second. He exhaled a breath he hadn't realized he was holding.

He pushed his hair away from his eyes. The bedside monitor's beeps were loud and irregular. The lines across the top of the screen grew more erratic with each passing moment. He reached for his father's lifeless hand. *Please, God, I've messed up these last few months. There are things I didn't get to say.*

From what he'd been told on the phone, he didn't think he'd make it here in time, but by the grace of God, he did. Now was his chance to say what he wanted to say.

"If you can hear me, I need you to keep fighting." Sam's voice was barely audible. *Pull it together. Stay strong.* "We haven't had enough time together." As cold as his own hand was, his father's was colder. His color was even worse than when Sam first arrived. Pale. No, not pale. Ashen.

Why can't I cry? Maybe the shock of the situation kept the tears at bay. Or maybe he was just ... numb. Regret replaced the tears. The period apart from each other had been a mistake, and time and distance made Sam see that.

"Sam." The weak voice registered above the beeping and whooshing of the machinery in the room.

He snapped his head up and stared into his father's half-opened eyes. "You're awake!" God had heard his prayer.

His father spoke again, but his voice was hoarse.

Sam lifted a cup to his lips and used a plastic spoon to place ice chips in his mouth. He smiled slightly.

"I ... have to tell you something." A deep, rattling cough racked his entire body.

"It's okay, you don't need to say anything." Sam grabbed the remote from the bedside table and pushed the call button.

"Yes, you need ..." The cough worsened, his face more ashen than before.

"Shh, it's okay." Sam prayed the nurse would hurry.

His dad's chest rattle became louder, and his cough was relentless.

"Have to tell you ..." His father gasped each word like it might be his last. "Closer."

Sam moved his head next to his father's. "I'm right here. What is it?"

His father whispered four words. Chopped, clipped words, but Sam understood them just the same.

His heart thudded, and he couldn't catch his breath. The words pierced him to the core. All he could do was stare. *Breathe, Sam. Just. Breathe.*

After a long moment, Sam opened his mouth to ask one of many questions running through his head, but his father gasped.

All the monitors blared, and the doctor and several nurses rushed in. An older nurse guided Sam by the shoulders and moved him away from the bedside.

He could no longer see his father for the action surrounding his bed. His eyes were glued to the monitor. He held his breath as the jagged lines flattened. All the beeping and varying tones grew monotone, flat, like the lines on the display.

The doctor called out the time of day. As if in slow motion, he turned away from the bed and walked to where Sam stood. Once again, he placed his hand on Sam's shoulder. "I'm sorry. He's gone." The doctor paused. Even he didn't know what to say. "You can sit here as long as you'd like."

Sam was unable to reply or even nod. And he still couldn't cry. Why couldn't he even now?

The nurses slowly unplugged the wires from his father's lifeless body, while Sam remained in his chair.

Eventually, the nurses left the room.

Paralysis gripped him. He had no idea how long he'd sat there, motionless. He replayed the man's last words at least a hundred times.

How do I move forward, Lord? What do I do with this information?

one

Twelve Months Earlier

Abbie Grayson counted the tables on the deck and then turned to the ones in the yard. More than enough to accommodate the nearly seventy-five people they expected. "Hannah, those chair covers you picked are beautiful."

"Thanks, Mom. Cassie and I had fun shopping for them." Her daughter straightened a chair cover. "I can't believe Sam's graduated."

Abbie shook her head. Where had his college years gone? It seemed like yesterday he graduated from high school and began his college career. Everything with Sam had moved fast since he'd only been part of their family for a few years.

"I can't get over the fact he has his theology degree." John sneaked up behind them.

"Were you eavesdropping on our conversation, dear?" Abbie asked her husband.

"Never." John kissed her cheek and laughed. "You've done a great job with these decorations. Sam's going to love this."

"I hope so, Dad. I'm so proud of him. Once again, Sam has

exceeded the statistics for foster kids graduating from college. How amazing is that?" Hannah said.

John flashed a smile. He still looked younger than his almost sixty-years, even though his hair had completely grayed. He liked to say it came from raising another teenager in their fifties. Even though he joked, he adored Sam. Their whole family did. And after thirty-eight years of marriage, they were happy and still each other's best friend.

But John was right about raising a teen later in life. It hadn't been easy, and Sam hadn't had an easy time getting to this point. He'd come to them as a sixteen-year-old foster child, broken and scarred from trauma. They'd gone through a lot together since then. And they adopted Sam on his eighteenth birthday.

"Where do you want these extra chairs, Mom?" Kyle asked. His wife, Cassie, followed him onto the deck with another box of party favors.

"Let's put them around the fire pit in case Sam and his friends want to sit there after dark. It's supposed to be a chilly evening for early June."

"It's sure beautiful today." Cassie smiled.

"The perfect day for a party." Abbie gazed at the view from their expansive deck. Rolling farm fields, blooming with wild flowers, crops, and green foliage. She loved their life in Franklin, Tennessee. They had the best of both worlds. A small town with a rural setting, yet just a few miles outside of Nashville and the home of Tennessee University, where John was a two-time national championship basketball coach. Abbie was beyond thankful for her life and her family.

"How do you think Sam is doing right now?" John asked quietly. "He told me he went back to therapy, but he didn't tell me much more."

Abbie's stomach dropped. She didn't want to think about it or talk about it today, but how could they not? The issue was front and center. "Oh hon, I wish I knew. Graduation has taken his mind off it."

To think it'd been a little more than four years since Sam's biological father, Andy Quinn, kidnapped him and was charged with drug trafficking. Of course, there was more to the story. Much more.

"The nightmares about the two girls started again. I think that's why he's going back to therapy," Abbie said. "I know his father and the others involved have denied those girls were there, but Sam still believes they were." Abbie chuckled sadly. "Did you hear what I said? Sam's father. We both know good and well that man isn't his dad anymore. Not since he gave up his parental rights."

"He never was any type of father." John pulled a chair out and sat at a table, gazing out at their property.

"You're right about that." Tears rimmed Abbie's eyes. Quinn and his evil associates wanted to force Sam to help lure girls for their trafficking scheme, but Sam refused and almost died because of it.

He talked about two girls—Amanda and Ava. But the police found no sign of any girls being held with Sam and suggested he'd been hallucinating. Even his therapist said it could be the way his mind dealt with the trauma.

"Way to drag the pre-party down, guys." Hannah groaned.

Abbie laughed, but there was nothing funny. Sam had already endured a lifetime of trauma before they adopted him.

"Well," Abbie said. "Let's pray the investigators will get to the bottom of it one day. And Sam's father, I mean Andy Quinn, gets years added to his sentence, and Sam can handle it all."

two

S am stood on the deck, his mouth wide open. His family had worked hard on this party, and everything was perfect. The tables were covered in navy and red, Belmont's school colors. Banners, balloons, and cutouts of guitars and Bibles were placed around the deck and on the tables. He laughed at the combination.

"What do you think?" his sister-in-law asked.

He side-hugged her. "I can't believe you guys did all this, Cassie. I love it!"

"I can't take much credit. Your mom, Hannah, and Wendy did most of it. Kyle and I got here a few hours ago."

He picked up the family picture from a table. "Who put this here?" He laughed. The photo had been taken at Kyle and Cassie's wedding, about a year after the Graysons adopted him.

"I think Hannah did. Hmm, you never lost your love of flannel shirts, did you?" She giggled.

"Hey now," he laughed. "At least I've ditched the ragged jeans. But flannel will always be my favorite."

He gazed at the photo. They all had dark hair, except him. His was blond and longer. They had dark eyes, but his were light. If he looked like any of them, it had to be Abbie with her shoulder length brown hair. Hers was a few shades darker and curlier. None of that mattered though. They'd always made him feel like he belonged. And this party was further proof.

All these people who he hadn't met until five or six years ago showed up to celebrate. His grandparents, his mom and dad's friends, and his good friends too. With one exception.

"Here's to Sam!" His best friend and fellow graduate, Nate, shouted as he raised his glass of cola.

"To Sam!" Everyone yelled. They raised their glasses and cheered.

Sam beamed and thanked them.

"Speech," a couple friends shouted.

Sam shoved his hands in his pockets and laughed, but the calls for him to speak only grew. He wasn't going to get out of this. He set his glass down and held up both hands. "Okay, okay. Thanks for not putting me on the spot or anything."

The crowd laughed.

A long piece of hair had come loose from his man-bun, as Hannah called it, and he pushed the strand out of his face. "I want to thank my mom and dad first." He pointed to his parents, and the crowd clapped. "None of this would be possible without you two. I hate to think of where I'd be without you."

Just about everyone here grasped what he'd been through as a foster child. "My life honestly didn't start until I came to stay with the Graysons when I was sixteen, and I thank God for them daily. It's an honor to be your son, and your brother." He nodded toward his mom and dad, and Kyle, Cassie, and Hannah. "And your grandson." He waved at Ed and Sarah, his mom's parents.

"And to all my friends, well, I wouldn't be here without you either. Thanks for sticking with me through everything. It's been a long road for all of us, but we made it."

They clapped and cheered. Nate and Tara, his first friends from high school, were engaged now. Michael, his high-school friend who attended college with him at Belmont was here, along with a handful of other friends from his time there. "I love you all." He exhaled. How had he survived this without shedding tears? "I don't know about everyone else, but I'm starving. Let's eat!"

Cheers erupted again as everyone rushed to congratulate him. Finally, he made his way to the outdoor kitchen where Abbie and her best friend Wendy had set up the food. Seeing Wendy made him think of his oldest and best friend, Lauren. She should've been here today.

He'd met her in middle school when he knew no one. The other kids avoided him because he was new and just the foster kid. But she ate lunch with him that first day, showed him around, and introduced him to others.

Lauren was popular in school. The cheerleader, the yearbook and newspaper editor, the student council and National Honor Society member. She knew everyone. Yet she chose him for her best friend.

Then she went away to New York City for college. *You should be here today, Lauren.*

He needed to shake off thoughts of her. Food and conversation would help. He made his way through the food line and grabbed a chicken salad croissant, pasta salad, and fruit, and then found a seat with Tara, Nate, and Michael.

"We're dying to know, how was your audition yesterday?" Michael asked.

Sam swallowed the first bite of his sandwich and shrugged. "I have no idea. I mean, I feel like it went well, but I couldn't get a read on them. There was a lot of whispering, but I don't know what that meant. They just thanked me, and that was it."

"We know you, Sam. You had to have blown them away." Nate popped the last bite of his sandwich into his mouth.

"I think you'll get it for sure," Tara added. "But we'll miss you at Franklin Community Church. They'll never find a high school worship leader as talented as you."

Sam laughed. "I think they'd be fine. But honestly, I don't

think I'm going anywhere. For one thing, Middle Tennessee Church is one of the biggest in the country. I can't imagine how many people they have to choose from." He picked up his sandwich and took another bite. His mom had fixed all his favorite food for the party.

"But how many people went to Belmont, studied music composition and theology, and can write songs *and* preach?" Tara shrugged. "And do they know other churches sing worship songs you've written? All because they've come here and heard you sing them and have taken them back to their home churches."

Sam's cheeks grew warm, and he focused on his sandwich. "That's only happened a couple of times."

His friends laughed. "You're hilarious. You have no idea how talented you are." Tara gazed at him and smiled, and asked if anyone needed anything from the food table. "I have to have more of that pasta salad."

Sam steered the conversation away from himself, and they discussed everyone's graduation plans. Michael graduated with an accounting degree from Belmont and planned to work for a firm in Nashville. Tara received her degree in website design and started her own business. And Nate was a budding musician like Sam. He played keyboard and guitar and even joined him in the church worship band. But Nate dreamed of being a studio musician in Nashville. He'd already had a couple of gigs.

Mom and Dad stopped at their table and listened to his friends talk about their plans.

He thanked God for the Graysons. *The Graysons.* He caught himself. Almost five years ago, they officially became his mom and dad. Over time, he'd stopped thinking of or referring to them as John and Abbie.

They'd supported his love of music since his seventeenth birthday when they gave him his first guitar. They wanted this job at Middle Tennessee Church for him as much as he did. With it, he could make a career out of writing and singing songs that would connect people to God—his true calling. Plus, the church job was a paid position.

His parents had more faith in him than he did. He didn't want to get his hopes up. Why would the church give this job to someone like him when others had more talent? It was okay. When he was seventeen, he'd made a promise he would honor God in everything he did. And when the right thing came along, God would make it happen. He believed that with all his heart.

three

Sam pulled into a spot in the large parking lot at Middle Tennessee Church. The clock on the dashboard read 9:45. Perfect. His meeting with Pastor Stephan Hayden was in fifteen minutes.

The pastor invited him to the church coffee shop to discuss his recent audition for the spot with the high-school worship team. But a rumor was going around that the church offered the position to another recent college graduate. Sam cringed. So, this meeting was to let him down.

He walked inside the coffee shop. The knot in the pit of his stomach tightened and turned. Why couldn't the pastor have just called to tell him he wasn't good enough? That would've been better than this.

"Hi, Sam." Pastor Stephan waved and motioned him over. "Good to see you again." The man stood and shook his hand. A second man, who appeared to be about thirty or so, sat at the table and stood and greeted him also. Great, not only the pastor, but also a stranger, would tell him how bad his audition was. He wanted to crawl into a hole.

"Sam, I'd like you to meet Kellen Sanders. He's our brand-new young adult minister. Kellen, Sam Grayson." Pastor Stephan offered to get Sam's coffee while Kellen and Sam chatted. Kellen had arrived from North Carolina a few weeks ago to start the young adult ministry. Sam immediately liked him. Kellen was personable and down-to-earth, and their conversation was easy. For a second, he forgot the letdown he was about to experience.

"Here's your coffee, Sam." Pastor Stephan sat the steaming cup on the table. "You're probably anxious to get to the point of this meeting."

"Well, a little." Sam took a sip of the way-too-hot coffee and burned his tongue. *Settle down before you make a total fool out of yourself.* "I'm guessing it's about my audition." He winced. As much because of the audition as the scalding coffee.

"It is." The pastor twirled his pen. "I wanted to talk to you about this in person. First, we selected someone else for the worship leader position." The man sat and smiled like that was good news.

"I understand. I appreciate you telling me in person, Pastor Stephan." He forced a smile.

"Please, Sam, call me Stephan." He leaned toward Sam, arms crossed on the table. "Here's the thing. You're too good for the high school spot. We want to offer you something bigger. I'll let Kellen fill you in." Stephan leaned in his chair and sipped his coffee.

Something bigger? They had his full attention. What could that even be? He was barely out of Bible college.

Kellen chuckled in a laid-back way that made Sam comfortable. "Like Stephan said, you're really good. Your audition tape blew me away. You're a natural, Sam."

"Umm, thanks." Sam looked away. He had no clue what to say.

Kellen continued. "I'm building my team for this new ministry. I'll be preaching, and I'd like you to be the worship leader. I've already picked a guitarist also, and from what I've heard, he's a close friend of yours. Nate Martin. He's my next call. We wanted to make sure you're on board first."

Was this truly happening? "You're serious?" Sam asked. "You want *me* to be the worship leader?" And his best friend would be on the team also?

"Yes," Stephan interjected. "But your title will be worship minister, because not only will you sing, you'll also be in charge of the music. You'll work with Kellen and select music to compliment his message each week. It's a full-time staff member position, and we'll even give you opportunities to preach later if you'd like."

"I don't know what to say. I'm completely humbled you think I'm capable. I just don't know if I'm qualified." He had to be honest.

"Here's what I know." Stephan laid his pen down. "If God calls you, He will equip you. And everything I've seen and heard tells me you've got the talent and the calling. If you're willing, God will do the rest."

"If you need to think about it, we understand," Kellen offered.

Sam's head spun, and he laughed. How was this his life? God gave him much more than he deserved. This wasn't just another dream. This was his life goal—his chance to fulfil his promise to God to live his life glorifying Him and spreading the name of Jesus.

"No, no, I don't need to think about it. I'll do it." Sam grinned and shook each of their hands. "Thank you. I won't disappoint either of you."

Stephan asked them to bow their heads, and he offered a prayer for this new, fledgling ministry, that God would use these young men to lead and guide the young adults in the congregation.

four

Andy Quinn cringed when the iron door clanked behind him. The sound of being locked in a prison cell or even a congregation room like this was something he still wasn't used to despite the nearly five years he'd been in prison. He doubted he ever would.

At least this big room provided a slight change of scenery. He walked to one of the cold steel benches and sat next to another inmate. Andy greeted the man and clutched his Bible.

"Good afternoon, gentleman," the minister began. "For those of you with us for the first time this afternoon, I'm Terrence from Grace Church here in Memphis. Welcome to Bible study. We're so glad you're here. Before we begin, who needs a Bible?"

Andy noted the new faces who raised their hands. What were their stories? Several were probably younger than his own son, Sam. What could they have done to mess up their life so badly they ended up in federal prison? Andy slumped forward. All these messed up people, and he was counted among them.

"If you've never opened a Bible before, that's okay. Right now, I want you to turn to the book of Psalms. It's at about the halfway point." Terrence held his Bible up to show the men.

Several men watched the minister, then fumbled through the

pages of their Bibles. Some asked for help from the person next to them. A few months ago, Andy was lost like the new men here today. Then, the minister had said turn to the book of Luke, and he had no clue whether Luke was the first book of the Bible or the last, or somewhere in between. But now, even he was getting the hang of it.

Terrence explained how to find today's chapter and verse. Psalm 69:33.

Andy found the verse and followed along as the minister read.

"For the Lord hears the cries of the needy; he does not despise his imprisoned people."

Hmm. He hadn't read that before.

The pastor looked out at the men. "If you confess your sins to Christ and proclaim him as your Lord and Savior, he'll forgive your sins. No matter how bad. But you must be truly sorry, repent, and accept Christ Jesus into your lives."

Andy had done all that, but he wasn't sure about all his sins being forgiven. He'd done things he'd never confessed to, not even to God.

Over the next few minutes, a couple inmates, one new, and one who'd been coming to the Bible study for a while, went forward and accepted Christ into their lives. Like Andy had done a few months back. He stood and clapped, just as others had done for him. Jesus held the keys to a new life and hope for a life outside these prison walls.

The guard walked him back to his cell and locked him in. Andy meandered to his small desk and set his Bible there. That's when he spotted the letter. He picked up the envelope, licked the seal, and pressed it closed. A guard would collect it later.

He sat on his cot. Had Sam even opened any of his letters? Almost five years in prison and not a word from his only son. Well, former son. He hung his head. The aches that filled his chest daily began. The feeling wouldn't let up until he fell asleep.

The minister in the Bible study said to pray for mercy and

grace, and to give it all to God. Andy sighed. He was new to all this God stuff. Yes, he believed, for the first time in his entire life. But he still didn't understand all of it. What did give it all to God even mean?

How could God forgive him for the things he'd put Sam through? He didn't expect Sam to forgive him, no matter how many times he apologized. He hoped but didn't expect to be forgiven for everything. The neglect and abuse from the time Sam was five. All the foster homes because of him. And worst of all, what happened in Alabama. How far from God had Andy been to make his son a pawn in a human trafficking scheme?

No, Sam would never forgive him. Why should he? Andy certainly would never forgive himself. So how could God?

five

Lauren pushed the cart from aisle to aisle, placing the books in their rightful spots. She loved her new job at Landmark Bookstore in Franklin. The shop was small and family owned. Maybe one day her book would be on a shelf here. Then she'd have a reason to call Sam. Her cheeks burned, and she brushed aside the thought.

This morning, the bookstore was quiet, and she had too much time to think. She clenched her teeth. Why hadn't she told Sam she was back in the area? It was already mid-June, and she'd been home for nearly a month. She needed to tell him soon before someone else did. But would he even care that she was back? After all, they were only friends.

"Hi, Lauren." Jan breezed into the shop. Her platinum hair and purple eye glasses made Lauren smile.

"Hi, Jan." The spring returned to Lauren's step. "Are you looking forward to the book signing tonight?"

"Oh yes, honey, I can't wait. All you new, young authors bring so much excitement to the book world."

That's why Lauren loved working for Jan.

The woman was in her early seventies but still came into the store every day to ensure it ran smoothly and to keep up with the times. She'd read every classic author from Charles Dickens to Jane Austen to Marcel Proust but also appreciated the up-and-coming authors too. And she took a special interest in Lauren's writing. Just like Sam did once.

"How's your book coming along, my dear?" Jan flashed her bright, white smile and tucked a piece of that fabulous hair behind her ear. She barely had wrinkles, wore stylish clothes, and didn't look anywhere near her age. "I'm surprised you have any time at all to write between your newspaper job and your time here."

"My work at the paper is just a features column, so I do that mostly from home. I have more time than you think."

"Will we see your first column soon?"

"In a few weeks." Lauren grinned, but then her stomach sank. Sam would see her column. How had she not realized that? She needed to tell him before he saw it. "I can't believe how hard writing is sometimes. I'm in a rut with my novel." She picked up *Jane Eyre* from her cart and put it back in its spot. "I bet Charlotte Bronte never had this much trouble coming up with a story."

"I bet she did." Jan arranged an assortment of books on the coffee table between two sofas in the center of the store. "Maybe you're trying too hard. The important thing is to simply get words on paper. The more you write, the more the words will come. Don't worry if it's a mess. Just write and edit later."

"I think I'll take your advice. I need to just write instead of staring at a blank screen."

Jan turned and gave a slight wave as she headed toward her office in the back room. "Maybe that old boyfriend of yours, Sam, can be your inspiration," she said over her shoulder.

"Oh, he wasn't, well, he was never my—" She sputtered the words, but it was no use. Jan was already out of earshot. Lauren exhaled. Why did everyone assume she and Sam had dated? Sure, they'd been best friends for years, but their relationship had never been anything more.

Sam's friendship meant the world to her. He was good and innocent. Kind of crazy considering all he'd been through. He'd supported her when she made the decision to attend college in New York City. She'd always wanted to become a writer, and in her mind, NYU was the best place to learn the craft.

But NYU hadn't been so good for her. Now, she questioned why it'd ever been her dream to begin with. Yes, their journalism and English lit programs were superb, but the fact the university was in New York and far from Tennessee and her strict parents had been a huge deciding factor.

Lauren pushed her cart to the children's section and straightened the small tables and chairs like every Sunday. She reshelved books left out yesterday, but the pep in her step from earlier left her as the bad decisions she'd made played out in her mind.

She'd moved away from her strict parents, that's for sure. If they found out how badly she'd rebelled, they'd be mortified. But no more than Lauren was. The past year had taken a toll. A lot about her had changed. But not quite everything.

Though she'd never admitted it to anyone, she still loved the one person she'd never be able to have. Sam Grayson.

six

Peeking through the side curtain, Sam took note of the crowd and swallowed hard. He'd been leading worship for the young adult service on Wednesday night for a few weeks now, and it was going great. But this Sunday morning, for the first time, he was filling in for the senior worship pastor at the main service. Instead of playing in front of about three hundred people, he would be leading a crowd of two thousand.

"It's time, Sam." Pastor Stephan tapped him on the back of his shoulder. "Don't be nervous. God's got this."

Sam nodded and walked to his place on the stage. Before the lights shone, he closed his eyes. *Please God, don't let me trip, fall off the stage, or forget the words. But most of all, let me get out of the way so they see You, and only You.*

"You're going to kill it, Sam," Nate whispered as he assumed his place at the keyboard. Tara touched his elbow as she passed him and took the stage as a backup singer. *And thank you, God, for putting Nate and Tara beside me.*

The lights came on, and peace washed over him as they played. But he avoided focusing on the size of the crowd. He sang a popular song by Chris Tomlin, followed by a song by Casting Crowns currently on the radio. He grinned as the church sang along and worshipped. But of course, they would. They'd often sung these popular songs during services.

What would happen when the third song began? One he'd written and only the band had ever heard. The second song ended, and Sam's heartbeat sped. His parents and Kyle and Cassie sat in the front row. Cassie gave him a thumbs up, and he lifted his chin. *Okay, here goes.*

He played his guitar and sang the words. He fixed his gaze beyond the crowd, to the parts farthest from his vision where he could only make out shapes. No one sang along.

As they entered the chorus, a few hands raised, and by the time they repeated the chorus, people sang along. He'd wanted so badly for the worshippers to connect with God through this song.

The song ended with applause.

Sam winced and broke in quickly with the meditation prayer that led to communion. He wasn't here to entertain but to lead worship.

He and the band exited the stage but came back to play "Amazing Grace" at the end of the service, and he thanked God for the chance to lead worship.

* * *

Sunday afternoon came as a huge relief. Sam went to lunch with his friends after the service and now was home for dinner. More than anything, he wanted to nap, but he didn't want to miss out on family time. He sat at the kitchen table while his father peeled potatoes at the stove, and Kyle talked about a case he was working on at the law firm. Cassie sat at the table with Sam and cut vegetables.

"I hate that I didn't make the service this morning." Hannah breezed in, her long, dark-brown pony tail flying. She set her purse on the kitchen island, washed her hands, and jumped in to help Dad peel potatoes for the soup. "But it was awesome online. You sounded great, Sam, and that song you wrote is amazing. Everyone's talking about it, you know."

Dad turned around from the counter and winked at Sam. "I told you."

Sam smiled. A nice sentiment, but they were biased. Mom and Dad thought everything he did was great. Hardly the case, but they were only being supportive.

"Thanks, but who is this 'everyone' you're talking about?"

"You haven't seen social media?" Hannah asked.

"You know I don't have any accounts." Sam yawned. He should have helped them get dinner ready. Maybe next time.

Hannah set the potato peeler in the sink and wiped her hands on a dishtowel. She grabbed her phone from her purse and scrolled. "See?" She turned the screen toward Sam. "There are about fifty more comments than an hour ago."

Sam grabbed the phone and scrolled. His cheeks heated up as he viewed the comments. "Great new song." "Love this new worship leader." "He's the most talented worship leader we've ever had." "Sam's a hottie."

Ugh. He scrunched his nose and handed the phone back to Hannah. "I could do without those last few comments."

"I agree." Mom entered the kitchen dragging a huge bag full of clothes but waved her phone in her free hand. "Some comments were inappropriate, but unfortunately, hon, I think that's something you'll have to get used to."

Sam stood and helped her with the overstuffed bag. He dragged it to the great room to sort through later. Mom and Wendy planned to open a clothes closet to benefit foster children, and the donated clothing poured in.

"I don't get that. Shouldn't Christians be in church to worship instead of flirting with pastors and worship leaders?" Kellen had received the same kind of unwanted attention even though married.

Dad turned around from the stove. "Remember, not everyone at church is there for the same reason. Especially kids who aren't choosing to go to church, or maybe they're attending for the first time. You have to use your judgment and follow your calling, not the social media comments. Right, Abbie?"

Mom's head snapped up from her phone. "Um-hum, sorry, what'd you say?"

"Mom, are you still scrolling through comments?" Sam asked.

"Sorry." She blushed. "I'm putting it away now."

The evening went on, and they ate dinner. Then Hannah and Dad cleaned up while Sam followed Mom to the great room in the center of their home—a huge two-story living room seldom used except for parties and Dad's team get-togethers where they'd watch games on the multiple big screen TVs. Sam had lived here for several years but still couldn't get over the expansiveness.

But today, clothes people had dropped off for Mom and Wendy's new business filled the room. Their new space wasn't quite ready yet, so in the meantime, they sorted and tagged clothes here. They'd even received donations of books, music, and jewelry for teens.

Mom pointed at the bags they'd accumulated but hadn't unpacked yet. "The goal is to sort what's good enough for the clothes closet and make other piles for things to give to another ministry instead."

She stopped and looked around the room. "And I guess we should start piles for things that are out of date or need to be washed. We might even need to toss some items."

"It's amazing what you and Wendy are doing," Sam said. "Back when I was in foster care, I never had enough clothes. What I did have usually didn't fit, was stained, or completely outdated." Not that he'd paid much attention. He had more to worry about back then. Until he came to the Grayson home and his life gradually became about more than simply surviving.

"I can't fault the foster parents. The stipends they receive aren't that much to cover everything needed for a new child.

Your dad and I were blessed not to have to rely on that money." Mom nodded toward Dad.

Sam's memories drifted to his first day here with only a few clothing items shoved in a trash bag. He hadn't even been sure of Abbie's name yet, but she'd been gracious and washed the clothes. The next day, she took him shopping and bought him some brand-new things, even though he was only supposed to stay for a few days. He smiled to himself. His emergency placement had become his forever home, even if it involved a roller coaster ride to get here.

Unlike average foster parents, his father's job as a college basketball coach afforded them many comforts. They could go out and buy new clothes for him, and many foster parents couldn't. His family was humble enough to realize that, and so, Mom and Wendy came up with the idea to start the clothes closet.

They'd leased a nice space near the Franklin town square. They wanted it to be a place with trendy clothing teens would want but at thrift store prices. He still wasn't sure how they could do that, but perhaps the donations from his friends and family were part of the equation.

Hannah held up a couple of teen dresses. "Look how cute these are. Mom, I agree with Sam. This clothes closet will be amazing and help so many people."

"Have you decided on a name yet?" Sam asked.

Abbie glanced around the room. "We have. It's going to be Sam's Closet."

"Oh, I love that," Hannah said.

"What do you think, Sam?" Mom asked.

Tears welled up inside. He didn't trust himself to speak. He nodded. "I love it," he whispered. *Thank you, God, for once again, turning ashes to beauty.*

* * *

"Sam, are you up?" Dad walked through the bedroom door without waiting for a reply.

Sam reached for the clock and squinted. 7:00 a.m. "I am now, what's going on?" Ugh, he'd hoped to sleep until at least eight.

"It's Richard Lacey. He's on the phone and wants to talk to us."

A single thud of his heartbeat forced him awake. Richard was the detective on the case when Sam's father and his associates had abducted him and taken him to Alabama. "What does he want?" The thought of him calling unexpectedly made his pulse quicken.

"I'm not sure. He said it's important he speak to all three of us. Throw some clothes on and come to the kitchen."

Sam jumped up, threw a T-shirt on with his shorts, and hurried to the kitchen. He didn't want to slow down to think about why the man would call this early.

"Okay, Sam's here now." John's phone was on the counter with the speaker on.

"Hi, Sam, how are you?' Detective Lacey asked.

"Umm good, I guess."

"I'll get right to it. Sam, what you've believed all along is true. Two girls were abducted with you, like you said. And now, they're safe and sound."

Sam gasped. Not what he'd expected to hear. He'd always known the girls existed. His family believed him, and he always got the sense Detective Lacey did too, or at least wanted to. But the police had told Sam over and over no evidence supported his claim.

Police searched the Alabama motel and found no evidence of anyone else held there except Sam. In the end, police charged his biological father, Andy Quinn, and his associates with parole violations and drug trafficking. Only Sam knew what they were actually up to.

His heart hammered against his ribcage. "So ... they're okay? Where were they?"

The detective paused. "We don't know a lot. Only that they're safe and were found in Miami a couple years ago."

"A couple years ago?" Sam's voice rose. He couldn't believe his ears. "And we're just now finding out?"

"I'm sorry, Sam. I just found out myself. It's complicated. The girls are cousins, and their parents thought they'd run away. But an undercover squad in Miami broke up a human trafficking ring and found them."

The floor swayed beneath, and Sam dropped to the kitchen stool. Even though he'd always thought that's what happened, he hadn't wanted it to be true.

"In any case," the detective continued, "the parents wanted to keep this to themselves since the girls were juveniles. They didn't want the attention. The parents got them into therapy and tried to get them back to normal life. But now, one girl is twenty, and she's bringing charges against Blaze to keep him in jail."

"And my father—er, Andy Quinn too?" The blood drained from Sam's face.

"Well, not exactly. The girl said nothing about Quinn. She blamed everything on Blaze."

Dad clenched his teeth. "You and I both know that's not true, Richard."

The detective sighed. "I know, John. Sam said Quinn was the one behind it all. But no one, not even Blaze, placed any blame on him. But we'll keep investigating. And don't worry, with Quinn's drug trafficking charges, he'll remain in prison for several more years. Oh, and Sam? Their names are Ava and Amanda. Just like you said."

Queasiness hit him, and he clung to the countertop.

"Are you okay?" Mom whispered.

He could only nod.

The call ended moments later, and the three sat at the kitchen table staring at each other.

"What are you thinking, Sam?" Dad asked.

He swallowed hard. "I don't know. I mean, I'm glad the girls are okay." But could they even be okay after what they'd been through? He doubted it. "I'm relieved. But I still know Andy Quinn did it." He still had a hard time referring to his birth father by that name. He'd known him all his life as Drew Keller. Even his own last name was Keller before his adoption.

"Yeah, I've got a big problem with that too." Dad rubbed the back of his neck.

Of course he did. John Grayson had been Andy's basketball coach before Sam was born. He'd tried, unsuccessfully, to keep him out of trouble even back then.

"But we need to be thankful Quinn is in prison and out of all of our lives forever," Dad said.

Sam was beyond thankful he was in prison and prayed he would indeed be out of his life forever. But he wasn't so sure that would be the case.

seven

Sam shoved the last of a granola bar in his mouth before he hurried out of the house to his new, or rather new-to-him, SUV Mom and Dad got him for graduation. He smiled every time he climbed into the driver's seat. Never had he thought he'd have his own car one day. He tossed his backpack in the back seat and headed to his meeting.

How had this become his life? With the help and support of his forever family, the nightmares had become less frequent, and he was able to move forward.

Maybe because the girls were safe and sound. He was thankful for his brother Kyle's advice. Sam had wanted to contact the girls, but Kyle talked him out of it. The younger of the two, Ava, wasn't quite eighteen yet, even younger than Sam thought. At least they were safe now. *Thank you, Lord, for answering my prayers.*

His life verse came to mind as he drove. *"And we know that God causes everything to work together for the good of those who love God and are called according to his purpose for them."* He loved how God put that verse on his heart whenever he needed it. Everything would work out. He had to get his head straight and think about the matter at hand. This meeting. On Music Row of all places.

Thankfully, Kyle would be there too. Not only would he be a calming influence knowing everything else Sam had dealt with lately, but he'd also represent him as his attorney. Apparently, someone in Nashville wanted to buy a couple songs he'd written. He'd sent several songs to a major recording label. With the recording equipment his parents had bought him over the years, he made demos of the songs he'd written.

He pulled up to the address, parked his car, and checked the time on his phone.

Kyle texted him.

Meet me inside.

Sam sucked in a breath and headed up the front steps of the building. *Thank you, God, no matter the outcome.*

The building wasn't a high rise like he'd pictured but much homier than that. More like a three-story house. He walked in, and the receptionist greeted him.

"Are you Sam Grayson?"

"Yes, I'm him, I mean, that's me." Ugh, why did he get tongue-tied in these situations? Hannah teased he could write song lyrics but couldn't carry on a conversation when he was nervous.

"I'll let Mr. Sawyer know you're here." She smiled and then disappeared.

Sam took a seat in the lobby. Kyle was nowhere to be found. Great. So much for preparing him.

"Mr. Sawyer will see you now, and your attorney, er brother, is here also. Would you like some coffee or water?" The receptionist asked.

"Water would be great, if you don't mind." His lips stuck together, and sweat beaded on his forehead.

She handed him a bottle of water.

He thanked her, and she led him to a small room. He'd pictured a much bigger, formal conference room. But this was nice. The space was homier and helped him relax.

A tall man with sideburns and a cowboy hat stood. He looked to be about John's age, but with less gray hair. He offered Sam a firm handshake.

"Sam Grayson, I've heard a lot about you. Glad to meet you. I'm Russell Sawyer."

"Nice to meet you, sir."

Kyle said hi but stayed seated. His brother had the appearance of an attorney today with his nice suit, short haircut, and briefcase. If he wasn't so nervous, Sam would've laughed at the image so contrary to the casual look he usually sported.

The big man chuckled. "Well, I guess you're wonderin' what we called you up here for." Mr. Sawyer motioned for Sam to take a seat.

"Yes, sir, kind of."

"I like your modesty, Sam. I'm gonna cut right to the chase." The man flashed a huge smile. "You ever heard of Caleb Hartley, the Christian singer?"

Was there anyone who hadn't? He was considered a pioneer in contemporary Christian music and was still in his thirties. "Yes, he's one of my favorites."

"How about Evan Cross, heard of him?" Mr. Sawyer grinned.

Sam laughed. "Of course, he's only one of the biggest country singers in the world."

The man laughed and hunched over the small table, uncomfortably close. "Well, I'm glad you know who they are, because they know who you are too." Mr. Sawyer pointed at him. "They've listened to your demos. Evan wants to record one, and Caleb wants to record ... get ready for this ... *four* of your songs."

Four songs. Was he serious?

His brother smiled and nodded.

"What? Is this real?" Sam's heartbeat thundered, and he forced himself to remain seated. His eyes darted from Mr.

Sawyer to Kyle. "They want *my* songs. Which ones?" His mind raced. At the moment, he couldn't remember what demos he'd sent.

"I can assure you this is real, son, and I've got paperwork to prove it." The man picked up papers beside him and slid them across the small table toward Sam.

Sam noted the songs listed and grinned, but other than that, he couldn't concentrate on the rest of the paperwork. He tilted his head back and laughed. "I'm just so shocked, I mean, I didn't think *anyone* would want these songs, let alone Caleb Hart and Evan Cross."

Kyle spoke through his own laughter. "It's okay, Sam, we understand. You don't need to sign the papers today. Take them home and read through them. I've gone through the papers line by line, and it's a really good deal. A great one, actually." Kyle nodded to Mr. Sawyer.

Mr. Sawyer from American Christian Music gave him some details.

Sam would retain all rights as songwriter and would receive a certain amount in royalties for digital downloads versus other media types. But Sam's head was in the clouds. He couldn't possibly sign the papers here and now. He was thankful to have his brother here to go over it again with him later.

"Sam, did you hear that last part?" Kyle asked.

His cheeks burned. Mr. Sawyer and Kyle both stared. "Oh, I'm sorry, I guess this is a little overwhelming."

Mr. Sawyer let out a deep, hearty chuckle. "That's okay, Sam. Once you digest this information, we'll talk again over lunch. It'll be less intimidating than right now."

"That sounds great." Sam exhaled.

"But I want to make sure you hear this part. I want to publish *all* your songs. We're an imprint of the biggest music publisher in Nashville, and we think you're a perfect fit. Any demos you have, we want to pitch them. And we want you to keep writing songs, and we'll publish them for you too."

He didn't know what to say. He was certain God had given him this dream, putting it on his heart that day when he was seventeen and chose to follow Christ. The day Jesus had saved his life.

Sam hadn't known what that dream would look like going forward, but at last, the picture was forming. This was all he could have ever dreamed. And more.

Thank you, Lord.

eight

"Five minutes, Sam." The stage hand hurried by.

"Knock 'em dead." Lauren said with a laugh, her green eyes twinkling. "Wait—I'm not sure that's the appropriate saying for a worship concert."

Sam laughed back. God had been good to him these last few years, but these last few months were over the top. He was pouring out His favor over him for sure.

He worked at Middle Tennessee Church as worship pastor but now spent more time songwriting than anything. The ink barely dried on his publishing contract before both Caleb Hartley and Evan Cross released their recordings of his songs. On top of that, church leadership sent him and Kellen on a worship tour of other churches. Kellen preached, and Sam and his band played worship music to young adult groups. Tonight was the last night of that tour—an experience nothing short of amazing.

He'd told Abbie recently all his dreams were coming true. He'd chosen to follow God, and God was making it all happen. Sam was beyond grateful. He'd suffered all throughout his childhood, but God had righted it and would surely shield him from future trials.

Abbie frowned and recited John 16:33. "Here on earth you will have many trials and sorrows."

Sam believed that, but he'd already experienced trials and sorrows. Surely, God wouldn't allow him to go through more.

Tonight marked the end of their first tour. They'd played Friday and Saturday nights and Sunday mornings for the last few weeks. But maybe even better than all this, he reunited with his best friend, Lauren. They hadn't seen each other in over a year, and she surprised him on this final weekend in Knoxville.

"Are you gonna hang out back stage or sit in the audience?" he asked.

"I think I'll hang back here tonight if that's all right."

Those green eyes made him dizzy. "Of course, whatever you want." He smiled and headed up the metal steps and onto the stage. The bright lights hit him, and the crowd cheered. Was this wrong? He was supposed to be doing this for God, but at times, he feared he enjoyed the spotlight too much.

He brushed away the thoughts, waved at the crowd of over two thousand, and launched into one of the most popular worship songs he'd written, "His Name is Jesus." The song was currently at number one on the worship music chart, thanks to the biggest name in Christian radio, Caleb Hartley. The crowd sang along, at times so loud he could barely hear himself sing.

After a few more songs, Kellen came on stage to deliver the message, based on the story of Joseph and his brothers. A story of family, envy, sorrow, fear, and redemption—one anyone could relate to. This tour had been a huge success, and Sam whispered a prayer of thanks as he exited the stage. *You've given me more than I deserve, Lord. Thank you for all You've blessed me with, and all You've trusted me with.*

After the show he found Lauren, and together with his best friends and bandmates, Nate and Tara, they ventured into town to eat. The city lights and the warm air contributed to the group's festive mood on this beautiful, warm October Saturday night.

"I'm lovin' this weather," Nate said.

"So much warmer than New York," Lauren added. "And the breeze feels wonderful."

Sam turned toward her as they walked. "Did I tell you how happy I am you joined us these last few days?"

He could've sworn she blushed, unlike the old Lauren.

"Only one hundred and seventeen times." Her smile was as bright as the downtown lights.

They'd known each other for well over ten years. Best friends from the day they met in middle school. But were they still best friends, or was that wishful thinking? They'd only seen each other sporadically throughout college. They'd texted and made an occasional phone call. When she arrived in Knoxville yesterday, things were awkward at first. She lived in New York, and her life as a *New York Times* journalist was different from his.

It didn't take long to find that old familiarness between them, although the awkwardness still slipped in from time to time. He couldn't quite put his finger on it, but she was different somehow. At times she cut her laugh short when they all laughed together, and she was quieter than normal. Not the life of the party like she used to be. He shrugged it off. It had been a while since they'd all been together. That was probably all it was.

They walked into a well-known burger place. The hostess seated them near the window with a gorgeous downtown view. She handed them menus, but his gaze was fixed on Lauren. She'd always been beautiful, but now she was striking. Her long, blonde, hair hung in waves just past her shoulders. And those eyes.

What was he thinking? He had to get her out of his head. He'd resigned himself to remain single, at least in this season of his life. Couldn't he do more good for God that way? He'd never imagined himself in a relationship before. He'd only ever wanted to serve God.

"You should've come out on the Atlanta churches tour,

Lauren." Tara's voice jarred him back to reality. "We had so much fun. You would've loved it."

"I wish I could have been there. It sounded like fun. I regret not seeing you all on your first ever tour." Lauren beamed at all of them, but when she got to him, her eyes held a different look. "I'm just so proud of you three."

What was that look? Regret maybe, although more serious than missing their first tour. Something else was going on. The past several months, they'd hardly texted. At the time, he'd chalked it up to him being busy with the band, songwriting, and his position at Middle Tennessee Church. And she was busy with her new job at the *Times*. But now, he didn't know. Something seemed off.

"This may be the best burger I've ever had." Nate took a bite, and Tara swiped some of his fries. "I don't know why you never order your own."

"Calories don't count if they don't come from my plate, right?" Tara laughed.

"Like you need to worry about calories," Lauren said.

The talk was light and fun as the four chatted throughout dinner. When they shared desserts afterward, it felt like old times. Back when Sam was a high school senior and became good friends with Tara and Nate. Lauren would join them for coffee after school or hang out with them on weekends. Always as friends. Sam thought nothing would ever split up the four of them. Not even Lauren moving to New York.

On the walk to the hotel, they discussed Nate and Tara's plans for their wedding next year. The girls talked about dresses while he and Nate planned a bachelor party. Sam was best man, after all. Their ideas ranged from zip lining to axe throwing. They'd have to hone in those details later.

They arrived at the hotel and stopped in front of the elevators. He and Lauren shared a quick hug—warm, familiar, normal. Maybe he'd read too much into this whole thing with her. Nothing was off, she was fine. He'd been looking for trouble where there was none.

Nate and Sam said goodbye to the girls and went to their room while the girls went to theirs.

Sam fell asleep as soon as his head hit the pillow and dreamed of traveling home tomorrow.

* * *

Lauren took her time showering and brushing her teeth. Hopefully, Tara had fallen asleep, and they wouldn't have to talk. Had Tara suspected something was going on with her? Lauren wasn't ready to talk about it. Not with Tara, and not with anyone.

She turned off the bathroom light and tiptoed to her bed, climbed in, and turned off the bedside lamp. *Good, Tara must be asleep.* She pulled the comforter up to her chin. As soon as she closed her eyes, the bed shook.

"Oh, no, you're not getting off that easily." Tara jumped up and down on her bed beside her.

"Do you *mind?*" Lauren squealed. "You're crazy! Why are you jumping on my bed?"

"I wanna know what's going on with you." Tara's face was right next to hers.

Keep it light, Lauren. "What are you talking about? Nothing's going on."

"Right. That's why you're all happy and talkative with Sam one minute, and you're quiet and sad the next. C'mon, I know we haven't seen each other for a while, but I feel like I still know you pretty well." Tara shrugged.

Lauren took a deep breath. Tara had always been nice even though Lauren attended a different school. Lauren genuinely liked both Tara and Nate. They were good and pure, the friends Sam truly needed back when his life was in a tailspin. Their life seemed simple and straightforward, whereas Lauren's had derailed. And for some reason, she couldn't get it back on track.

"There's nothing wrong. You're imagining things." Lauren turned over and yanked the comforter up to her chin again, but Tara had other ideas.

"Oh no, you don't." Tara switched the light on. "I'm not giving up."

"Ugh." Lauren sat up and laughed. She'd have to say something to satisfy Tara so they could both sleep. "Okay, you're right. It's been a little weird. That's all."

"Weird how?" Tara scrunched her eyebrows together and stared into Lauren's eyes.

"I guess I've been away from home for so long, but I've also been away from church for a long time. Things have been awkward between Sam and me, and on top of that, I feel weird in the churches you guys play in. Like I don't belong." That wasn't a lie. Just not the whole truth.

"You didn't go to church or Bible study when you were in New York?" Tara's voice held no judgment, only curiosity.

So why did Lauren feel ashamed? And why couldn't she bring herself to tell Sam she was living in Nashville? She took a deep breath and closed her eyes for a brief second. "Things were so different. Most of my friends weren't Christian, and I didn't have my parents and Christian friends as examples. I fell away big time." She searched Tara's face for judgment but still found none. "But I'm trying to get back." And she was. That was the truth.

Tara tilted her head. "I get that. I felt the same way at TU. Even though it's in Nashville, with so many people with different beliefs. I found myself falling away, too, during my freshman year. But Nate and my parents, and even Sam, reeled me back in. They showed me I could be friends with people from different beliefs yet still stand strong in my faith."

Lauren lacked that strength. She gave in too easily to other people's ideas. It'd taken her a while to admit it, but she'd rebelled against her strict parents. "That's where I went wrong. I didn't keep in touch with Sam, or you, or any of my other friends. Even my parents. I made it too easy to fall away from what had always grounded me." Again, the truth.

"Well, I want to stay in touch. Let's text and call when you get back to New York. We can keep each other grounded and accountable. Deal? And I'm so glad you confided in me."

Sure. Except I didn't tell you or anyone else I failed at my job at the Times and moved to Nashville two months ago. But other than that ...

"Deal."

nine

"Anybody home?" Sam dropped his bags in the laundry room and headed toward the kitchen.

"Sam!" Mom exclaimed. "We didn't expect you until later." Even at twenty-three, he missed his mom's hugs.

"We left right after the morning service and drove straight home. Where's Dad?"

She thumbed toward the hallway. "He's in his office talking to Coach Wes. Problems with a player."

"That's not good. The season hasn't begun yet." John Grayson was one of the winningest and most respected coaches in all of college basketball. His long tenure at Tennessee University produced more wins than losses and two national championships.

"I thought I heard your voice." Dad beamed as he came up the hall from his office and wrapped Sam in a bear hug.

He stepped back and observed his mom and dad. How fortunate he was these two adopted him after he'd spent most of his childhood in foster care or with his negligent, criminal, father. His biological mother died when he was five, and he barely remembered her. The Graysons were the family he'd always wanted but never realized how much he needed.

"Now sit down, I made your favorite soup last night. I'm going to heat it up, and you're going to tell us all about the tour." Mom walked to the refrigerator and showed him the crock of chicken pot pie soup. Indeed, his favorite.

"You mean all the details I've already told you on our phone calls every night? You do realize I've only been gone for two weeks." Sam teased them. This would call for coffee. He walked to the coffee cart, and his favorite dark roast was stocked up. Mom had prepared for him to be home. He brewed the coffee while Dad told him about his problem player, and then Sam walked with care to the kitchen table with three mugs of coffee.

"He reminds me of your father when he played for me." Dad frowned and stared at the coffee Sam brought him. "I'm afraid he's headed for disaster."

Sam's mouth hung open, and he closed it. His dad rarely said anything about his birth father. After the trafficking scheme in Alabama, his parents were shocked to find out Sam's birth father, who had many aliases, had played for his adoptive dad years ago. The school dismissed him from the team and expelled his biological father because of drugs and arrests. But not because of his adoptive dad's lack of trying.

Dad had always been bothered by what happened with Andy Quinn. He'd told Sam adopting him brought closure to the situation. What a series of events only God could've woven together.

Dad's head snapped up. "I'm sorry I said that. I don't know what made me bring his name up."

"It's okay." Sam shrugged, but based on the concern on his dad's face, he wasn't buying it.

"No, it's not, I'm sorry. The last thing I want is to smack you in the face with something that brings up bad memories. I spent today dealing with the same things from back then, and I just blurted it out."

"Hey, it's okay." Sam reached out and touched Dad's arm. "If

I can't handle the mention of his name, then I haven't come as far as I thought. Seriously."

Dad met his eyes. "Sometimes I forget how strong you are."

Mom brought three bowls of soup to the table, and Sam was grateful not only for the soup but for her lightening the mood.

"Did you and Lauren have fun together?" Mom asked.

"We did. It was great hanging out after all this time. Plus, I think Tara was happy to have another girl around instead of us guys." Sam blew on a spoonful of soup before tasting it. He had dreamed of this soup while he was gone.

"So, what's going on with you two?" Dad asked.

Sam choked on his soup then laughed at his dad's bluntness. For some unexplained reason, he couldn't stop laughing. He must be more tired than he realized.

"What's so funny?" Dad asked.

He and Mom stared like Sam had lost his mind, which made him laugh harder, until they started laughing too.

"You know we look like a bunch of lunatics." Tears of laughter rolled down Mom's face.

"And we don't even know what we're laughing at." Dad failed to stifle a laugh.

Sam got ahold of himself. "I'm just slap happy. I've had six hours sleep over the past two nights." He sighed. "You're always the peacekeeper. But then you bring up Andy Quinn, and next thing I know, you're trying to figure out if there's something between Lauren and me. It just hit me as funny."

Dad chuckled and set his spoon on the table. "I guess I was a little blunt."

"I think what your father is trying to say is we're glad you and Lauren got to spend some time together." She winked at Dad. "We know you think God is calling you to remain single. And maybe he is. But if not, there's nothing wrong with having a girlfriend."

Sam got his laughter under control and stirred his soup. "Things aren't like that with Lauren and me."

"We're just saying the two of you are deeply rooted in your faith and doing the right thing before God, but that doesn't mean you can't carry that deep faith into a godly relationship."

"I get that, I do. But we're *only* friends, that's all."

"I guess I'd hate to think you're remaining single because of all you've been through. That the trauma you've experienced would keep you from having a family of your own someday."

"Mom." He grimaced. "I just turned twenty-three. I'm not saying I'll never have a girlfriend or a family. I'm just saying *not right now*. I need to focus on God and what He wants for me."

"Okay, I get it." Mom put her hands up. "We're sorry to pry."

"We?" Dad laughed. "I merely asked one question. But your mom's right. We just want to see you happy."

"Thanks, I know you mean well. *Both* of you." Sam turned back to his soup. It was good to be home.

Monday morning rolled around too soon, and he still hadn't caught up on sleep. Coffee would help. He hit the drive-through at the coffee shop across from church and walked in at exactly 9:00 a.m. as the staff meeting started.

"Welcome back, Sam," Pastor Stephan shouted from the front of the room. Everyone turned and welcomed him.

Sam smiled and lifted his coffee cup, greeting the large staff group of about one hundred.

"We won't put you on the spot since you got back late yesterday, but maybe you can provide an update at next Monday's meeting."

"Sure thing." His voice was thick as he took in all the smiles and waves from his coworkers at his new home church. With the latest tour over, he could focus on music programming for church and still have time left for what he loved most. Writing songs.

After the meeting, he talked to a few friends on staff on the way to his office on the second floor. He threw his backpack on the corner chair and switched on his computer to see how many emails were waiting for him. He probably should've checked them while gone, but he hadn't thought about it.

The news homepage popped up, and he pointed his mouse toward his email account. But something else caught his eye. A feature by Lauren Asher ... How had she written something for the *Tennessean* when she was in New York?

He stared at the link for a moment. A writer could work for a Nashville paper even while in New York City. Many people worked remotely these days. That had to be it.

He clicked the link, which opened an article titled, "Seasons of Change," and Lauren's picture and byline were at the top. Why hadn't she told him she was writing for the *Tennessean*? No sensible reason came to mind.

He skimmed the article. She wrote about the change from summer to fall and compared the change in seasons to life changes, such as her moving back home to Tennessee. *What?* He read that again, and his head spun. Apparently, in the last couple months, she'd moved from New York City back to Nashville.

She'd been back for two whole months. And she hadn't told him. Sure, they weren't as close as before, but they'd spent three days together in Knoxville. He couldn't think of a single reason for her not to tell him. This was a major life event. How could she not share that with him?

He didn't know whether to be mad or concerned. He tensed his jaw, snatched up his phone, and his fingers flew over the keyboard.

> What's going on? I see an article you wrote for the Tennessean and find out you're in Nashville. 20 minutes from Franklin. Why didn't you tell me?

He hit Send without thinking and then re-read it. It definitely came off that he was mad. Well, good, he had a right to be mad, and he couldn't wait for her explanation.

ten

anic set in. She re-read Sam's text and set her phone screen-side down on the table. He had every right to be upset. She'd put off telling him, and he found out accidentally. Exactly what she didn't want to happen. But she hadn't been able to figure out how to tell him without him asking a lot of questions.

She sat paralyzed by her laptop at her table in the small downtown Nashville coffee shop and tried to read the few paragraphs she'd typed for her novel. But Sam's text screamed at her from her phone.

Calm down and think. He deserves an answer. What could she possibly text back that would make sense? Especially when she didn't have a good reason. They needed to talk in person. She picked up her phone and forced herself to breathe while her fingers typed out the words.

> I'm so sorry you found out this way. I meant to tell you but didn't. Can we talk in person? Lunch or coffee today? I'll come to Franklin.

Her heart pounded in her ears as she hit Send. She exhaled and waited. Of course, he'd be mad. What kind of best friend didn't tell the other she'd moved back and lived twenty minutes away? As her heartbeat steadied, her phone vibrated, causing it to speed up again.

Merridee's, 12:30.

Yep, he was mad. His texts were never that short and to the point. She hesitated and then hit the "thumbs up" emoji.

It was 10:30 a.m. Two hours was too long to sit there and think, yet not enough. She slipped her computer and phone into her bag, placed her empty coffee cup on the counter, and ordered a large ice water to go. She needed to clear her head before meeting with Sam.

She drove to Franklin and strolled through the park. The warm, late-October air and sunshine washed over her. What would she say? She couldn't tell him the whole story, at least not yet. But she'd tell as much as she could about what led her back to Tennessee.

* * *

Kyle Grayson walked out of the deposition with his head held high and a smile on his face. His job as an entertainment law attorney had become more interesting lately. AI had come to the forefront and could be viewed as a potential threat to every client. Every singer, actor, and writer, including his brother Sam. In a few months, he'd become one of Christian music's most notable songwriters. Today's deposition was a move in the right direction.

He stepped into his office. A pile of messages caught his attention, but he checked his cell phone first. The first text was from Sam asking if it was okay to reschedule their lunch. Huh? Kyle picked up the phone and hit Sam's number.

His brother answered on the first ring. "Hey, sorry about cancelling on ya."

"No worries, little bro, just wanted to make sure everything was okay."

"I don't know, man. It's Lauren. I don't know what's going on with her. I'm meeting her at Merridee's to figure things out." He didn't sound excited about it either.

"Why, what happened?" Kyle's administrative assistant handed him two documents to sign. He handed the papers to her and mouthed, "Thank you."

"You're not gonna believe this. She's moved back here. She's living in Nashville and working for the *Tennessean*, and she didn't even tell me. I found out by accident. I opened my computer this morning, and there it was right in the center of the news page, a feature in the *Tennessean* by Lauren Asher." Sam sounded exasperated.

Kyle tapped his tablet screen and pulled up the article and saw the words on the screen written by Lauren herself.

"Wow, I don't know what to say." Kyle paused and scratched his chin. "But look, I'm sure you've both changed over the past year. Afterall, you're both older and out of college and have real jobs now. Things are bound to be different. When I run into old friends from high school now, things aren't usually the same because of all the time spent apart. That's just natural."

"Right, I get that. But how do you explain her not telling me when we just spent three days together in Knoxville?" Sam sighed.

Kyle took a deep breath. No, he wouldn't tell Sam what he'd heard about Lauren. It was just a rumor, after all. And a hard-to-believe rumor at that. Not a credible source, either. It was a friend-of-a-friend-told-me situation.

"I can't explain that. But it sounds like maybe she wants to when she meets with you. Just keep an open mind, and give her some grace. Think of all you've been through in the past four years since you two have spent any real time together. My guess is she's probably gone through some things of her own."

There was silence on the other end of the phone. "Sam, you still there?"

"Yeah, just thinking. You're probably right. She probably has a good reason for not letting me know she's moved back. I just pulled up to Merridee's. I'm early, but I'm gonna go on in and wait for her."

"Cass, me, and Hannah are all coming over for dinner tonight, so I'll check in with you then. Good luck, bud."

"I don't know what to expect at this point. But thanks for talking to me. I'll let you know how it goes tonight."

Kyle put his phone away and exhaled. He said a silent prayer that the rumor he heard wasn't true, and that God would work out all the details.

eleven

Sam strolled into Merridee's in downtown Franklin at 12:15 and ordered a large, iced tea. A grilled cheese sandwich was tempting, but he decided to wait. He wasn't that hungry and honestly didn't even know how long he'd be staying.

He paid for his tea and walked through the warm, homey coffee shop and bakery, to a back booth where they'd have a certain degree of privacy. He was early, but if he knew Lauren, she'd be early too.

But that was it. He didn't know her like he used to. That thought had crossed his mind while they were in Knoxville, but he'd brushed it aside. Afterall, it was bound to be weird after not seeing each other and having little communication for over a year. His instinct was right. Something was different about her.

He glanced up in time to see her walk in. She wore a pink hoodie and jeans, her hair in a ponytail. She spotted him right away, and Sam waved at her without smiling. As she approached, he could tell she didn't have any makeup on but was more beautiful than ever. His resolve melted, but he had to press her for answers. The pain of her withholding information from him crept back in and helped get his resolve back.

"Hi." She barely made eye contact, and her weak smile hardly curved her lips.

"Hey. Do you want something to eat or drink?"

"Umm, maybe just an iced tea." Her eyes still didn't meet his.

"I'll be right back." He stood and approached the counter, and a minute later, returned with her glass of iced tea.

He placed the tall glass in front of her. "Lemon and two sugars still?" Or had that changed too?

"Yeah." She smiled a little more. "Thanks."

He tapped his fingers on the table. "Look, I'm sorry I came off so gruff in the text messages. I was just shocked."

"It's okay." She stared at her lap. "You had every right to be. I meant to tell you in Knoxville. Even before that. Honestly, I did."

"Then why didn't you?" Sam swallowed hard. At least, she was here now.

Her eyes met his for the first time since she'd come in the door, and suddenly, she teared up. "Sam, I need you as a friend now more than ever. I want our friendship back. More than anything, I want to get back to where we were before I left Tennessee."

His heart melted. He couldn't stand to see her cry. "I want that too, Lauren. More than anything."

She dabbed her eyes with her napkin. "The reason I didn't tell you is because I'm a colossal failure. And here you are, so successful. I guess I'm embarrassed."

"A failure?" Sam sat back in his booth and watched her. "You're anything but a failure, Lauren. I mean, you graduated from NYU, you're a newspaper writer, and you're working on a novel. How is that a failure? You have nothing to be embarrassed about. In fact, you've accomplished a lot."

She bit her lip, on the verge of tears again. "Things weren't great for me in New York. I didn't fit in at the *Times,* and I felt like I was drowning. Sam ... I quit my dream job after a few months. How is that not a failure?"

Sam breathed deeply and rubbed his chin. How could she ever think she was a failure? "Okay, New York wasn't for you. And so what if you quit the *New York Times?* Mabe it wasn't *the* dream, just another dream of many. You had no way of knowing what it'd be like to work there. I don't care where you work or what you do. I'm so glad you're back. I wish you'd told me."

"I'm so sorry, Sam."

"It's okay," he said, lost in her green eyes again.

She took a sip of her tea. "I know I don't look like it, but I'm glad to be back home. Back here with you, even my parents."

They laughed. Lauren loved her parents, but they were extremely strict. That had to be a major factor in her going to New York. Sure, she wanted to attend NYU, but also she wanted to live life out from under her parents' rules.

"I'm sorry New York didn't work out for you, but I'm glad you're back."

"You really forgive me for not telling you?"

"Of course. I could never stay mad. Let's move on. I want to know all about your job at the *Tennessean.*"

She managed a true, happy smile. "Well, I'm writing a weekly features column, and I love it. Oh, and I almost forgot. I'm working part-time at Landmark Bookstore also." She hid her face in her hands playfully.

"What? Lauren!" He threw a wadded-up napkin at her. "You're killing me! Are you married with kids now too?"

"Of course not." She laughed, but something in her expression changed. The same sadness he'd seen in Knoxville. What was that about?

"I'm just kidding. Landmark, that's awesome. I'm glad you told me before I ran into you there." He gazed at her for a long moment. "Do you have time to order lunch and talk some more?"

"Yeah, that sounds good." Her sadness disappeared.

They ordered grilled cheese and chili. The conversation remained light, and they talked and laughed through lunch.

His old friend was back again, and he was grateful.

twelve

"Hannah's here with the desserts," Abbie turned around from checking the chicken roasting in the oven as Hannah barged through the front door and walked across the great room to the open kitchen. "Thanks for picking these up." Abbie took one of the bags from her daughter.

"Let me help you." Sam jumped up from the table where he, Kyle, and Cassie had been chatting.

"Take the bag hooked around my thumb." Hannah laughed. "Otherwise, I'll be off balance and lose everything."

"Got it." Sam grabbed the bag from her. "I can't let you drop that apple cider cake."

"Don't anyone dare drop that cake." Kyle shouted.

"Wow, the farmer's market was packed." Hannah huffed as she dropped the rest of the bags onto the kitchen island. "But I got the cake and some caramel apples."

"Don't eat without me." John came out of his office. "Sorry, that call ran a little long."

"You're lucky we didn't start with these desserts," Kyle said.

The sound of everyone chatting made Abbie smile. They'd been through some hard, dark times in the year before Sam's adoption, and before that, Sam and Kyle didn't get along. Back then it wasn't even possible for everyone to be in the same room together. Looking at this family now, no one would ever guess they'd gone through all those hard things.

Everyone pitched in and set the table. John prayed, and then they all dug into the roasted chicken, potatoes, and carrots Abbie had whipped up with her daughter-in-law's help.

"Sam, I heard you say Lauren was in town. I thought you might invite her tonight," Abbie said.

Sam met Kyle's eyes briefly.

"What? Something I said?"

"Um-hum, no, it's just something weird happened today." Sam put his fork down and sipped from his water glass. He went on to explain the surprise about Lauren being back in town.

Sam shook his head. "I still don't know the whole story. Just that New York City and the *Times* weren't for her."

"I can see that." John shrugged. "Either you like a big city like New York, or you don't."

"I get that. It's just ... she kept it a secret. And I don't know, I guess we're just not as close as we used to be."

Abbie detected the sadness in Sam's voice. For years, Lauren had been his only friend. Not only that, he hadn't really dated anyone all through college. Oh, maybe coffee or dinner with someone here and there, but never anything that lasted more than one date, let alone anything serious. She worried he would end up alone because of his trust issues. "Maybe you two will be able to see each other more and reconnect," she suggested.

"Yeah, I hope so."

Abbie thought the world of Lauren. She was a good Christian girl, and she and John had always thought maybe someday she and Sam would end up together. Now that she was back in Tennessee, maybe there was still that chance.

* * *

After dinner, Sam waved goodbye to Kyle and Cassie, and Dad went to his office. Sam helped Mom and Hannah sort through more items for the clothes closet.

The store would officially open in a couple of weeks. Mom and Wendy now had the keys to their new retail space near the square in downtown Franklin. Some remaining items left behind needed to be organized, washed if necessary, tagged, and moved to the shop.

After a while, Hannah left for her apartment in Nashville. She had school to teach tomorrow.

Mom excused herself and said she was going to drag Dad away from his game tapes to watch a movie.

"I'm going to stay in here and sort a while longer," Sam said.

One after another, Sam held up articles of clothing and looked over them, searching for signs of wear or stains. There were none. And those labels. His eyes widened. The majority of these items had come from high-dollar stores, and some even had store tags still on them. Either they'd never been worn, or people had bought and donated new clothes. Once he got to the end of the bag, he picked up his phone. 10:15. Time for one more bag before bed. He got up from the floor and ambled to the other side of the room where bags covered the floor. Uh-oh. He was out of tags.

He walked down the hallway and peeked into the family room where his parents were watching a movie. "Mom, do you have any more tags?"

"There's a whole shoe box full in the closet," she answered without looking up.

Sam meandered toward his parents' room and opened the door to their walk-in closet. Or wait—did she mean the closet in the great room? He got ready to close the door but then spotted a bag of clothes and some shoe boxes on the top shelf of his dad's side of the closet. Maybe more clothes they needed to go through?

A blue stepladder stood in the corner, and Sam brought it near the boxes on the highest shelves. He climbed to the second rung from the top. This shelf was out of reach. Why had Mom even put labels here? He pulled the first box out and opened it. It wasn't tags at all. The box contained family pictures from when Kyle and Hannah were in their early teens.

The box contained some funny photos of his brother and sister. He thumbed through them and laughed, then closed the box and shoved it back in its spot. He pulled out another. Same thing, more family pictures. He'd love to look through them, but not tonight. His eyes blurred, and he couldn't stop yawning.

A quick peek into the bag of clothes told him those were John's, probably going to charity. He was in the wrong closet after all. He put the bag back on the shelf, took one step down the ladder, and out of the corner of his eye, he spotted a box with the letters AQ written on the side. A shiver ran down the back of his neck. Those initials could stand for something other than Andy Quinn, right? He chastised himself for being paranoid. More than once, Hannah had told him, "Not everything is about you, Sam."

He laughed and climbed down the ladder but paused at the bottom rung. What if AQ did stand for Andy Quinn? His biological father had played for his adoptive dad many years ago, maybe the box contained basketball items related to him? It was on Dad's side of the closet.

Curiosity got the best of him. He climbed back up the ladder and pushed the bag of his dad's clothes aside. Then he carefully slid out the AQ box and carried it down the ladder.

He sat on the carpet in the middle of the huge walk-in closet and removed the lid from the box. Envelopes were stacked inside. Were these Andy's recruitment letters? What else would they be? But the number of letters didn't make sense.

Sam pulled the first one out. Most were unopened, but this particular one had been. When he turned it over, his eyes had trouble reconciling with his mind what was written on it. The envelope was addressed to Sam Grayson, in care of John Grayson, and the return address was the Memphis Federal Correctional Institute, Inmate Andy Quinn.

thirteen

S am had no idea how long he'd held his breath, but it probably explained his dizziness.

His hands shook as he sifted through all the unopened envelopes. Twenty-five or thirty at least, all addressed to him. Why had his biological father even written to him? On top of that, his adoptive parents had hidden the letters from him. But why?

He sat with the opened letter in his hands and stared at it. How long had his parents kept these from him? He pulled the box toward him and thumbed his way back to the earliest postmarked letter. Almost three years ago. They'd been hiding these for that long.

Even when they'd learned Sam's biological father had been on his adoptive dad's basketball team many years before, they'd told him right away, hadn't they? Suddenly, his mind was spinning, and he questioned everything they'd told him, and when. If they'd hidden these letters, what else could they be hiding?

His heart pounded, and he gritted his teeth. He didn't know if his anger was directed toward his adoptive family or his birth father. What business did Quinn have writing Sam anyway?

He stood and paced the room. Perhaps he should call Lauren. He pulled his phone out of his back pocket and started to text her but then stopped.

Maybe he should read this one letter first.

He studied the opened envelope once more. The man's small, careful handwriting scrolled across the front the way Sam remembered it. The letter tugged at his soul. He had to know what it said. He pulled the letter out of the envelope and carefully unfolded the single notebook page. Several paragraphs were on the front page, nothing on the back. He drew a deep breath and began reading.

> *Dear Sam,*
>
> *I understand why you don't answer my letters, and I can't blame you. If somebody put me through everything I put you through, I wouldn't wanna hear from them either.*
>
> *I hope, no I PRAY, that you'll reconsider.*

Sam's breath caught. Wait—his biological father prayed? He didn't think the word or concept was something the man even knew.

> *I have changed, no thanks to myself but all thanks to God above. But I won't continue to bug you. I've done that enough. Just know that if you ever change your mind, I'd love to see you. Or, if nothing else, a phone call. I want to tell you I'm sorry in person. I don't expect you to ever forgive me, but I need you to see how I've changed and how truly sorry I am.*
>
> *Sincerely,*
> *Andy Quinn*

Sam could barely breathe, but at the same time, he had to know more. He'd have to start at the beginning. He pulled out the one with the earliest postmark and opened it.

Dear Son,

I know I don't have the right to call you son anymore, and I'm sorry for that. I have so much to tell you I don't know where to start. I'm going to a Bible study here in prison. At first, I only went to get out of my cell once a week and get good behavior points. But after a few months, something changed inside me. The pastor here says it's the Holy Spirit. I don't know about that because all this is new to me.

I feel different, though. For the first time in all my years on earth, I know I've lived my life all wrong, and I've treated people wrong. Especially you. I've asked God to forgive me for all I done wrong, and all the things I did to you and put you through. I think God forgives me, but I don't expect you to. I just need you to know how sorry I am.

All your life, I let you down and only used you for stuff like getting food stamps or cheap housing. I've talked to God about the horrible things I done to you, and I feel his mercy. But that doesn't change things for you, does it? You needed a parent, and I wasn't one.

I really hope you're happy with John Grayson and his family. By now you know the connection I had with them. They are good people who I hated for no reason, especially when they got involved and adopted you. But I feel different now. I'm thankful they could offer you peace and a stable life that I couldn't. Or wouldn't. That hurts me to say.

This is a lot to take in, I know. It would be great to hear back from you, and maybe sometime talk in person. I don't deserve that at all. I'm just asking you to think about it.

Sincerely,

Andy Quinn

PS. I had no idea how to sign this letter. Dad? Drew Keller? But I decided on the truth.

Sam reached the end of the letter but couldn't stop staring. And yet he couldn't put it down. His heart pounded harder than ever before. He sat like that for what seemed like forever.

"Sam?"

He jerked his head up.

His Mom stood in the doorway of the closet.

"Umm, what are you doing there?" Her smile was forced.

His father walked in and stood next to her. He looked at the box on the floor in front of Sam, and he froze in place.

Mom repeated her question, glancing from the box to the space on the shelf it had come from, and back to Sam again.

He followed her stare. "Why? Why did you hide these from me?"

"Sam, we can explain." His father's perpetually tanned face paled a few shades.

"I'm so sorry, Sam. We never meant for you to find these," Mom said.

"You never meant for me to find these?" The words came out much more forceful than intended. "What kind of answer is that? These were addressed to me, not you!"

"Sam, don't yell at your mom. This is my fault. She wanted you to have them, but I didn't. It was my idea not to give them to you." His tone was matter-of-fact, no apology in his voice.

Sam took a step back and glared at John. "Is that supposed to be some kind of apology, because it sure is lame," he shouted.

Dad held his hands up. "Let me explain."

If anyone would've ever told Sam he'd feel this much animosity toward his adoptive father, he wouldn't have believed it. "Go ahead, I can't wait to hear it."

"We didn't think you could handle whatever was in those letters."

Sam waited for him to continue, but he didn't. "That's it? That's all you have to say?"

His dad flinched. "Now wait a minute—"

"No, you wait a minute," Sam shouted again. "This wasn't your decision to make. Were you ever going to give them to me?"

"I don't know," his dad's voice was straightforward again.

Sam glared at his dad. He stooped to the floor, shoved the letters in the box, and slapped the lid on top. "I can't be here right now." He stormed past them with the box under his arm.

"Wait, Sam, where are you going?" His mom yelled.

Ignoring her, he slammed the door.

fourteen

How could they do this? He'd always believed their relationship had been based on truth and honesty. Now he didn't know. And what about trust? How many times over the years had John said, "You can trust us," and Sam always had. But this was different. How could he trust them if they'd hid the letters?

Well after midnight, rain pelted his windshield. He parked his car, jogged to the front door of Kyle's home, and rang the doorbell. His brother wouldn't be happy to see him this late on a Sunday night. Especially without calling.

After what seemed like forever, the door opened, and Kyle stared at him. "Sam, what's going on? Are Mom and Dad okay?" He grabbed Sam and pulled him in out of the rain.

Cassie came down the steps wearing a robe.

Sam glanced at the clock on the wall in their great room. Nearly 1:00 a.m. What was he thinking coming here so late? Except he'd left and had no place to go.

"They're fine. Everyone's fine."

"Okay, next question. If everyone is okay then why are you waking us up in the middle of the night?" Kyle gritted his teeth and huffed.

Yep, his brother was angry.

"Kyle!" Cassie said. "Have a seat, Sam. It's okay, tell us why you're here. And it's not the middle of the night." She glared at Kyle.

"Well, it is when you have to get up at 6:00 a.m. But come on in, tell us what's going on." Defeat rang out in Kyle's voice.

His brother was right. They had to get up early, and here he was, disrupting their sleep. He should've just gone to Nate's apartment. But Nate didn't know everything Kyle did, so it hadn't made sense to go there.

He took a deep breath and told Kyle and Cassie about the hidden letters, then handed the first to Kyle. Both his brother and sister-in-law sat with their jaws hanging open. They must not have known after all.

"They really hid these from you?" Kyle asked.

"Yeah, can you even believe it? What right did they have?" Sam huffed.

Kyle read and re-read the letter. He rubbed his chin, then handed it to Cassie.

She hesitated. "Is it okay if I read it, Sam?"

"Sure, I want your opinion too." Exhaustion kicked in, but he wanted to hear their thoughts. He needed their help to make his parents see why hiding the letters was so wrong.

Cassie read the letter and then handed it back to Sam. She and Kyle sat and didn't say anything.

"So, what do you think?" Sam asked.

Kyle's expression had softened from when Sam first arrived. He cleared his throat. "Well, I don't know what to think about the letter itself. I mean, whether he meant those things or not, and if he actually turned to God. I just don't know. But ..." Kyle's voice trailed off.

"But what?" Sam asked. "Go ahead and say whatever it is."

"I can understand why they didn't give the letters to you," Kyle blurted out.

Cassie stared at the floor without saying anything. She obviously agreed.

"What?" Sam flew up from the sofa, forgetting about his exhaustion.

"Sam, hear me out. Please, just sit back down." Kyle's voice was gentle.

Sam didn't know what to think. But he trusted his brother. They'd had a rocky beginning when they first met. But Kyle had helped pull him through various situations over the years and had never led him in the wrong direction.

He swallowed hard and sat on the sofa facing them.

"Let me ask you something. Do you think Dad or Mom have ever steered you wrong? Or have they ever done anything to intentionally hurt you?" Kyle asked.

Sam didn't even have to think about that. "No."

"I'm not saying I think hiding the letters was the right thing, but I know they'd never intentionally hurt you. Not ever. They must have reasons that make sense to them. My guess is they didn't want to see you hurt again by a man who's harmed you repeatedly throughout your childhood."

He didn't want to admit it, but Kyle had a point. His adoptive parents had proved they only wanted the best for him. They'd been nothing but supportive. "I guess you're right. But one thing I don't understand about that letter. That one had been opened, so they'd read it. Andy Quinn says he's changed, and he's following God now. How would that hurt me?"

This time, Cassie spoke. "How many times has that man lied to you over the years, Sam? To get what he wanted or needed."

He slowly exhaled. She was right. They both were. How could he not see it? "I get it. I guess I didn't think it through. I was just so shocked to see these letters."

"I can only imagine." Kyle agreed. "Look, it's late. Stay here tonight, and tomorrow, you can talk to Mom and Dad."

Sam exhaled. "Okay, thank you. That sounds good."

"I'm going to text them and let them know you're here.

They're probably worried. I'll tell them you'll talk to them tomorrow."

"Thanks." Sam was grateful to have a brother and sister-in-law who would take him in and hear him out in the middle of the night. But what about Andy Quinn? He'd always wanted to be as far as possible from the man. Why was he so confused about that now?

fifteen

Abbie poured coffee for her and John, then set out some muffins she'd bought yesterday.

"Do we even know if he's coming back here this morning?" John asked.

"I figured he would since he has to change clothes for work. I know he's scheduled to go into church today for meetings later this morning. I'm grateful Kyle called us last night, otherwise I wouldn't have been able to sleep."

John reached for a muffin. Not the blueberry crumble one he wanted but rather the high fiber, multi grain one he should have. "Same here. I hope he's cooled off some. And I also hope he forgets about those letters."

"I'd prepare yourself just in case he wants the rest." Abbie sighed. "He only found the box. A big envelope contains a few more."

John stopped mid-bite and put his muffin back on his plate. He'd never understood why Sam longed for connection with his birth father. All that man had ever done was hurt him. "I know, I have it right here." He pointed to the bar stool next to him. "I guess we'll give it to him since he has most of them already. But it makes no sense to me, Abbie. I mean, we're his parents now."

Abbie shook her head. "Hon, we talked about this in family therapy. Adoption doesn't erase the trauma, no matter how close he is to us."

"I know, I remember. But I can't wrap my head around that concept. Look at the life he's had with us compared to the life he had with Andy Quinn. There's no comparison."

"Right, but—"

"Anybody home?" Sam's voice, softer than normal, interrupted Abbie mid-sentence.

"In the kitchen." John's eyes met Abbie's.

"Hi," Sam said then gave a sheepish grin as he rounded the corner, stopped, and leaned against the wall.

"Hi, sweetheart." Abbie walked to him, hugged him lightly, and he hugged her back.

He followed her to the kitchen island where John sat.

John stayed in his seat but said, "Good morning."

"You want some coffee?" She went ahead and pulled a mug down from the cabinet before he even answered.

"Sure." Sam pulled out a bar stool across from John and sat, and Abbie placed the hot mug in front of him.

The silence was deafening. John spoke first. "I'm glad you're here, and I hope you'll give us the chance to explain."

"Yeah, I don't want to fight. I'm sorry about last night. I was in shock. But that's no excuse."

"It's okay, kiddo. I know it was a shock. We're sorry too," John said.

Sam nodded. "I kind of understand."

"We thought we were doing the right thing. But now, your mom and I agree we went about it the wrong way, and we're sorry. Those letters belong to you, not us. And it was my idea not to give you the letters, so please don't blame Abbie. Here's the rest." John picked up a large envelope from the bar stool and put it on the kitchen island between him and Sam.

Sam stared at the envelope with his mouth open and didn't say anything at first. "Thanks." He looked at John then Abbie.

John gave a quick nod but didn't say anything. He still didn't want Sam to have them. What good could they bring? But he couldn't continue to hide them.

"After talking to Kyle and Cassie, I understand why you didn't want me to have them." Sam paused and bit his lower lip. "But I do feel like I need to read them."

"You're going to read them all?" What could Sam be looking for in those letters that he didn't have here with them? Hadn't they provided a family that supported and loved him? And more than that, John was his father now. Not Andy Quinn.

"Well, uh, yeah. I just need to see what he said in them."

John clenched his fists as the anger building inside him caught him by surprise. He bit his tongue. *I need your strength, Lord.*

"You know we're here for you, hon," Abbie said.

"Thanks, Mom, I appreciate that. And yeah, I know."

John clamped his mouth shut. Better not to say anything.

* * *

Abbie made a quick stop to pick up coffee and pulled into a parking spot at *their* shop. Hers and Wendy's—the new clothes closet for foster kids. They were fortunate to get prime retail space on Main Street in Franklin—the street led to the town square, where the theater and shops were located. The area had high rent for sure, but she and Wendy had decided they didn't want to skimp. The rent was their donation.

This shop showcased items for teens in foster care. They wanted these kids to feel special. They'd refer to the store as vintage, but the prices would be thrifty. This would be their ministry to foster kids.

Opening day was around the corner, and they still had much to do. The signage would arrive next week, and the grand opening would take place the week after that. Today their clothing racks were being delivered and assembled, and she and Wendy would finally start setting up the shop.

She opened the front door, and Wendy wasn't there yet. Abbie almost turned around because she didn't want to admire the freshly painted walls for the first time without her, but she quickly brushed aside that thought. She held her breath for a moment as she took it all in, then smiled. The walls were all painted in trendy colors. Rose gold for the girls' side of the store, blues and grays on the boys' side. And of course, silver and gold mixed in here and there.

The unique shop catered to ages twelve to eighteen but had a small area in back for smaller kids' clothing. Still, she and Wendy had decided to devote this shop to teens. After all, baby and toddler hand-me-downs were easy to find. In their research talking to foster families, they all said the same thing—they could usually manage the smaller kids' clothing, it was the older kids' items that were harder to find. And of course, more expensive.

Abbie slowly released her breath and stood motionless as she soaked it all in. They even had an area in the back for donated books, CDs, jewelry, and other things teens might like. The donors had been so generous, and Franklin Community Church had made a large donation to help them get started.

"Hey, will you look at this? I could cry right now." Wendy squealed.

She and Abbie hugged and laughed. "I didn't even hear you come in. I was so amazed by these walls."

Wendy took the coffee Abbie handed her and spun around, slowly taking it all in. "Wow, those friends of Sam's sure did a great job painting. I love how the little kids' area is purple and pink. We should get a little table to put back there so kids can look at books or color while their moms shop."

"Great idea." They walked to the left front side of the store where their cash register would be in a couple of days. The only thing there now was the checkout counter and a couple of stools, and they both sat for a moment and sipped their coffee. It was a lot to take in.

"This is a dream come true," Abbie whispered. Saying it too loud might make it not true. "And I get to do it with my BFF."

Wendy teared up. "A dream we didn't even know we had. I never thought that you taking in a foster child would change my life as well."

"Speaking of Sam ..."

"Uh-oh, the letters still? I thought you and John resolved that."

"Kind of, sort of." Abbie sat her coffee cup on the glass counter. "I think Sam is okay, and I'm okay with the letters, but John really isn't."

"What? Why? John is always the most level headed of you two. I mean, um ..." Wendy placed her hand over her mouth.

"Hey now!" Abbie laughed.

"You know what I mean." Wendy blushed. "He's just so in charge all the time."

"That's the problem." Abbie waved her hand. "He's always been in control of every situation, except for one. Andy Quinn. And he thinks Quinn is still trying to control Sam by way of those letters."

"Mm-hmm, I can see that. John's jealous of what might happen when Sam reads the letters. Maybe even afraid he might want to see Andy?"

"Yes, and worried Sam reconnecting with Andy would bring back trauma and memories he's worked so hard to get over. John also feels it's a slap in the face after all we've done for Sam." Abbie paused and shifted on her stool. "We met this couple a while back who'd been through a similar situation. I never old you about them before now because I tried to put them out of my mind."

"I'm listening." Wendy leaned forward across the glass countertop toward Abbie.

"John and I met this couple at church a couple of years ago.

Maggie and Ron. They went through a similar situation. They adopted their daughter when she was a teenager, and then when she was nineteen, she reunited with her biological mom." Abbie paused. "She moved in with her and eventually cut off contact with Maggie and Ron. The story has haunted us ever since we heard it."

The two remained silent for a moment.

"That's awful," Wendy spoke first.

Abbie nodded. "Thinking about that story has always made me sad, but it made John mad because of everything that couple did for the girl, and she ended up turning her back on them. That's why he's mad now. I'm kind of beginning to see his point."

Wendy exhaled and took a sip of her coffee. "Andy Quinn has been messing with you all for a long, long time. It's so crazy."

"Isn't it? Who would've thought the player John couldn't help in college would turn out to be our foster son's biological dad."

"That's all God, and it's for a reason," Wendy said. "Even though it seems crazy to us, and we can't imagine why."

"Mm-hmm, that same verse pops into my head a lot. *'For my thoughts are not your thoughts, neither are your ways my ways, declares the Lord.'* I've been trying to figure out His ways when it comes to our family for a long time now. I've finally decided it's best to leave it all in His hands."

"Amen," Wendy added. "Just like our clothes closet. I pray every day our shop blesses someone. I honestly believe God led us to do this for a reason, and I can't wait to see what that is. Just like Sam's story as part of your family. God's not done with that either."

Abbie smiled at her friend and nodded. She wanted to believe that, but she just wasn't sure.

sixteen

Sam fumbled for his phone on the headboard in a blind attempt to turn off the awful buzzing noise. Hadn't he turned all his alarms off last night? He wasn't going into work until noon because he'd have practice with the worship band until 8:00 tonight. He stared at his phone alarm. The time displayed was 8:30 a.m., but he didn't want to be awake yet.

He continued staring. It wasn't his alarm but his phone buzzing with calls and text messages. He couldn't make sense of all the notifications, and the number kept increasing. If this was an awful group text, he was going to be mad.

> I'm so proud of you. Call me!

Sam squinted to make sure he was reading that right. What on earth had he done while he was sleeping to make his dad proud?

> So happy for you, little brother. Call me when you get a chance.

> Congratulations Sam! You deserve this. I can't wait to celebrate with you.

Okay, now they had his attention. As he scanned the dozens of texts, most included a variation of congratulations. He picked up the phone to call Dad to see what this was all about, but an incoming phone call rang first.

Sam tapped the phone to accept the call, but before he could even say hello, Nate shouted into the phone. "Wow, Sam, can you believe it? Well, actually, I can. You deserve this, buddy. And I can't wait —"

"Wait, stop!" Sam exclaimed. "*What's* going on? I woke up to a million texts, and I have no idea what anyone is talking about."

"Stop it, Sam!" His friend Michael laughed in the background, apparently on speaker phone with Nate. "Be serious. You haven't heard?"

"Heard what? All I heard was my phone going off, waking me up too early." Sam's voice rose, and he threw his free hand up. He moved to his walk-in closet and searched for adequate pants and a shirt, his phone speaker turned way up. Fully awake, he might as well get dressed.

"I guess we get the privilege of telling you then. Are you sitting down?" Tara asked.

"Tara is there too? Umm, yeah, I can't wait to hear about this wonderful thing I've done that everyone knows about except for me." He wanted to start this whole day over by getting the sleep he'd planned for.

"Okay, maybe you won't be so grumpy after we tell you." Tara laughed.

He ignored her comment.

"Are you ready?" Nate asked but didn't wait for Sam's response. "They just announced the American Christian Music Awards, and you're up for songwriter of the year."

"Right, uh-huh, now tell me the real reason you're calling me so early."

"He's serious, Sam!" Michael shouted. "Plus, song of the year for the song you wrote that Caleb Hartley recorded. It's a songwriter's award."

Sam ran his hand through his hair and held it back, away from his forehead. No way. He'd only been writing seriously for a couple of years. Sure, some of his songs had been picked up by big name artists, and Christian radio and streaming were playing them. But still.

"Sam, you still there?" Nate asked.

"Uh-huh, yeah, I'm here. Are you sure? Songwriter of the year? And song of the year?" Sam asked.

"Yes, yes, yes!" Tara and Michael yelled in the background. "Do you think your phone is blowing up right now because we're all mistaken?"

Sam dropped to his bed, pants half on, half off. He couldn't wrap his head around it. "I can't believe it. You're serious?"

"We wouldn't kid you about this, buddy." Michael said.

"We're so proud." All three chimed in.

"Thanks, you guys. I can't believe this." Sam ran his free hand through his tangled bed-hair. *Should I even be happy about this, though?*

Almost six years ago, God had rescued him and told Sam to live for Him. And that day, Sam promised God he would spend his life doing just that. He was determined to make his life point to Jesus.

"I'm not sure about this. How do accolades fit in with doing work for God?" he asked.

"I get what you're saying," Nate said.

His friend knew him well. They'd had several discussions about keeping God front and center when performing.

"Sam, you're the humblest person I know. You don't even realize you deserve this nomination, but you do. The key is to stay humble, like we've talked about."

Sam agreed with the staying humble part, but it still struck him as weird. The nominations made his heart soar, but he struggled with that. He needed to talk to Mom and Dad—the most devout Christians he'd ever met. Besides, Dad had received his share of accolades over the years as a college basketball coach.

"Yeah, you're right. I'm grateful, for sure." Sam forced his bubbly voice and positive words and thanked his friends for calling him. Then he hung up and called Dad.

* * *

Lauren settled onto the deck of her Nashville apartment to work on her next feature for the *Tennessean*. Another unseasonable, seventy-one-degree day in early November, and she intended to take full advantage. She situated herself at the round table on her deck with her peppermint tea. Her wire-haired dachshund, Daisy, lay in her little dog bed near the corner of the deck. From there, she could watch all the happenings below and get sun on her little belly.

Lauren lifted her face toward the light breeze blowing through her hair. Life was getting better. She still had to work through some things, but she felt like her old self again. In fact, perhaps she should ask Sam over to her apartment. He hadn't been here yet. Plus, he loved dogs, and he'd never met Daisy.

Her phone chimed, as if on cue. An incoming text from Sam. He thanked her for calling him earlier about the American Christian Music Awards and asked if she wanted to get together one evening.

She flipped the phone over on the table and stared at the back. But why? After all, she was just thinking about asking him over, so what was the problem? Before she could spend time pondering that question, she picked up her phone again and texted him.

> Do u wanna come over and see my apartment tonight? And meet my DOG?

She hit Send before she could change her mind.
Sam texted back.

You got a dog? Yes! I'll pick up a pizza.

They settled on a time, and Lauren turned her attention to her feature story. But she couldn't concentrate and squeezed her eyes shut. What if Sam asked questions about her time in New York, or worse yet, why she left? She wasn't ready for that.

But she'd have to come clean, especially if she wanted to be best friends again. And she did. But the truth was, she yearned for more than that. She'd always wanted more, but Sam had been through a lot, and the timing was never right. Yes, if she wanted any kind of relationship with him, she'd have to tell him everything. She'd do it in little pieces, starting tonight.

seventeen

Sam entered the lobby of the athletic center on the TU campus and followed the sounds of basketballs bouncing, then a whistle blowing and his dad yelling. He laughed. Like the first time he'd visited his dad on campus back when he was a foster kid and he had no clue how big of a deal his dad was in the college basketball world. Now he was aware, but not because Dad had ever told him or even hinted. The man was the ultimate in humility. And Sam's role model for sure.

After slipping in unnoticed, Sam climbed to the second level of bleachers, sat, and watched. John Grayson was well respected and set a great example as a Christian. If Sam could be half the man Dad was, he'd be grateful. His thoughts wandered to his birth dad, and a chill ran down his spine. Another letter from him arrived today. This one was marked Urgent—Please Open on the front. He could sense the man begging him to open the letter.

So far, Sam hadn't opened any of the other letters. Ever since he talked to his mom and dad, he hadn't been too tempted to read them. It was wrong for them to hide them, but he understood a little better why they did. Now he had the letters in his possession so he could read them if he wanted. And the one marked Urgent beckoned him.

What could the man have to say to Sam that could be so urgent? His biological father was a drug dealer, a child abuser, a human trafficker, and he'd stolen Sam's childhood. The only good thing that came of it all was Sam being fostered and adopted by the Graysons.

They were the family he wouldn't allow himself to dream of when he was a kid. And now they were his mom and dad. God gave him more than he ever asked for, more than he ever dreamed. There was the verse again. It'd been on his heart ever since the American Christian Music Award nominations. *Now all glory to God, who is able, through all his mighty power at work within us, to accomplish infinitely more than we might ask or think.*

"Hey." The voice startled him back to the present. Dad climbed the bleachers toward him, and the players walked off the floor. Practice was over.

"Oh, sorry." Sam chuckled. "I was in my own little world."

Dad punched his shoulder lightly. "C'mon, let's get out of here and get something to eat."

They trekked to Dad's car and drove to a local deli off campus. His dad generally liked to go there when he wanted to sit and eat without being bothered. People on and near campus were used to seeing him around and didn't pay much attention, which was nice.

They ordered sandwiches, sat at a quiet table in the corner, and ate. "Are you doing okay? You've been quiet since those awards were announced." His dad sipped his cola.

Sam took a deep breath. He didn't want to appear ungrateful for the nomination. But he needed his dad's take on the whole thing. "It's been weird, I guess. I don't feel right about it."

Dad tilted his head and shrugged. "What don't you feel right about?"

Sam wasn't sure he could put his feeling into words, which was ironic. "On the night at church with Hannah, when I gave my life to God, I audibly heard God say He would give me a life that would glorify Him. So, I guess my dilemma is I'm being nominated for awards, and I don't feel like the attention should be on me. It feels wrong. All the attention should be on God."

His dad slowly nodded. "I can understand. I guess I hadn't thought of it that way. You want my opinion?"

"Of course."

Dad swallowed the last bite of his sandwich and guzzled more cola. "I think this nomination is an opportunity for you to honor God."

Sam tilted his head. "What do you mean?"

"Over the last few years, before you became a professional songwriter, we've watched as your music has spread. Worship leaders have come to our church and then went back to their own churches and played songs you've written. Do you remember on vacation we attended that church in Florida last year, and they sang one of your songs?" Dad flashed his brightest smile.

"Yeah, I almost passed out. I couldn't believe it." Sam beamed.

"I remember. You were still in college, long before you published any songs," Dad said. "So just think, your music, which honors God, is now being sung by the biggest names in Christian music. *And* a big-time country music singer. Your worship songs are being sung all over the country, and even in some other countries, because of that."

"I'm good with all that. I feel like the songs honor God. It's the awards I'm unsure about."

Dad shifted in his chair and leaned toward him. "Think about it this way. If your songs are nominated or win awards, your name gets out there even more. Those songs spread farther and farther. Which means the knowledge of our God, who you sing about, spreads even more."

He'd never thought about it that way.

"The key is to stay humble," Dad continued. "We just studied a verse in the book of James. It says, '*God opposes the proud, but gives grace to the humble.*'"

"I love that. I need to write that one down." He thought about what Dad said about the name of God and spreading knowledge of Him. "Wow, that's pretty amazing when you put it like that."

"And don't you worry, your mom and me will keep you accountable in being humble." John laughed.

"I'm counting on it."

eighteen

Sam pulled up to Lauren's apartment building and scanned the numbers. Apartment number 211. In the right corner of the building facing the woods. He looked up at her deck. Something moved beneath her table and chairs, and he squinted. A very long, low-to-the ground, brown and tan dog with a ferocious bark. Sam laughed.

He walked around to the passenger side of his SUV, retrieved the pizza from the floorboard, and picked up the flowers he'd bought at the grocery store this afternoon. Nothing fancy, just wildflowers Lauren might like.

He headed up the stairwell and took several deep breaths. He'd never been nervous around Lauren before, but she acted differently since she'd returned from New York. Still. Even after her confession about her move home, there had to be more she was hiding. He shook off the feeling and pushed the button beside the door. The doorbell rang followed by ferocious barking.

The door opened, and there she stood. Even in jeans and a sweatshirt, she took his breath away.

"C'mon in." She flashed that same bright smile he'd known for years.

Sam relaxed his shoulders, handed her the yellow and orange fall bouquet, and followed her inside.

"Aww, thank you. These are beautiful." She reached above her refrigerator for a vase. "You remembered I love wildflowers."

"I did." He placed the pizza box on her kitchen counter and reached down to scoop up the long, short-legged dog.

"That's Miss Daisy." Lauren raised an eyebrow and laughed.

"Well, hello, Miss Daisy." He petted the fluffy pup while she licked his face. She tried to wiggle out of his arms, and he placed her back on the floor. The little dog zoomed around the apartment while they laughed. "I've never seen a hairy dachshund before."

"She's a wire hair. Often their hair is bristly, but hers is soft. And she's a lot of fun." Lauren laughed while her dog completed her round of zoomies.

"She's super cute. Leave it to you to get an abnormal dog."

Lauren punched him lightly on the arm like she used to do. "C'mon, I'll show you the rest of the place."

Lauren seemed more like her old self as she showed him her two-bedroom apartment. She was proud of the spare bedroom she'd turned into an office to do her work for the *Tennessean* and a novel she was writing.

"This is great, Laur. I love your desk in front of the window and all your bookshelves. It's a great office."

"Thanks. I spend hours at a time in here. C'mon, let's eat before the pizza gets cold."

They lounged on the living room sofa and ate their pizza while a Christmas movie played on TV.

"You're like my mom. Christmas movies before Thanksgiving." He teased.

"Well, it *is* November." Lauren shrugged.

They finished their pizza, and Daisy fell asleep on the sofa between them. The conversation was easy. He hadn't known what to expect.

"Hey, Laur." He didn't want to spoil the mood, but he had to know. "Why'd you leave New York?"

The smile left her face. She turned away for a second before meeting his gaze and took a deep breath. "You know, at first, I loved New York. It was exciting there. Always something to do, anytime day or night. And NYU ... it was my dream ever since I can remember. But now I can't remember why."

"I know. Because you wanted to write, and NYU and New York City seemed like the best place."

Lauren grabbed her water bottle. "I guess it was, for a while. But to be honest, it was hard to be myself there. I didn't have many Christian friends. Even the church I joined didn't seem truly invested, and I quit going. I kind of rebelled."

Was that why she'd stopped texting and calling him? Even when he texted her, the replies were shorter and less frequent. He wanted to ask, but he let her talk.

"And I met a guy there."

Now we're getting somewhere. "I wondered if you were involved with someone when you stopped texting me."

"Yeah. I was." Her face fell. Would she cry?

"So, you miss him."

Her head snapped in his direction, her mouth open. "No, not at all. In fact, I wish I'd never been involved with him."

He didn't understand. "Did he hurt you in some way?"

"No, nothing like that. It's just that ..." She breathed in deeply. "It's so hard to tell you this."

Sam's heart thudded in his chest, and he didn't know what to say. He questioned whether he wanted to know what was so bad she didn't want to tell him. "It's okay. You know you can tell me anything, right? But if you're not ready, that's fine too." In a way, he hoped she wouldn't.

"I feel like I need to tell you in order for our friendship to move forward." She blew out a breath and peered at the ceiling. "By not telling you, I'm lying about who I am." A tear slid down her cheek, and she turned away.

"Hey." Sam reached for her hand. "Whatever it is, it's okay. You know I won't judge you, don't you? No matter what, you're still my friend. Look at all the stuff I've been through, and you've never judged me."

"But none of what you went through was your fault. I deliberately made poor choices that were no one's fault but my own."

Ideas formed in his mind about what she may have done. *Don't jump to conclusions.*

She gazed at the ceiling, as if trying to compose herself. "You know, I thought I was so grounded in my faith. But when things got tough, I stepped away completely."

"What do you mean?"

"I forgot everything I ever stood for." Her shoulders slumped. "I started dating an older man."

Sam's heart sped up at the older part. "Okay, well that's not so bad. Was he like seventy-five? Eighty?"

"No, Sam. When I said older, I meant thirty." She laughed, but a single tear trickled down her cheek. Daisy stirred and looked up but then laid her head back on the sofa and sighed.

"Well, see, I told you it wouldn't be so bad." Sam said, even though thoughts about her relationship with the thirty-year-old hijacked his mind.

"There's more to the story." As hard as she tried, she couldn't make eye contact. "He was married."

That actually wasn't one of the scenarios in Sam's head. He wasn't sure whether this one was better or worse. "So, you began dating this man and didn't know he was married?"

"No, that's not it." Lauren slowly shook her head and studied the floor. "I knew he was married when I got into the relationship. I knew ... from the beginning."

Sam sucked in a breath and wrapped his head around what she'd said. Back when he'd been living with his birth father, something like this wouldn't have shocked him. But being a Christian and seeing marriage the way John and Abbie lived it, and even Kyle and Cassie in their new marriage, this was a shock. He didn't know what to say. He couldn't say he understood because he didn't. "So, what happened?"

Lauren stayed silent for a few minutes. Would she even continue? After a moment, she put her hand to her mouth and spoke. "His wife found out about us. She confronted me in a restaurant in front of others. At a work event with coworkers from the *Times*. I was horrified."

He stared at her and didn't know what to say or ask. The scenarios in his head all ran cold.

"But what happened after is what I'll regret most."

He couldn't imagine what was next, but she didn't shy away. She met his gaze this time.

"I begged him to leave her." Tears flowed down her cheeks. "They had a baby, Sam, and I *begged* him to leave his wife. What kind of person does that?"

His shock gave way to sorrow. Only one kind of person who'd do that, and it hurt him to say it. "The kind that's in love."

Lauren wiped her tears with the back of her hand and stared at the floor. "You know, at the time I thought I was, but now that I'm separated from it, I know I wasn't. I was so mixed up. He broke up with me, and for a few weeks, I was devastated. That's when I decided I needed to be back here in Tennessee. Back with my parents, and back to my faith."

It was a lot to take in. "Where are you in your faith now?" He'd sensed her slipping away for a long time now. This explained her behavior, but he wanted to know which way she was heading. Closer, or farther away.

She wiped the tears away again and attempted a smile, but it fell short. "I'm trying to get it back, but I need your help. I need your friendship more than ever, Sam. But I'd understand if you don't want to be friends anymore after what I've told you, and how I treated you."

How could she even think he wouldn't be her friend because of this? "Of course, I'm still your friend, Lauren." He wanted time to process everything Lauren had said about her faith, and that guy. "I'll always be your friend."

She sniffled. "Thank you. You're still the best friend I've ever had."

Her green eyes still dazzled him, even through the tears. And despite everything she'd told him. "And you've always been mine, and you always will."

They chatted more about her decision to come back and how she loved writing for the *Tennessean*. Even if it wasn't as elite as the *New York Times*, she felt grounded there, and she was glad to reconnect in a good way with her parents. She'd always thought they were too strict, but now she understood why.

When Sam rose to leave, he and Lauren shared a hug. Like old times. "Think about coming to Bible study tomorrow night. Nate and Tara will be there and other girls I think you'd like a lot. Only seven of us total."

"I'll text you tomorrow." She led him to the door.

Sam tilted his head and gazed at her. His heart was lighter, not so much because of her words, but her smile—the one he'd missed so much.

* * *

Sam came home and marched straight to his room. On his desk, staring him in the face, was the letter. The one marked Urgent—Please Read. He picked it up and examined it closer. He turned it over and started to open it but had second thoughts. The ones he'd already read confused him and still clouded his mind.

Instead, he pushed the letter aside and picked up his journal and guitar. He opened the journal and read the lyrics he'd written last night. A decent start, but only halfway done. He strummed the chords and quietly sung the words, stopping occasionally to erase and change a word.

Who was he kidding? This song wasn't going anywhere. It didn't feel genuine. Something prevented him from giving his full attention. Something on his desk. He swallowed hard and set his guitar aside, closed the journal, and snatched the letter that begged him to open it.

The envelope felt thicker than the others he'd skimmed over in the box of letters. He rested on the edge of his bed and turned it over and over in his hands. What was he so afraid of? His father was in prison, and these were mere words on a page. He couldn't hurt him anymore.

After removing the letter from the envelope, Sam unfolded it and drew a deep breath.

Dear Sam,

I don't know whether you read any of my letters or are even getting them. So, I'll start from the beginning like always. I'm sorry, Sam. I'm sorry for all the horrible things I've put you through. I don't expect you to ever forgive me, but I have to let you know I'm sorry.

I've been following your music career. I'm so proud of you. Not so much for the music part of it—although I am so proud of that—but more because of your faith in God and the way it comes through in your music. I'm amazed you can do that after all you've been through. I guess more than anything I want to talk to you about how you have that kind of faith.

I've been going to a Bible study here, and I got saved. I still feel like my faith is so small compared to yours. I'm sure you been through things I don't even know about, but your faith is strong, and you share it with others. I'd like the chance to talk to you about God and faith and everything going on with you. And I want to tell you I'm sorry in person.

I pray someday I'll see you again and you'll see me as more than a deadbeat dad. You don't owe me anything, that's for sure. But I'd sure like to see you.

Take care,

Andy (Drew)

Sam gripped the letter and shoved his head between his knees. *Just breathe.* He faintly heard a knocking sound but couldn't figure out where it came from.

"Hey, I didn't hear you come home—Sam, what's wrong?"

Mom asked. Her voice sounded far away, but she touched his arm. "Are you all right?"

"Uh-huh, yeah." He lifted his head in time to see Dad enter the room.

"What's going on?"

He had to pull himself together. If they thought he was this upset about one of Andy's letters, that would prove his dad's point about hiding them. He reached for the water bottle on his desk and guzzled it.

"Are you not feeling well?" Mom placed her hand on his forehead.

Sam shook his head, which made him dizzy again, but he strained a smile. "No, I'm fine, just tired." But he followed her gaze to his own hand, which clutched the letter.

"A letter from Andy Quinn." She frowned.

He took another swig from his water bottle. "I want you both to read it and tell me what you think."

Dad pulled out Sam's desk chair and sat. Once he read the letter, he passed it to Mom.

Sam bit his lip and tried to steady his breath.

She finished reading it and handed it back to Sam.

"Well, what do you think?"

Neither said anything for a long moment. Dad cleared his throat. "I don't know if I believe him. He's been trouble for many years. I'd like to think he's changed, but I doubt it."

Sam flinched and had no idea why. Was there part of him that wanted Quinn's words to be true so he could reconnect with his biological father? He stared at the floor and tried to gather his thoughts.

"I don't know, honestly, but I agree with your dad."

"Don't you think God can turn him around?" The desperation Sam heard in his own voice surprised him.

"Of course, I do, hon. Nothing is impossible with God. But we don't know Andy's heart. Only God does."

"Your mom is right," Dad said. "But knowing Andy like I

have for years, I've never seen anything in him to think he might change."

Sam's head hurt, and his parents' words confused him even more. They always saw the good in people. Maybe they were right, and there was no good whatsoever in his birth father.

He needed to be alone with his thoughts. And most of all he needed to pray for direction concerning Andy Quinn.

nineteen

L auren submitted her article to her editor and waited. She walked to the counter and ordered a second cup of coffee. She'd work on her novel at the coffee shop while she waited to hear back from her editor. It could be an hour, or several, depending on how backed up her editor, Chantal, was today.

She re-read the text from Sam asking her about Bible study tonight and sighed. After Sam came over and they'd cleared the air, things were a lot better. She'd told him about her ex-boyfriend, and Sam had been so sweet about it. She sensed more of a connection with him than ever before.

She started to text him but stopped. She placed her phone on the table and put her head in her hands. How could she possibly go to Bible study with him? Her presence would be an insult to God. She shook her head, and her eyes brimmed with tears. Someone as entrenched in sin as she was couldn't sit before God in a Bible study.

Still, she wanted to see Sam. Maybe she could see him afterward. A plan formed. She texted and said she was busy tonight but could meet up with him tomorrow for a walk at their favorite park. She waited for his reply.

He agreed. They'd meet tomorrow at lunchtime at the park near Middle Tennessee Church where he worked, and they'd eat sack lunches at a shelter house. It was going to be another unseasonably warm November day, a beautiful day to be outside. And it would get her out of Bible study tonight. But what about next week? And the week after?

* * *

The following day, Sam sat with Lauren at the small shelter house by the pond, and they ate turkey sandwiches from the local deli. The warm fall breeze and filtered sunshine thawed him after being in his air-conditioned office. It was nice to be with her like this.

She was almost back to her normal self. Almost. Something was still off, but he chalked it up to them being apart for so long. Each time they got together would be less awkward. And what he was about to ask would either make it less or more uncomfortable. He was unsure which way it would go.

She talked about her article that would be published tomorrow and how excited she was about it. He couldn't stop smiling. She found what she loved to do, just like he had with writing of a different kind. Songwriting.

They threw their trash away and set out for a short jaunt around the pond. The fall colors were past their peak. Most leaves were deep shades of burgundy or brown. He loved this time of year, and wished he could hang out here all day. But a quick glance at his watch told him he needed to leave in twenty minutes to make it back to church for a 1:30 ministry meeting. It was now or never.

"Hey Lauren, I wanna ask you something." He came to an abrupt stop.

After stopping too, she turned toward him. She removed the rubber band from her wrist and twisted it around her long, blonde hair.

"Sure, what is it?" Lauren continued to fight with her hair. She laughed, but he thought she'd never looked prettier.

"Okay, so you know the American Christian Music awards are coming up in February." Sam paused.

"Yeah, I'm so excited for you. Are you getting nervous?"

Her question derailed his train of thought. "Umm, I don't know, a little. People keep telling me I need to write an acceptance speech in case I win." He grimaced. "I can't imagine I would, but everyone says that's a speech you don't want to improvise. So, I'll have to get something ready." He shrugged and stuck his hands in his pockets.

"I think you're going to win." Her smile was genuine. "So, you'd better get that speech ready."

Heat rose to his face. "I don't know about that. But I wanted to ask you if, umm, well, if you'd be my date for the night." There. He said it.

"What night?" She stared blankly.

He'd messed this up so badly that she didn't even know what he was talking about. "The night of the American Christian Music Awards. Will you go with me? Of course, we'll also go to dinner. It'll be a whole night. I guess like a date," he stammered.

"Yes, I'd be honored." Her cheeks turned bright pink, probably matching his.

He didn't realize he'd been holding his breath until he let it out. "Okay, great. When it gets closer, I'll figure out what time we need to go to dinner and all that and let you know."

"That sounds amazing. And I guess I'll go shopping for a dress." She grinned.

They chatted as they finished their circle around the pond, and he walked her to her car.

"Thanks, this was nice."

"Thank you for saying yes." He swallowed and then remembered to smile. He'd actually asked Lauren on a date. For a second, he thought about kissing her, but instead he hugged her like he'd done a thousand times before.

Driving back to church, it occurred to him that this would be their first ever date in the more than ten years they'd known each other. He hoped he wouldn't do anything to mess it up.

twenty

"Here's the last of it." Kyle said.

"Thanks for doing that for me. I don't like going up and down that ladder." Abbie was thankful he'd gotten the Christmas decorations out of the attic for her. John was in Florida preparing for a basketball tournament, and she'd meet him there this weekend. But first, she wanted to get her Christmas decorations up.

"You shouldn't be going up on that ladder at all, Mom. That's what I'm here for, or Sam. Where is he anyway?" Kyle asked.

"He's at church. They're practicing their Christmas set."

"Ah, that makes sense." Kyle brushed the attic dust off his pants. "It's hard to believe Christmas is in three weeks. By the way, I've been wanting to ask about the letters from Andy Quinn. Has he read them, not read them, what's going on with that? I haven't really talked to Sam any more about it."

"Let's go sit at the bar, and I'll tell you." They walked to the kitchen together. Kyle got water for them both and sat on the bar stool. "And here you go, chocolate chip cookies I made last night." She slid the platter in front of Kyle.

"With nuts, my favorite." He grabbed two and put them on a napkin.

Abbie winked, crossed her arms on the counter in front of her, and told Kyle what the letter said. "Your dad and I both said we didn't think he'd changed. That it would be hard for him to make that radical of a change."

"Yeah? And what did Sam say?" Kyle asked between bites of cookie.

"He didn't say a lot that night. But since then, anytime we've brought the letters up, he changes the subject. It's clear he doesn't want to discuss them with us anymore."

"Mm-hmm. Do you think he's read them all?"

"That's what we were wondering. Last night during dinner, your dad asked him if he'd read any more, and Sam didn't answer. Instead, he shocked us." She twirled one of her long, brown curls around her index finger. This next part was hard to say out loud. "He's decided to visit Andy."

Kyle stopped mid-chew, his mouth full. "What? He's going to the prison to visit him?"

"Yes, tomorrow." Abbie grimaced.

"Tomorrow? Wow, I don't know what to say." Kyle's mouth was still full, but he slowly started chewing again. "What did you and Dad say when he told you?"

"We were shocked like you are. We thought he might decide to write to him, but visit? We never dreamed he'd want to visit Quinn. Neither of us is happy about it. Especially your dad. Honestly, he feels betrayed."

Kyle pushed the cookie platter away and sat back in his chair. "I can see that, after all the bad stuff he's gone through with Quinn, even before Sam came along."

Abbie nodded. "That, and I think he feels like it's a slap in the face after all he's done for Sam trying to save him from Quinn, you know?"

"Yeah, I get that. Does it feel that way to you too?"

Abbie sat back, her eyes focused on the space between her and Kyle. She went on to tell him about the couple at church, Maggie and Ron. "Yeah, I do. But I also understand why he's doing it. He just wants answers. Answers about everything that man put him through, the girls in Alabama, and whether he's truly changed."

"And I'm guessing one of his biggest questions is why his father never loved him and gave him up as easily as he did."

"Yes, I'm sure that's *the* big one."

"I hope he gets the answers he's looking for."

Abbie hoped and prayed for Sam and John to find peace no matter how things played out between their youngest son and Andy Quinn.

* * *

Nothing about it felt like the week before Christmas. Not the weather, not his family, and not what he was doing today.

Sam turned off the radio station and clicked on his music app playlist. No Christmas music today. He'd drive three hours to FCI Memphis to visit Andy Quinn. That was way too much time to think.

Sam had pulled out of the driveway without his mom and dad's blessing.

Since well before his adoption, he'd lived and breathed by their advice and guidance. But this time, they were wrong. Perhaps they thought Andy Quinn was incapable of turning his life around. But didn't that go against everything they'd taught him about God, and how the Bible taught that with Him, everything is possible. For some reason, they didn't think that applied to his birth father.

Sam clenched his teeth, glanced at his side mirror, and merged onto I-40 West. He needed to see Andy in person to find out if the man had changed. They hadn't called each other lately. That would have been too awkward. Instead, Andy had written with possible visitation dates, and they'd settled on today.

At least Lauren supported his decision. They'd talked about

it at length. She didn't know everything Andy had put him through in his childhood, but he'd told her some of it. She was hesitant at first when he told her about the visit, but the more they talked, the more she understood Sam's need to see him.

Why couldn't his parents do the same? Lauren thought maybe they were threatened by a relationship forming between him and Andy. He couldn't understand why they would feel that way. No matter how this turned out, John would always be Sam's father in every way that counted, and of course, Abbie would always be his mother.

But Sam longed to know why Andy had never wanted him, had never wanted to be a parent to him. His mind drifted back to the day when he was seventeen, a few months before his adoption by John and Abbie. They'd told him Andy Quinn wasn't going to contest the adoption. He signed over his parental rights instantly when asked.

Sam would've been eighteen in a matter of months, and they wouldn't have needed his consent. It wouldn't have mattered. But the fact Andy had signed off without a second thought had hurt him to the core. No matter how much his parents loved him and how much he wanted to be part of their family, it still hurt. And that hurt had burned a hole inside of him.

He'd always needed answers, and, hopefully, this was the start of getting them.

twenty-one

After a short stop to gas up and grab a cola in Lexington, Tennessee, Sam made it to the prison in a little over three hours. He pulled into the visitors parking lot, got out and stretched, and then left his jacket in the car. One less thing. His stomach was in knots. He'd love to turn around and go back home, but he couldn't. He needed to do this.

Once inside, a prison guard approached and asked to see his identification and his approved visitation paperwork. Next, he asked Sam to stand behind the gate while the guard walked the items over to a computer. The man came back and gave him a tag with his name and Andy Quinn's and directed Sam to walk through the metal detector. Just like at the airport, he put his keys and his shoes in a container. The guard gave his scanned items back, and then Sam followed him through several sets of automatic doors.

Sweat beads rolled down his forehead. Maybe he wasn't prepared for this visit after all. How would he feel when he stared into the face of Andy Quinn? The man he'd known as Drew Keller, or simply his father. Sam stopped in his tracks. This was a bad idea. He should've listened to his real mom and dad and not come. What on earth was he doing here?

"You okay?" The guard turned around from about ten feet ahead.

Sam remained frozen, yet he wanted to turn and run. What had made him want to come here anyway? "I think I need a minute."

The guard, who appeared not much older than Sam, stepped toward him. "Your first time here, huh?"

All Sam could do was nod.

"Well, I can't tell you what to do, but I saw you came from Nashville. You drove at least three hours. Just to remind you, there'll be several guards in the room. And you can leave any time. But if you don't want to go in, I can take you back now."

He was right. There would be guards present, and he could leave whenever he wanted. The first step would be the hardest— the part where he met his birth father for the first time in nearly six years. Since those days in Alabama. No, he couldn't let his mind go there, or he wouldn't go in. *Please God, tell me what to do.*

A strength from within him propelled him forward. "I'm going." He nodded to the guard.

Sam entered the visitation room, and the door locked behind him. He searched the room, and at a table near the concrete wall with a barred window at the top sat the man who used to be his father. His biological father. He swallowed hard.

The man appeared a lot older than his forty-three years. His short, cropped hair was mostly gray, and he seemed smaller than Sam remembered.

Please be with me, Lord. Sam willed himself to put one foot in front of the other until about five feet separated him from Andy Quinn.

"Sam." Andy smiled, an unfamiliar look for him. "Can I give you a hug?"

"Umm, how about a handshake?" Sam extended his hand.

Andy reached to shake his hand, squeezing it as if he didn't want to let go, but Sam pulled away.

"Umm, I'm not sure what to call you." Sam sat at the table,

careful to maintain his distance. "I can't call you Dad because you're not my father anymore, and I feel weird calling you Andy because I never knew you by that name."

Andy hung his head before looking into Sam's eyes. "Thank you for coming here. I can't tell you how much it means. I know the name thing's weird, but why don't you just call me Andy?"

Sam tried to ignore his thundering heartbeat and the sweat that beaded on his forehead. *Calm down, Sam.* He was at a loss, unable to remember the things he wanted to say and all the questions he wanted to ask. He exhaled a held breath. "I don't know. Maybe it wasn't a good idea for me to come."

"Don't say that. I'm glad you came. I wanted you to see I've changed in my time here." Andy said.

"Changed how?" Sam tilted his head and folded his arms across his chest. At least the man spoke to him. He couldn't remember a single conversation they'd had when Sam lived with him. Ever.

"You changed me, Sam. I've been following your worship ministry, and your songs. When I first heard your songs, I couldn't believe they were about God, and to God, after all the things you went through as a kid. Because of you, I attended the church service here, and a Bible study. I even go through my Bible to find the verses your songs refer to." Andy's voice quivered.

Sam studied him intently. He seemed sincere. He had to be, or he wouldn't even realize the songs were based on Bible verses, right?

"What I'm trying to say, I guess, is I've given my life to God." Tears flowed down the man's face.

Sam had never seen him cry, and he wanted to believe him. He had never heard him even speak the name of God until the letter. *Is this real, God? I have to know.*

But this time, no Bible verse came to mind. No answer from God in any form. "How do I know you're telling the truth?"

"All I can tell you, Sam, is if we can stay in touch after today,

I'll prove to you through my words and actions I'm telling you the truth. And I want to start by apologizing. For everything," Andy said. "Did you read my letters?"

Sam shrugged. "Only a couple."

"Well, they were all about the same since I wasn't sure whether you were getting them. I was a terrible father, the worst. I was so wrapped up in the drug business and schemed to get money. I made that my priority. Actually, I made it my whole life and neglected you because of it." Andy hung his head and appeared to compose himself. "It's my biggest regret. And I'll spend the rest of my life trying to make it up to you if you'll let me."

Maybe I'm being too harsh. But no, he wouldn't let sympathy toward the man take hold. "Well, you know you're not my dad anymore, so I'm not sure how you're going to do that."

Sam wasn't about to let him off easy, and he wasn't going to tell him he'd long ago forgiven him. He had to, or it would've eaten him up. His counselor had told him forgiving his father was for Sam's sake, not his father's. Sam needed to forgive him to move on with his life.

"I don't know either, but if we can stay in touch, maybe we can be friends."

"Friends?" That word sure hit wrong. Sam laughed and slapped the metal table with both hands. Anger surged from a place he'd forgotten existed. "How do you expect me to be friends with you when you used to be my father, but you decided you didn't want to be that anymore, so you just signed me away?"

Andy turned his head as if he'd been slapped, then quickly hung his head. "Look, kiddo, I've made a total mess of my life. Back all the way to my first memories, I was always messing everything up. But with God, I feel like I'm on the right path now. That's all I know to tell you."

"Don't ever call me kiddo." Something in him snapped. That's what John, his real father now, called him.

"You need to wrap it up in the next five minutes." The guard interjected then returned to his spot near the back of the room.

Sam didn't need five minutes. He'd heard enough. He stood and motioned for the guard. "I need time to think about things."

"I understand." Andy stared at the table. "If I can ask one thing, would you please go back and read all my letters, especially the ones from the past year. I think you'll see more clearly how I've changed."

Sam wasn't ready to commit. He turned and walked toward the guard.

"Have a Merry Christmas, Sam," Andy yelled.

Sam paused, but didn't turn around, and the guard led him out of the visitation room.

twenty-two

Sam's Closet wasn't normally open on Saturdays, but Abbie and Wendy decided to open for half days on Saturday during the Christmas season. And they were glad they did. Their business was booming, and it wasn't just clothing that was selling.

It was heartwarming to see some of these kids come in and buy books and CDs for their family and friends. And they were so proud they could do it with just their allowance money, or what little cash they had from an after-school job. As an added plus, the shop was extremely busy, and that helped get her mind off Sam and his trip to the federal prison in Memphis today.

She and Wendy closed shop at noon and drove to the Cool Springs Galleria together for last-minute Christmas shopping. On the way, Wendy commented on all the beautiful Christmas decorations downtown. Garland and lights adorned the storefronts and lamp posts. But Abbie had so much on her mind she wouldn't have even noticed if Wendy hadn't pointed them out.

They arrived at the Galleria to find impatient shoppers standing shoulder to shoulder in line at every store, while Christmas music piped in through speakers. It took much longer than they counted on to make the few purchases they each wanted to make. They laughed at each other for being surprised by that. Finally, they finished and made the long trek back through the parking lot to Abbie's car. The weather was nice for December. Sunny and mid-fifties, although Abbie would've preferred snow. But that hardly ever happened in middle Tennessee.

The car beeped as she pointed her key fob at it, and the trunk popped open. She and Wendy loaded their packages. Abbie had bought a pair of pants for John, some boots for Sam, a casual dinnerware set for Kyle and Cassie, and some personal care items for Hannah. Nothing any of them needed for sure. Technically, she'd already finished her shopping, but like every year, she added a few last-minute items.

She started the car, and they headed toward Newk's for lunch and some girl talk before they stopped for the day.

"You know, with us having a shop together, I envisioned us chatting all day long. But I think we talk less now than before." Wendy reached toward the dash to adjust the heat vent.

Abbie glanced at her friend. Wendy was her lifeline. They'd been friends for over forty years, and best friends for much of that time. There was hardly anything they hadn't been through together.

"I thought the same thing, and boy, were we wrong." Abbie laughed. "But it's a good reason, at least. I mean, did you ever imagine the shop would've taken off like it has so far?"

Wendy pointed up. "It's all God. You and I couldn't have done this."

"Mm-hmm, you're right about that." They pulled into Newk's and were fortunate to get a close parking spot out front. When they walked in, they even found their favorite booth empty.

"Wow I'm tired! I can't believe we had people lined up at both registers all morning." Wendy yawned once they were situated at the table with their drinks. She was stunning with her purple jacket and her dark hair newly highlighted. "Thanks for lunch. It's on me next time."

Abbie waved her off. "It's the least I could do based on the number of texts you've had to read from me lately."

Wendy's expression transitioned to concern. "I hadn't wanted to be the first to bring it up. Today's the day, huh?"

"Yes," Abbie sighed. She peeked at her watch. "He should be there by now."

"How are you feeling?"

Abbie paused while the server brought their soup and sandwiches. "Hmm. For starters, worried about our relationship with Sam since we spoke out against him visiting Quinn. Honestly Wendy, you know everything there is to know about the situation. Do you think John and I are wrong?" She could count on her friend to answer truthfully.

"Honestly," Wendy hesitated, "no, I don't think you're wrong. If I were in your shoes, I'm certain I'd feel the same way."

Abbie nodded.

"But," Wendy began.

"But?" Now she was concerned.

"My only *but* is, I think I understand why Sam wants to see the man."

"You do?" Abbie asked, a little too loudly. "Everything about this just feels like what that couple from church went through with their daughter. Look at everything Quinn put him through. Sam will probably never get over the trauma of his childhood, which all stems from that man."

"I know you're right about all that. But I think abandonment runs deep. Even though the man did terrible things, he was still Sam's father, and he abandoned him."

Abbie laughed through the tears trying to form. "I forgot about your psychology degree."

Wendy shrugged and sipped her iced tea. "I can't imagine how hard it is. How's John dealing with it?"

"The same as me. Worried. He feels his father-son bond with

Sam is threatened. Last night, he was talking about all the nights he sat up with Sam when he had nightmares caused either directly or indirectly by Andy Quinn. He's hurt and angry." Abbie put her sandwich down and slumped back against the booth.

"That's so hard. I understand where he's coming from too." Wendy opened her mouth to say more but didn't.

"What were you going to say?" Abbie asked.

Wendy clasped her hands in front of her and rested her chin on her hands. "I think the best thing you can do is be supportive of Sam. He's confused right now, and you might just have to let him get hurt."

They finished their lunch, and Abbie thought about her best friend's words all the way home. She was right. Sam was twenty-three years old. He'd been through things she and John couldn't even imagine. And probably things they didn't know about. They needed to let him do this, and they needed to support him. They'd be here for him if it all came crashing down.

twenty-three

Snow in Franklin was rare, but an inch of the white stuff overnight made this Christmas Eve breathtakingly beautiful. They celebrated in the large two-story great room at Sam's parents' house. The opened window coverings combined with the moonlight and landscape lights made their little winter wonderland sparkle.

The whole family was there. Kyle and Cassie, Hannah, and even Abbie's parents. Sam laughed at something Kyle said, but otherwise, the tension in the air was palpable. Dad especially had not been happy about Sam's prison visit. And in the last six days since Sam had returned, he'd read every letter Andy had ever sent him.

When he left the prison, he had no intention of reading the letters. But by the time he arrived home, he'd had time to run through everything in his mind and had calmed himself. What if his father had truly changed? It'd be wrong not to at least hear the man out. Not because Andy had asked, but because Sam needed to see for himself.

"We'll be ready to eat in five minutes," Mom shouted from the adjoining kitchen.

"And then we'll open presents!" Hannah bounced on the sofa adjacent to Sam.

"You sound like a little kid, sis." Kyle laughed and threw a sofa pillow at her.

Sam wished he felt like joining in the fun, but he didn't. He usually loved Christmas with the Graysons, but this Christmas was different. His heart was troubled. If only he could talk to Dad about it, but he couldn't be objective when it came to Andy. He'd already proven that.

They made their way to the table. Dad led them in prayer, and they all talked and laughed and then ate their ham, scalloped potatoes, and green beans.

"You've been awfully quiet, Sam." Cassie elbowed him lightly. "What do you think Santa's bringing you?"

The more he'd gotten to know his sister-in-law, the more he liked her. She was a combination of Kyle and Hannah. Playful like Hannah, but also serious like Kyle.

"Well, I'm hoping for notebooks, pens, and guitar picks so I can keep writing." Sam laughed. And he seriously would've been happy with only those things, but his mom tended to go overboard with Christmas.

They continued chatting, but Sam's thoughts focused on the letters. Every one of them proclaimed Andy's faith, his apologies to Sam for everything he'd ever put him through, and most of all his regret for signing the document that severed his parental relationship with Sam.

The more letters Sam read, the more he believed the man. He prayed and asked God to guide him. Lately, a verse kept running through his mind. "Guard your heart above all else, for it determines the course of your life." He'd need to be careful.

The night wore on, and they opened their gifts. Everyone chatted happily and held up their gifts for the rest of the family to see. There was no shortage of hugs and thank-yous.

Sam received a piece of recording equipment, some clothes,

boots, notebooks, pens, and guitar picks. He hugged his parents, but the tension remained, especially between him and his dad.

That was okay. Sam made some decisions that would ease the awkwardness after the first of the year. He needed to keep moving forward the best he could, even if forward meant seeing less of his parents.

twenty-four

"I'm twenty-three years old. It's time." Sam stood in front of them with his hands in his pockets and shrugged.

Abbie gawked at Sam. This wasn't how she'd expected to spend the day after Christmas.

John sat with his mouth open, holding his coffee cup in midair. "Sam, we don't care you're twenty-three and still living here. Please don't let that drive you to move out." He paused and placed his cup on the end table. "Listen, I'm sorry. I know I haven't been supportive of you visiting Andy Quinn, but I can't help the reservations I feel about the man. But I promise, I'll do a better job of supporting your decision to see him."

Sam shrugged. "See, you're bringing him up now, and we aren't even talking about him. This has nothing to do with him. You don't get it. I want my own place, so I have breathing room to make my own decisions. I think it's time. I make my own money now, and I can easily afford to get an apartment, where I can write and live my life."

Abbie bit her lip and held back the tears. She and John had talked about it recently. They'd always told Sam he could stay for however long he wanted. They enjoyed him being here. He didn't officially become part of their family until he was eighteen, so they'd never wanted him to be in a hurry to move out. They wanted time with him since they didn't have him through most of his childhood.

But he worked as the worship minister at the area's newest megachurch, a paid position, and that wasn't even a fraction of what he made now as a songwriter. They'd guessed it was only a matter of time before he'd want to move out. They hadn't expected it to happen like this. Even though Sam denied it, the move was a direct result of his burgeoning relationship with Andy Quinn. And, of course, the mounting tension between Sam and John over that relationship.

"We knew this day would come eventually," she said quietly. "And hon, if this is what you want, then we support you one hundred percent. I know things have been, well, strained lately." She made a point not to look at John when she said it. "But we want you to know you can always come home. Always, no matter the circumstances."

"Thanks, Mom." Sam smiled.

Abbie was thankful their connection was still intact, even if his and John's was unraveling. "I'm putting my deposit down tomorrow at an apartment on Columbia Avenue. They told me I can take possession on January first, so I guess I'll start packing."

All Abbie could do was nod while Sam left the room. "Why didn't you say anything to encourage him, or tell him he can always come back?" She couldn't hide her irritation with her husband's attitude.

"I nodded. I agreed with everything you said."

"You have to get over your animosity toward ... whatever this is between him and Quinn. That's not helping things, you know." Abbie didn't raise her voice often, but today, she couldn't stop herself. "Is it because you're jealous?"

"Jealous? That's what you think?" John scoffed, rose from his recliner, and paced the room. "No, I'm not jealous. I'm worried, Abbie. Think about everything that man has put him through over the years, and I'm sure there are plenty of bad things he did to Sam that we don't even know about. And now Sam's letting him back into his life? I'm telling you, nothing good will come of this."

Abbie stared at John. "Haven't you learned anything from raising Kyle and Hannah? The more you speak out against something, the more they want to do it. That's exactly what you're doing here. You're practically pushing him toward Andy Quinn."

John breathed in deeply. "This is different. Don't you realize Quinn is a dangerous man? Even from prison he has influence. Surely, you've thought about that. Sam's not being smart. I don't like it, and I'm not going to support it." He huffed.

"I disagree," Abbie said. But it didn't matter. Her husband had already stomped out of the room, down the hall, and slammed his office door.

* * *

"Honey, are you awake?" John shook Abbie's shoulder and knew good and well she wasn't. It was 3:00 a.m. Their argument was hours ago, but he wouldn't sleep until he talked to her. He'd spent the last several hours in his office, thinking, praying, and admitting his hurt and jealousy to God. Now he needed to admit it to his wife.

"I'm awake. What's wrong? What time is it?" Abbie yawned.

John slipped into bed beside her. "Nothing's wrong. It's a little after three. Can we talk?"

Abbie scooted into a sitting position and turned the bedside lamp on low. "What is it?" Her annoyance seemed to be gone.

"I'm sorry about our argument. It was my fault. I wanted to tell you that, and that I've figured out some things."

"Thank you." Abbie didn't hesitate. "I'm sorry too. What have you figured out?"

John adjusted the comforter around them both. "I'm more hurt by this thing with Sam and Quinn than I realized, and I'm angry with both of them." He was relieved to finally admit that to Abbie and hoped she'd understand.

"I don't understand." She nixed his hopes. "I mean, I get your anger toward Quinn, but toward Sam?" She asked, no judgment in her voice.

"Don't you see, Abbie? That man tore Sam's life apart, and who picked up the pieces? You and I did. Over and over. Quinn's the one that did all the damage, and we did all the fixing, and where did that get us?" He'd let some of his anger out, and Abbie sat and stared at him. "Haven't you thought of it that way?"

"Well, not really."

I must be some kind of monster. Was he wrong to feel this way? "It's just, we've done so much for him, and you know what's going to happen in the end, don't you? Sam's going to get his heart shattered, and we're going to have to pick up the pieces again." The fight had suddenly left him.

"But John, isn't that what we do as parents?" She twirled a long brown curl. "I don't want to see him hurt either. You know that. But don't you think there's a chance the change in Andy is real? I mean, it's what we prayed for back when he played for you, long before Sam was born."

John sighed. To think how long thoughts of Andy Quinn had consumed his life. First, as a player of John's nearly twenty-five years ago, then later, when they fostered the man's son, unbeknownst to him and Abbie. "Yes, it's what we prayed for, and God *can* change him. I have zero doubt about that. My concern is whether God has changed him. Has Andy Quinn truly come to faith in the Lord?"

Abbie shrugged and bit her lower lip. "I guess there's no way for us to truly know. All we can do is pray it's true, and if not, that he'll come to faith. We need to put this in God's hands and ask God to guard Sam's heart."

John agreed, although he was afraid Sam's heart was already wide open for Andy Quinn to step right in.

twenty-five

Sam walked around his apartment and picked up a few things lying around and put them in their rightful place. He'd been here about a month now and took pride in keeping it neat. But today, it had to be pristine.

He put a few glasses in the dishwasher and looked around. Everything was nice and neat. His finger was ready to push Start on the dishwasher when the doorbell rang. No, he'd wait until after she left. This was Mom's first visit to his apartment, and he wanted everything perfect.

His pulse quickened as he walked to the door. He shouldn't be nervous. This was his mom after all. But this was her first visit, and she was coming without John. And on top of that, he hadn't seen either of them since he moved out.

He put a smile on his face and opened the door.

"Sam!" she shouted. In less than a second, she'd closed the distance between them, wrapping him in a hug. "Oh, I'm so happy to see you."

After a long moment, she let go, and Sam laughed. "I'm glad to see you too." He caught his breath. "Come on in, and I'll show you the place."

He hung her coat on the horizontal coat rack on the wall, and she hurried in and put her purse on the kitchen counter.

"This is beautiful. I love this granite. It all looks brand new." She moved her hand along the cool granite countertop as she took it all in.

"It's new construction. I'm the first tenant." He led her through the combination living room and kitchen, and then into his bedroom with an attached bathroom and walk in closet. Then he led her out to the deck. "Of course, it's only a fraction of the size of yours, but I know I'm going to use it all the time when the weather gets warmer. It's peaceful back here."

"I love that there's nothing but trees out here behind your deck. You'll be able to hear the birds singing in the springtime."

They went inside, and Sam showed her the second bedroom near the entrance to his apartment. "I use that room for my office, but I'm going to put a bed in there in case anyone stays over."

"I'm so happy for you, Sam, it's perfect. I miss you like crazy, but I'm glad you're doing well." She gave him a genuine smile.

"Thanks, I am. And I miss you too." He jumped to his feet. "I was going to get us water. Would you rather have coffee?"

"You know, coffee would actually be great."

He started the coffee and returned and settled onto the sofa. The silence between them made it awkward for a moment before she spoke up.

"Are you excited about the American Christian Music Awards next week?"

The smile plastered on her face made him think she felt awkward too. "Yeah, I am. Kinda nervous too, I guess." He got up to get two mugs out of the cabinet and poured the coffee. "I told you Lauren is going with me, right?" He returned and set the mugs on the coffee table.

"Yes." She grinned. "Has she found a dress yet?"

"Yeah, its blue, that's all I know." He laughed and sipped his coffee. This was going to stay uncomfortable until he addressed what was unsaid between them. And she was going to make him be the one to do it.

"So, how's John?" he asked, but immediately wanted to take it back. Why had he called him John, and not Dad? He didn't mean to call him by his first name. He grimaced and wanted to say he meant Dad. That might make things worse though. But if Mom realized he'd said John instead of Dad, she didn't let on.

"He misses you."

Sam tilted his head. "He does?"

"Of course, he does, hon. I know you two disagree about these visits to your, uh, Andy Quinn. But Sam, your father only wants what's best for you."

"And he doesn't think Andy is what's best for me."

Mom placed her mug on the coffee table. "How are your visits going?"

She hadn't answered the question.

"They're going well. I know Dad doesn't believe he's changed." Thankfully, he'd said Dad this time. "But he hasn't seen him or talked to Andy, and I have. Mom, he's changed, and for the first time in my entire life, I feel a connection with him. I don't understand why Dad doesn't want me to have that. I feel like I'm healing, finally."

"I want to believe that, I really do. And I pray every day that Andy Quinn is being truthful with you. But please be careful, Sam. Promise me that," she pleaded.

Sam groaned. He wanted to yell at Abbie, but he respected her too much. She didn't understand. She hadn't talked to Andy like he had, listened to his apologies, or his story of salvation. Her mind was made up, and so was John's. Nothing he could say would sway them.

He calmed himself, and they made small talk for the next thirty minutes—about his job at church and his songwriting and then about Kyle, Hannah, and Lauren, and the American Christian Music Awards again.

Sam flopped onto the sofa when she left. Abbie and John

didn't understand him and what he was going through, and they'd never support his pursuit of a relationship with Andy Quinn.

But he didn't need their support. He had Lauren, and he had Andy, and he had God. That's all he needed right now.

twenty-six

Sam parked his freshly washed and detailed SUV in front of Lauren's apartment building and stepped out. He left his suit jacket in the backseat to avoid wrinkles. His palms sweated, and there was a pounding in his chest as he walked up to the second floor and knocked on her door. The door opened, and there she stood.

"Lauren, wow, uh, I mean, you look beautiful." He stepped closer and hugged her, careful not to mess up her perfectly arranged hair. Completely stunning, she wore a long, fitted, icy-blue dress with silver sparkles and had a few silver sparkles in her hair. Her jewelry was simple, yet perfect. Like Lauren.

"Thanks." She blushed. "You look amazing too."

He responded with a blush of his own. He'd gone with a simple, black trendy suit with a gray shirt and no tie. "Umm, thanks." It dawned on him there was no crazy little barking dog running around. "Where's Daisy?"

She laughed and pointed to her dress. "This is one of the few times she's banished to her crate for a few hours. I couldn't have her jumping on my dress."

"I totally get that." He laughed, but he couldn't quit staring.

She was beautiful. "So, are you ready to go?" They were going to dinner first at Etch in downtown Nashville.

"Yes, but I want to get a picture of us first." She picked up her cell phone, and they posed for the selfie. She snapped several for good measure. "I'll send them to you."

They made small talk until they arrived at the restaurant. Sam went around to her side of the car and opened the door for her, then took her hand to help her out of the car. He gave his keys to the valet but never let go of her hand as they walked into the restaurant. He hoped she wouldn't notice how clammy his hands were. *Why am I so nervous? It's just Lauren.*

Once the maître d' seated them, they both giggled. This was fancy for them. Sure, they'd both been to fine restaurants with their parents, but Sam had never been to one by himself or on a date. "I feel like a little kid playing grown up," Sam said with a twinkle in his eyes.

Lauren's cheeks turned a rosy-pink color, and she giggled. "Me too. I went to prom but it wasn't anything like this." By the time his venison and Lauren's porcini chicken arrived, they'd settled in and were able to make conversation without giggling. It dawned on him why he was so nervous. She meant more to him now than she ever had. And it wasn't only because of how close they'd become over the past month. It'd been an ongoing process ever since he'd met her, all the way back in the eighth grade.

"Thank you for being my date tonight," he whispered.

She blushed again. "Thank you for selecting me out of the hundreds of girls you have to choose from."

Sam laughed out loud. "Oh yeah, right."

She studied him for a moment. "That's what I like so much about you, Sam Grayson. You don't even realize how people admire you and talk about you."

He tilted his head. "What do you mean?" He couldn't imagine what she was talking about.

"See what I mean? Do you even realize the number of girls

that call the church wanting to talk to you? You forget my good friend Regan works in the front office. They screen your calls, you know, so you don't have to deal with that. And all the chatter about songwriter of the year, and you being one of the brightest new songwriters in Nashville?" She smiled at him. "You're so humble. How do you stay that way?"

He didn't know what to say. He didn't know about girls calling the church but doubted that was true. And as far as all the other stuff, he'd heard bits and pieces, but he didn't dwell on those things. His only goal was to serve God.

"Well, I don't listen to all that stuff because it's probably not even true." He reached for his wallet, counted out the cash, and laid it on the tray with the check. The whole time she beamed. "What are you smiling at?"

"You have no idea how talented you are, do you?"

Sam squirmed a little. "Thanks for saying that. But this isn't me doing any of this. It's all God. I asked him to use me to glorify him, and that's all I want." He hoped she understood. He wasn't looking for a life of being center-stage, or a so-called Christian celebrity.

"I know." Their eyes locked. "That's what makes you so special."

Sam left the tip on the table, and they exited the restaurant the way they entered, hand in hand. They drove the short distance to Lipscomb University, the site of the American Christian Music Awards.

* * *

Lauren walked into the auditorium next to Sam, and he held her hand again. *What was happening?* Whatever this new stage of their relationship was, it had moved fast. Here they were, hand in hand, during a defining moment in Sam's life and ministry. They sat in the same room with the biggest stars in the

Christian music world, and she and Sam were right up front with all the other big nominees.

The performances were phenomenal, and every once in a while she had to glance at the stars, some of whom were legends, sitting near them. She'd seen many in concert over the years. But if Sam was in awe, he didn't show it. The only inkling he might be a little nervous was his jiggling left leg.

They cheered as Caleb Hartley won multiple awards for singing Sam's song, "His Name is Jesus." And each time Caleb accepted an award, he thanked Sam for writing the song. Now only three awards remained, and Sam was nominated for two of them. Songwriter of the Year and Song of the Year. Both were songwriter awards.

She and Sam shared a long look as the announcer read his name as nominee for Songwriter of the Year. He appeared calm, cool, and collected. Maybe he didn't care whether he won this award, but she wanted it for him. He had no real awareness of his own talent, and she wanted him to have validation he was good at something. That he was the best at something. Because he didn't have that confidence in himself.

The room fell silent as Matthew West opened the sealed envelope. "And the winner is ... Sam Grayson!"

The auditorium erupted in applause. Sam stood then bent down to whisper in Lauren's ear. "Thank you for always believing in me."

She smiled, tears blurring her vision. He turned and walked up the steps to the stage and gave an acceptance speech she'd never forget.

twenty-seven

"Commercials are over, hurry up." Hannah shouted from the family room.

Abbie had run to the kitchen to refill the snack bowls. "Coming." She gazed at her family watching from their great room. Hannah was here, along with Kyle and Cassie, and even Abbie's parents, Ed and Sarah, had come over to view the award show with them.

"This is so exciting." Sarah beamed. Abbie didn't have the best relationship with her mom and dad, but they sure loved their grandkids, including Sam. "You know, it's an honor just to be nominated."

"Grandma, don't you think Sam will win?" Hannah asked.

"I most certainly do." Sarah declared. "I'm just saying, if he doesn't, it's still a huge honor."

"What do you think, hon?" Abbie nudged John. He'd been quiet tonight. His and Sam's relationship had gone from strained to practically nonexistent, and every time Abbie thought about it, her stomach hurt. All because of Sam pursuing a relationship with Andy Quinn. She understood where Sam was coming from to a certain extent, but John didn't understand it at all.

"I think he's gonna win." His eyes held a glimmer she hadn't seen in a while.

Abbie smiled. No matter what was going on between him and Sam, John was beyond proud of his son.

"Oh, here it is, songwriter of the year!" Cassie exclaimed.

"Everybody, shh." Hannah grabbed a throw pillow from the sofa and hugged it to her chest. "I'm so nervous for him."

Kyle picked up the remote and turned the volume up. The room was quiet while the nominees were announced. When Sam's name was called, they flew out of their seats and jumped up and down, hugged each other, and screamed. Even Abbie's parents danced and hugged.

The camera focused on Sam getting up from his seat in the audience. "Oh wow," Hannah gasped. "Look how gorgeous Lauren is."

"They're stunning together," Cassie exclaimed. "So, was this like a real date?"

"Shh," Kyle turned up the volume. Cassie punched him lightly on the shoulder.

"Quiet everybody, he's on stage." John shushed them this time.

Abbie's eyes filled with tears as Sam gracefully accepted the award from the hands of the presenter. He stepped to the podium, and she smiled at how much poise he showed. Besides his two nominations, four songs he'd written had all won awards tonight by the singers. He had truly earned this songwriter award.

You could hear a pin drop in the room as Sam reached into the inside pocket of his black jacket and pulled out a piece of paper.

"He's so handsome." Abbie beamed.

He looked up at the audience and laughed. "Wow, I'm stunned right now. To be mentioned in the same breath as the other nominees has been an honor. I mean, wow."

The audience chuckled kindly at his use of the word *wow*.

"I want to start by thanking everyone who was involved with these songs, from the producers to the managers and artists who picked my songs to sing. I especially want to thank Caleb Hartly, who took these songs way beyond anything I could've ever imagined."

He went on to mention his band mates, Nate and Tara, and several producers and managers, and Abbie couldn't contain her tears. How far Sam had come! He'd taken his passion for words and music and created this career, this gift that glorified God. But to anyone who asked, Sam would credit it all to God.

"I want to thank my parents, John and Abbie Grayson, who've supported and encouraged me throughout this journey, my brother Kyle and sister-in-law Cassie, and my sister Hannah, who I credit with my love of Christian music. Also, to Andy Quinn for believing in me, and for my beautiful girlfriend here in the audience, Lauren, who never stopped believing in me."

"Above all, and more than anything, I thank God Almighty for sending his son Jesus to save me and for giving me this wonderful life I'm so unworthy of." Sam's voice quivered as he spoke those last words. He held up his award and pointed straight up. "Thank you, God." The music came on, and the broadcast went to a commercial.

Tears of pride streamed down Abbie's face, but in the back of her mind, something didn't feel right. Sam mentioned Andy Quinn in his acceptance speech. She wiped the tears away and smiled to hide the shock. Did John and the others catch those words? Of course they did. They'd hung onto his every word.

John closed his eyes, head tilted toward the floor as if praying. Or maybe trying to collect his emotions.

She prayed he wouldn't say anything to ruin the evening. Sam's mention of Andy bothered her, too, but she wasn't going to let it ruin the moment.

"Did you hear that?" Hannah exclaimed.

Abbie's heart thudded in her chest. *Oh Hannah, please don't bring up Andy Quinn's name now.*

"I sure did." Cassie grinned. "His *girlfriend* Lauren? When did that happen?"

"Right? That's what I want to know." Hannah laughed, and the two girls walked to the kitchen with their water glasses, giggling like high schoolers.

Abbie breathed a sigh of relief.

John put his arm around her shoulder. "I'm so proud of him," he whispered in her ear. "You know that."

"I do. Let's celebrate, and we'll talk about the rest later. There's still one more nomination left. Song of the year."

John joined everyone else in the conversation, which flowed in several directions all at once. The topics included how proud they were, how stunning Sam and Lauren were, and when did she become his girlfriend?

Abbie laughed. She wanted to know too.

They settled around the TV, and everyone was quiet for the Song of the Year nomination. And once again, Sam was declared the winner.

Abbie couldn't stop the tears. She thanked God for the beautiful life He'd given Sam and for choosing John and her to be his parents.

Please God, let us remain his parents, no matter what life throws at us. And no matter what Andy Quinn throws at us.

<h1 style="text-align:center">twenty-eight</h1>

Lauren beamed as Sam held onto her hand after the ceremony. Some guests made their way out, and others stood in the aisles talking. Several award winners, including Sam, were interviewed by different media personalities. She hung back a few feet as he answered questions from an on-air radio personality.

The night had been a dream come true for Sam. Knowing him, a dream he probably never acknowledged. He would never lose his humility, and she was proud he was firmly rooted in his faith.

But that speech. Each time she tried to push his words aside, they occupied an even bigger space in her mind, until she couldn't ignore them any longer. He called her his *girlfriend*. Not that she minded.

Yes, they'd gotten close since she returned to Nashville. Lately, they'd spent all their free time together. But they'd never discussed being a couple. He'd never asked her to be his girlfriend. He'd told her more than once he planned to remain single, at least for the near future.

She'd wanted to define the relationship for the past few

weeks, but she didn't want to scare him away. Had he just defined it?

As soon as he finished the interview, another media person grabbed him and asked him to sit for a moment and talk. He followed the man, smiled back at Lauren, and mouthed the word "Sorry."

She laughed and shook her head. "It's okay," she mouthed back.

Her stomach fluttered. His straight posture, the smile on his face, and the ease in which he chatted with the media were awe-inspiring. When did he become such a professional?

He flashed a quick smile.

She thought back through all the years she'd known him. When she'd first befriended him in the eighth grade, he was definitely closed off. He'd put up walls. But the more she talked to him, the more he opened up to her, and it didn't take long for them to become best friends.

All through high school, Sam had been in and out of foster homes. That meant he switched schools a lot, but even so, they remained best friends. It wasn't until she moved away to New York they eventually stopped communicating. That was completely her fault. Thankfully, they were back in that place of comfort and friendship again. And maybe more.

She shook off the thoughts of her years in New York, the relationship that was a mistake, and all the ways she would never be what's best for Sam. But even with all the competing thoughts in her head, one thought overrode them all—she loved Sam. She always had.

* * *

"Sorry about that." Sam reached for her hand, and she jumped. "Are you okay?" He laughed.

"Yes." She giggled, eyes wide. "I guess I was in my own little world, thinking about how proud I am of you."

"Thank you." The heat rushed to his face again. "And thank you for being here with me tonight. There's no one else I'd want by my side." He gazed into her eyes and thought about kissing her. But then he turned away for a second before facing her again. "I, umm, I'm sorry I called you my girlfriend up there."

"You're sorry"? Her face fell.

He could've kicked himself. "Oh, no, I don't mean it that way." He squeezed her hand and looked into her green eyes. "What I meant was, I'm sorry I blurted it out like that. I intended to ask you tonight. But I didn't mean to declare it to the world without asking you first."

Her eyes widened, and she didn't say anything.

How did he always mess these things up? The room became hotter, and beads of sweat appeared on his forehead. "So, umm, will you? Be my girlfriend, that is?"

At last, a huge smile lit up her face. She wrapped her arms around his neck, hugged him tight, and whispered in his ear. "I thought you'd never ask. Of course, I will."

He held her, and their eyes locked. They'd never kissed, and he wanted to kiss her. Was this an appropriate place with people bumping into them as they stood in the middle of an aisle? He wasn't sure. But she didn't look away from him even with all the bustle around them. He leaned in, framed her face with his hands, and brushed her lips with his.

"Sam Grayson!"

They snapped their heads up to see who shouted his name. His pulse raced from the kiss. Whoever interrupted them better have a good reason.

The voice sounded familiar, but he couldn't place it until his mom's best friend, Wendy, waved. The voice belonged to her husband, Roger. It made perfect sense they'd be here. Roger Nelson was one of the biggest music producers in Nashville. Sam never realized he was involved in Christian music though.

"Hi, Mr. and Mrs. Nelson," Sam smiled.

"Hi, Sam, congratulations, honey." Wendy hugged him. "I've been texting with your mom. Your family is so proud of you."

Yeah, and I'm sure you'll be texting Mom about the kiss you just saw. He'd always liked Wendy. She was like a sister to his mom. Sam didn't know her husband as well, but he'd always been nice. "Thanks, I can't wait to talk to them later."

Roger Nelson stood behind his wife and stuck out his hand. "Congratulations, that was an impressive sweep tonight. Two awards for a first-time nominee, and other artists receiving awards for songs you've written. It doesn't get much better." For a smallish guy, Roger had a strong handshake and a big presence.

"Thank you, sir, I appreciate that." The heat returned to his cheeks. "You remember Lauren?" Wendy had met her before, but Sam didn't know what, if anything, Mom had told her about their relationship as of late.

After pleasantries and small talk, he hit a wall and was ready to get out of there. "It was nice seeing you both. I think we're gonna get going," he said with a polite smile.

"I won't keep you, Sam." Roger reached for his wallet. "I want to give you my card, and I'd like to talk to you sometime next week. I've watched Middle Tennessee Church online, and I've heard you sing. You shouldn't be giving all your songs away. You have a great voice in your own right, and I think you can record some songs for radio and streaming. What do you think?"

What had he just said? Sam didn't want to appear stupid, but he thought the man had asked if he wanted to record his own songs for radio. No, he must've misunderstood.

"You heard me right, Sam." Roger laughed as if he'd read Sam's mind. "Call me and we'll get together over coffee and chat. How's that sound?"

"Yes, sir, that sounds great. Thank you so much."

He and Lauren left the auditorium and made their way to the parking lot. What happened tonight? The awards he'd won were mind-boggling enough. And on top of that, a major record producer had wanted to talk to him about recording his own songs. He could barely wrap his head around it all. *Thank you, God. This is truly from You because I couldn't do this myself.*

But the biggest event of his life happened *after* the awards ceremony. Lauren had said yes, and they kissed.

twenty-nine

The next few days were a whirlwind for Sam. Congratulations poured in from all over. He alternated between being overjoyed and overwhelmed. He understood now why everyone had always told him to stay humble. During fleeting moments, pride attempted to creep in. At least he realized it, right? That way, he could correct it.

Over and over, he replayed the call he'd received from his family on awards night. His mom gushed and said repeatedly how proud she was. Even Dad congratulated him, told him he was proud, and sounded genuinely excited. Sam smiled. He didn't want tension between them. Maybe Dad had even come around to the idea of Sam visiting Andy Quinn.

Besides, he didn't need Dad's approval. Sam sighed. Except the truth was, he did. He loved his adoptive dad, and for the last few years, they had a solid, special relationship. If Sam were honest with himself, he missed talking to him. But Dad made it clear he didn't want to discuss Andy. Not only that, he didn't approve of Sam visiting the man. What if this was the first sign of him changing his mind?

He parked his car in the Main Street garage and walked to Landmark Bookstore.

Jan manned the front counter. "Well, if it isn't my favorite award-winning songwriter. How are you, Mr. Grayson?" she asked in a playful tone.

He loved this woman. She acted much younger than her seventy-plus years and was fun to talk to. "Thank you, Jan. I appreciate that. And you're my favorite bookstore owner for sure. Have you seen my girlfriend around?"

Jan pointed up. "I think she headed upstairs to set out some new cookbooks. Tell her to take a coffee break. I've got this." The woman winked at Sam.

"Will do." He winked back and turned toward the steps. After he sprinted to the second floor, he found Lauren where Jan said she'd be. In a room with a stove, refrigerator, and a kitchen table and chairs. Like an actual working kitchen but also filled with bookshelves full of cookbooks. Such a cool room.

"Hi there." Lauren flashed him a huge smile from behind a stack of books on the table.

"Are you up for coffee? Jan said you could take a break." Sam approached her from the other side of the table.

"When have I ever turned down coffee? Especially with you?" Her face turned red and she turned from him, and Sam's pulse quickened. Things had been perfect between them ever since he'd announced on live television she was his girlfriend. It wasn't lost on him it could've gone a different way since he hadn't asked her first. He was blessed it hadn't.

"Let's grab your coat on the way out. It's cold today." They stopped in the back office, and he helped her with her coat. On their way out, they asked Jan if she wanted anything. She declined as she was doing a special juice cleanse to get swimsuit-ready for spring break.

"How old did you say she is?" Sam said with a laugh as they ambled along the sidewalk to Meridee's.

"She's seventy-three, but she sure doesn't dress or act like it. I hope I'm like that at her age."

They held hands as they strolled into Meridee's and ordered coffee. "Do you have time to sit for a few minutes?"

"Sure, we're not real busy, and Jan doesn't care." She tilted her head. "Speaking of not being busy, how is it you have time to meet for coffee between work at church, songwriting, and mulling over your meeting with Mr. Nelson?"

Sam took a deep breath. "That's what I wanted to talk about." His thoughts turned serious. "I think I'm going to do it."

Lauren's eyes widened, and a huge grin gradually curved her lips. "You're going to sign the recording contract?"

Sam nodded. He'd thought and prayed about it, and his brother had gone over every detail with him. "Kyle said it's not only legit, but it's a great contract." Since Mr. Nelson was married to Abbie's best friend, he figured the man wouldn't take advantage of him. But it was nice his brother was an attorney who could help him with these things.

Lauren went from looking stunned to shrieking in less than a second. She flew out of her side of the booth. Without warning, she wrapped both arms around Sam's neck and kissed him. Neither could stop laughing.

After a few moments, she let go and went back to her side of the booth, breathless. "I'm so happy for you. I don't even have words." She brushed a tear from her eye. "I'm so proud of you."

Her reaction touched his heart. "You don't know how much I appreciate that."

"What happens next?" She blotted her eyes with a tissue.

"This morning, I sent him ten songs—demos—and he'll listen to them and let me know. But the best part is Nate and Tara can be with me—Nate on keys or bass and Tara on background vocals." He'd been worried about that. They'd been with him from the beginning, supporting him in every way, and he wasn't about to leave them behind.

"That's incredible. I know how much you wanted that."

They talked for a few more minutes, and then she needed to return to work. He walked her back to the bookstore and then hurried to his car. Everything with Lauren had been great the last few weeks. They got along well and supported each other in everything they did.

He started his car and thought about his next stop. The discussion he'd planned with his mom and dad. Hopefully, the conversation would be as supportive as the one he'd just had with Lauren. He couldn't think of any reason they wouldn't support him in this. But these days, it was hard to guess how they might react.

thirty

A bbie made tea, removed the Italian cream cake from the bakery box, and carefully cut it.

"Oh, is that the cake you 'won'?" John was overly dramatic in his use of air quotes.

"Okay, so I paid twice what I would've from the bakery at the church bake sale yesterday. But I don't think I'll hear you complain while you eat it since it's your favorite." She took three plates from the cabinet. "And I didn't hear you complain that all the proceeds went to the adoption weekend event."

"Well, you're right about that. I just love teasing you, honey."

She was glad about the teasing. Apparently, John hadn't noticed her shaky hands. Sam was coming over for the first time since, well, she didn't exactly remember the last time. At least well before the American Christian Music Awards, when everything went even farther downhill between John and Sam.

If he was nervous, he sure didn't show it. Abbie understood his position. They were both afraid Sam would end up getting hurt.

"You need any help?"

"No, tea's on, and the cake is cut. He should be here any minute." She peeked at her watch.

"What do you think this is about?"

Abbie shrugged. She honestly didn't know. "If I had to guess, it's something about Quinn. Sam's been visiting him regularly. But I don't know." She paused and bit her lower lip. "Hon, please promise me that whatever this is about, there won't be an argument."

John sighed. "I haven't wanted to argue about any of this. But all I can think of is every awful thing that's ever happened to Sam has been either directly or indirectly caused by that man. It eats me up. I try to get Sam to understand, but it turns into an argument. How can he ignore all that man has put him through? I just don't understand."

The front door opened. "Please promise me you'll try," she whispered.

"Hey." Sam slipped into the kitchen, startling them both.

Abbie immediately went over and hugged him. "It's so good to see you."

John stepped forward to say hi and gave him a hug. "I'm so glad you're here, son."

"Thanks, me too. I'm sorry it's been so long." Sam sounded relieved.

"From what we hear, you've been very busy." John winked.

Abbie grabbed their favorite mugs, and they carried their tea and cake into the cozy family room. They talked about the weather, the clothes closet, and Kyle and Cassie's new dog. And then Abbie got to the thing she really wanted to talk about. "Wendy told me she saw you and Lauren kissing at the awards."

Sam's slid down in his seat. "Mom!"

"We're thrilled for you. You know we love Lauren. We always have," Abbie said.

"Ditto what your mom said."

Abbie winked at John. She hadn't known whether to bring it up or not, but she was glad she did. It reminded her of all the cozy and easy conversations they'd had over the years. They needed to get that back with Sam. Well, maybe not embarrassing him like she'd just done …

They finished their cake, and Sam spoke up. "I have some big news."

John tensed up beside her.

"What kind of news?" she asked.

He broke into a huge grin. "I've signed a recording contract. I'm going to start recording my own songs instead of giving them away."

Abbie looked at John. Her husband grinned from ear to ear. It melted her heart to see him so proud of Sam.

"We've always thought you should do that." John smiled.

"I'm so excited for you. How did this even come about?" Abbie asked.

"You really don't know?"

Abbie and John both shrugged. "No," Abbie finally replied.

Sam chuckled. "Roger Nelson offered me the contract. He approached me after the awards, and then we met a few times after that. Kyle reviewed it for me and said it was a great contract."

Abbie laughed. Her best friend's husband had offered Sam a recording contract. How long had Wendy been forced to keep this a secret? "Oh my, I bet Wendy has been about to explode. Wait til I talk to her."

"And Kyle too." John laughed. "I'm glad you had him check it out for you."

"Me too. And I'm glad I can finally tell you." Sam acted more relaxed and at home with them than he had in a long while.

They discussed what all this meant. Sam would be recording ten songs for release to radio and streaming services. He'd go on a college campus tour that would focus on his worship music, and a young pastor Sam had met would preach. It'd be more like a worship service than a concert.

Abbie was so proud, and based on John's grin, he was too. It felt good to have Sam back. Today had gone better than she could've imagined. Why had she been so nervous? *Thank you, Lord.*

Sam got up to leave and hugged them.

"Does Andy know about this?" John asked.

* * *

Sam stopped in his tracks and turned around. What was this? Had he been wrong to think John was okay with him seeing Andy?

Abbie glared at John. "Why did you have to bring Andy Quinn up today? It's been a perfect afternoon."

But John didn't pay any attention to Abbie. Instead, he stared at Sam and asked the question again.

What was happening? A moment ago, John had been proud and glad to see him, and just like that, he wanted to start an argument. For the first time, Sam considered lying to his dad, but he wouldn't do that. "Yes, he knows."

John grimaced. "So, you told him before you told us?"

He hadn't thought about it like that. "I, umm, visited him yesterday, so I went ahead and told him."

John's face turned red. "I guess that's why you didn't come to our game last night. You went to see him, and that's a six-hour round trip. You told me you were coming to the game. The last home game of the season."

Oh no. How had he forgotten? "I'm so sorry, Dad, I forgot."

"I'm right, aren't I? You went to see *him,*" John accused.

Sam took a deep breath and gazed out the family room window. How had this afternoon turned bad so quickly? He wanted to kick himself for his part in it. John probably wouldn't understand that. "What do you want me to say? Yes, I went to see him, and I forgot about your game. I'm *so* sorry I forgot. I really am. I wanted to be there. But I won't apologize for my visits to him."

"You wouldn't have forgotten the game if you hadn't been so

wrapped up in Quinn. You should have been at the game. I think you owe me that." John folded his arms.

Sam laughed wryly. "I owe you? Do you want to know why I've been visiting him? It's because he's been way more supportive lately than you have."

"What?" John's face turned an even darker shade of red. He was about to blow up. Sam had never seen him like this. "He's been more supportive than I have? Well, let me ask you something. Where was he when you were a kid going from one foster home to another? And where was he when you came here and had nightmares every night? Was it him or me calming you down then? And if I remember correctly, a lot of those nightmares were due to him."

"John—"

"Abbie, I'm sorry, but it has to be said. Sam, we did everything for you to get you through all the pain and trauma caused by that man over the years. Have you forgotten all that?" John shouted loud enough for the neighbors to hear.

Abbie pleaded with him to stop.

"It's called forgiveness." Sam whispered and turned to leave. "You should try it."

Sam stomped out of the room and John followed him, but Abbie stopped him. "Please, John, stay here."

Abbie caught Sam outside the front door. "Sam, wait."

He turned and exhaled, shoulders slumped, utterly defeated. "Mom, I'm sorry. I know you don't believe Andy's changed either, but I do. And if John can't support that, well then, I can't come around anymore."

Abbie hugged Sam, tears filling her eyes. "Please don't write John off. He loves you. But he's having a really hard time with this."

"Don't leave, Sam." John's voice rang out from inside, and he ran out into the driveway.

Sam turned away and got into his car. He'd had enough, but John rushed to his window.

"Wait, please. I'm sorry."

Sam hesitated, then lowered his car window but didn't say anything.

John apologized again. No longer red, his face softened. "I guess I'm not handling this very well."

"Thanks for saying that." Sam exhaled. "And I'm sorry too." But he wasn't sure why. What did he have to be sorry for? Not about seeing Andy. "I'm so sorry I missed your game." He truly was. The event was important to him, and Sam wanted to be there.

"Look, maybe we can have lunch or breakfast in a couple of days." John shrugged. He was trying.

"Yeah, that would be good." Sam forced a smile. John reached out and touched him on the shoulder briefly through the open window, and then Sam drove away.

thirty-one

Sam and Nate worked with their bandmates to get their instruments and sound equipment set up in the common room. Not once did Sam doubt they were doing the right thing. The men's prison ministry first approached him about performing at the Memphis prison months ago, but he turned them down. He wasn't up for it then.

But after he reconnected with Andy and learned how worship music changed him, Sam reconsidered. He needed to do this. In a few minutes, his father and the entire Bible study group, as well as other men who received a pass for good behavior, would come to this room to see them perform.

He and Nate agreed it wouldn't be best for Tara to come. Instead, they brought men from the church worship team who volunteered. They were set up and ready to go, and they took their places as the prisoners filed in. Some talked in hushed tones as they entered. Some even carried Bibles.

"Which one is him?" Nate asked.

"I'll tell you as soon as I see him. Oh, there he is." Sam waited until Andy saw him and gave a slight wave.

Andy returned the gesture.

Nate waved at Andy, too, in a show of support, which Sam

appreciated. Not everyone thought it was impossible for him to change.

The prison chaplain, a large man in a suit and tie, trekked to the front of the room to speak. But first, he turned to Sam and Nate and the rest of their band. "On behalf of these men, we can't thank you enough for being here. These men need all the exposure to Jesus they can get." He shook Sam's hand then proceeded to shake hands with Nate and each man in the band, then faced the crowd and turned on his microphone.

"Good evening, men. I'm glad you joined us for this special evening of worship. I'd like to introduce you to someone. You've heard the songs he's written on the radio, and you've sung some of his songs in Sunday morning worship here. Men, please welcome Sam Grayson and his band."

The room erupted in applause, and Sam's mouth dropped open. Did all of them know his songs, or were some here just to get out of their cells for a while? He didn't know, but did it even matter? God would find a way to these men's hearts if it was His will. *Please, God, use these worship songs to point these men to you.*

"Oh, and for those who don't know, Sam's father is an inmate, Andy Quinn. Andy, where are you?" Andy gave a little wave from the crowd of about a hundred, and the man beamed when other inmates clapped.

Sam didn't expect it, but he was proud. Although he didn't understand how he could feel proud of his father, an inmate. He let that roll around in his mind as he and the band started out with a song everyone knew, but one he hadn't written. "Amazing Grace."

The entire room erupted in singing, and they sang every word. *Amazing grace, indeed.*

The band continued playing and sang all Sam's songs, as well as some by other artists. One was Lauren Daigle's "Rescue," which God had used to touch Sam's soul on the night he was saved six years ago. They ended the evening with "How Great Thou Art." Again, the men sang all the words.

In between songs, Sam talked about the biblical inspiration for his songs, and the men who'd brought Bibles with them, marked those passages. The chaplain took the microphone after Sam and his friends completed their last song. He asked the band to play something quietly.

Understanding what was about to take place, Sam told his guys to play "Come to the Table." The chaplain asked for anyone who wanted to receive Jesus Christ to come to the front where he would lead them individually in prayer to accept Christ in their lives.

Sam's heart soared as a line of at least a dozen men formed. One by one, they walked to the front, and the chaplain led them in prayer. His father didn't come forward, but he'd told Sam he'd already accepted Christ.

Nate caught Sam's eye. "I wish Tara were here to see this."

Sam wished Lauren were here as well.

* * *

Sam's spirits still soared the next day when he met John and Kyle for breakfast not far from the TU campus. He'd been leery about this meet-up since the argument they'd had last week. Even though John apologized, Sam was unnerved by what happened. That day, everything had gone so well until John flipped a switch and went off on him.

Regardless, he missed hanging out with him and the talks they used to have. Maybe that's what was wrong. He and John hadn't hung out in months. This breakfast might be what they needed to get back on track.

Sam recently asked Kyle to represent his business interests since they exploded overnight into something Sam could no longer manage. Thankfully, his brother was happy to oblige.

The negotiation of Kyle's fees had been tough since his brother refused to exact his regular rates. He wanted to charge him next to nothing and much less than any other attorney Sam could've retained. Sam insisted on a certain number and threatened to walk away before his brother finally agreed.

It was only fair. This was business, and besides, Sam wanted to take care of him like his brother had done for him these last few years. Kyle was always on his side.

The two discussed business when John showed up. "Sorry, I'm late. I couldn't get off the phone."

"What's new?" Sam laughed.

"He's right, Dad. You're not known for short calls with recruits." Kyle joined in the teasing.

John chuckled. "My boys know me too well."

John sat and looked over the menu. The conversation was happy and lively. Gratitude filled Sam. This is exactly what they needed. Time together to laugh and talk. He'd make a point from here to get together with John more often. This made him realize even more how much he missed him.

The server came to their table to get their order. They chatted while they sipped their coffee and waited for their food.

"Oh, hey Sam, tell us about the show you did yesterday," Kyle said.

The air left Sam's lungs, and he shot Kyle a look. Didn't he know about it? If he did, he certainly wouldn't have brought it up here. "Nah, I'd rather hear what y'all have been up to."

"C'mon, Sam. I ran into Roger Nelson last night. He told me what an amazing show you put on, but I didn't get any details."

Great. His brother didn't know where this would lead, but Sam sure did

"I'd love to hear too." John's smile was genuine. The one Sam had grown to love over the years. Today, he felt more at ease with John than he had in quite some time. Well, that was about to be ruined.

Sam exhaled. Maybe he'd tell the story and leave part of it out. "Okay, well," Sam fixed his eyes on the coffee mug in his hands. "You know Mr. Ramirez at your church, right? With the men's ministry?"

John nodded. "Yes, of course. I know him well. He's a good guy."

"Yeah, he is. He asked me a while back to do a worship night for their prison ministry, so we did that yesterday. Not all of us, we didn't take Tara, but Nate and me and the rest of the band." Sam smiled, but it quickly faded as his nervousness got the best of him. But he was also proud of how well it went. "It was awesome. At the end, fourteen men received Christ."

"Wow, seriously?" Kyle asked.

"That's wonderful, son. I'm so proud of you and what you're doing." John beamed. His comment warmed Sam's heart. Their relationship had been rocky to say the least over the past several months, but John's face glowed with pride. Sam was glad he could share this with him after all. He breathed a sigh of relief.

The server brought their plates of bacon, eggs, and pancakes. Sam hadn't realized how hungry he was until now. He scooped up a forkful of scrambled eggs.

"Was this at the Nashville city jail?"

Sam almost spat out his eggs but attempted to regain his composure. He glared at Kyle. "Can you pass me the salt, please?" Sam hoped Kyle would understand and drop the conversation.

"No? Where then?" No such luck. Kyle handed him the salt shaker.

Sam sat back and exhaled.

John's posture changed immediately. He put his fork down, crossed his arms, and stared at Sam.

No use hiding. Kyle certainly wasn't thinking and didn't get the hint. He'd likely continue the questions. "The federal prison in Memphis."

"Oh, man." Kyle lowered his head and focused on the napkin in his lap before turning to Sam. "I'm sorry."

John's face turned red, like the other afternoon. "And I guess Quinn was in attendance? I mean, that's the whole reason you did the show, right?" Thankfully, he didn't shout like he had last week.

"Yeah, he was there, but he's not the sole reason we played. Dad, fourteen men accepted Christ. Do you know how amazing that was?" Sam realized his own voice rose with every syllable, but he didn't care.

"Yes, it is amazing. And I'm proud of you for your part in that. But I'm worried you can't seem to see that man for who he is." John huffed. "And I can guarantee Quinn isn't saved."

"How can you know for sure he isn't? And how can you claim to be a Christian and say that? I'm beginning to think you're the one who's insincere." The words flew out before he had a chance to filter them. He winced. He hadn't intended so be so harsh, but it was too late now,

"I can't believe you'd talk to me like that after everything I've done for you. Don't expect me to pick up the pieces when he destroys you again." John tossed his napkin on his plate.

"Hey, both of you, please, stop." Kyle pleaded. "I'm sorry. I shouldn't have pressed this conversation. If you two can't get along, then we need to go."

John pushed away from the table, stood, and threw some cash from his wallet onto the table. "I'll make it easy. I'll go. Sorry I ruined your morning, boys. I'll see you around." And with that, he was gone.

"I'm sorry, Sam. I don't know what I was thinking. I guess I wasn't."

Anger competed with the tears that burned the back of his eyes, but Sam fought them back. "It's not your fault. But do you see how he is? I know you didn't believe me because you'd never seen him act like that. Can you even believe him?"

Kyle took a swig of his coffee. "He definitely over-reacted, for sure. But—"

"But what?" Sam nearly shouted. "What could you possibly say to defend him?"

Kyle rubbed his chin and struggled to find the words. "I

believe he only has your best interest at heart. And he thinks Andy Quinn is not in your best interest. Dad loves you. You know he does."

Sam ignored that last part. "But how does he know a relationship with Andy's not in my best interest? He doesn't know Andy. Or his relationship with God."

"You're right. He can't know those things. But he does know how much that man hurt you in the past, and he'd do anything for that not to happen again. That much I know."

"He'd rather run me off then?" Sam threw his hands in the air.

Kyle leaned toward Sam. "I think if it came down to it, he'd rather lose you than see you hurt by Quinn again."

Sam didn't know what to say. How did that even make sense? He shrugged it off. They paid for their half-eaten meal and left, and not a moment too soon. How had this breakfast turned into such a debacle? The situation reinforced what he'd been thinking.

Maybe he didn't belong in the Grayson family anymore.

thirty-two

"That sounds awful." Lauren handed a bottle of water to Sam and sat on her sofa next to him.

"He was terrible. I mean, how can he keep treating me like this?" He said through gritted teeth.

"What did Kyle say?"

"Oh, a bunch of stuff about how John only has my best interest at heart and thinks Andy's going to hurt me again. It's getting old that none of them understand."

The doorbell rang, setting off a barking frenzy from Daisy. "Pizza's here." Lauren chuckled lightly.

Sam smiled halfheartedly. "I've got it." He paid the delivery guy and returned with the pizza box. Lauren handed him a plate from the coffee table, and they each put a slice of pizza on their plates. They took a few bites before Lauren decided to dive back into the conversation.

"I kind of see Kyle's point."

"What point?" Sam's expression was blank.

"About not wanting to see you get hurt again. I mean, you really haven't been around Andy enough to know for sure."

Sam put his plate on the table and stared at Lauren. "I haven't been around him enough to know what?"

She'd thought long and hard about whether to say anything. Despite everything Sam had recently told her, she had doubts about Andy Quinn. And not just doubts—fears.

She remembered things Sam told her about Andy over the years. Things the man was involved in, people he ran with, and things he didn't protect Sam from. Some things she didn't know for sure, but she read between the lines. Andy Quinn wasn't a good man. How had Sam forgotten all that man put him through?

This wasn't the night she planned to have this conversation. It could change everything between them. But she dove head first into those waters, and now, he stared and waited for an answer. "I don't think you've been around him long enough to know his true motives."

Sam stood. "You too, Lauren? Does no one believe anything I say?"

She stood and faced him. "It's not you I don't believe. Of course, I believe everything you say. And I know you believe him. It's just, I have to wonder if he's actually changed."

"Why would you think he hasn't?" Sam's voice rose. "Does everyone think I have no judgment skills at all? I think I would know if he was lying. And how could someone lie about being saved?"

For all he'd been through in his life, most of it due to Andy Quinn, Sam was still so naive. Or maybe he had wanted that man to love him so badly over the years he was willing to believe anything. Maybe she should agree and let him think the best. Quinn still had several years behind bars, so what would it hurt?

"You're right, Sam, I'm sorry. Please believe me. Of course I don't question your judgment. You know I'm gonna support you in this." She closed the distance between them and put her arms around his neck, and he pulled her into a hug.

Sam exhaled. "I'm so glad. I need you on my side. There's something I need to tell you I haven't told anyone."

She backed up from the embrace and looked into his eyes. "From your smile, it seems like good news."

"It is. He's going before the parole board in a couple months. He might get early release for good behavior."

Lauren's heart thundered in her chest. She dropped her arms and backed further away. No, she couldn't have heard him right. "Andy Quinn might be getting out soon? Sam, are you serious?" The blood drained from her face, and she turned away quickly.

"Yeah, what's wrong?"

"Nothing, I mean, do you think he *should* get out?" She looked at him, her head tilted.

"Well, yeah. He's served almost six years. And he admitted he didn't do anything with the girls. I asked him directly. He said the idea was all Blaze, and Andy protested. Once Blaze caught the girls anyway, Andy talked to him about letting them go. When he wouldn't release them, Andy refused to participate."

Lauren couldn't believe what she'd heard. "But Sam, I remember you telling me he was in the coffee shop where the girls were kidnapped. And you remembered him drugging you." Had he forgotten? Andy Quinn was the mastermind, and he lied to Sam. How could he not see it?

"Just because he was in that coffee shop doesn't mean that was his plan. He was there to sell drugs." Sam held up both hands. "And I know, that was bad enough. But I'm not sure he drugged me. I was so out of it, I can't be sure anymore."

What? Sam was mixed up right now. He'd conveniently forgotten everything that man had ever done. But she couldn't lose this relationship with him over Quinn. Especially right now when he was so ... confused. He needed her on his side now more than ever.

"I guess I'm just shocked, that's all. I trust your judgment. I do."

Her stomach churned, and her head hurt. In the past, she'd withheld things from Sam. Things she should've told him but didn't. But this was the first time she'd flat out lied to him.

* * *

"I'm so sorry to show up without calling first," Lauren said as Abbie led her into the foyer and hung her coat.

"Don't be ridiculous. You're welcome anytime. C'mon in." Abbie hoped her confusion and concern weren't obvious. "Are you okay? Is Sam okay?"

"I'm sorry, yes, we're both fine," she said, but her face and eyes were red. "I'm just worried about Sam."

"Is it okay if I get John?"

"Mm-hmm, yes. It would probably be a good idea." Lauren shivered.

"Have a seat here in the kitchen. I'll get John and then make you some hot tea."

Abbie's pulse sped up as she went down the hall to John's office. "Hey, hon, Lauren's here and wants to talk."

John tilted his head and gave her a blank stare. "Lauren?"

"Yes, you know, Sam's Lauren. I don't know why she's here, but she looks upset."

John rose from his desk and followed her to the kitchen.

"Hi, Lauren," John said while Abbie turned on the tea kettle. "How are you?"

Lauren stood and hugged him. "Hi, Coach Grayson. I'm okay." Once again, she apologized for showing up unannounced.

Abbie set the steaming mug on the table in front of Lauren. They were quiet for a moment while Lauren sipped her tea.

John spoke up at last. "I guess you know Sam and I haven't been getting along great lately."

"I know." Lauren blew on her tea. "I'm not judging you, believe me. If he finds out I told you this, he probably won't be talking to me either." She slumped her shoulders and explained what Sam had told her about Quinn going before the parole board.

"What?" John jumped to his feet. "How can that even be possible? The man got fifteen years."

"Sam said something about good behavior, mentoring other men, I don't know. Honestly, I was in shock," she said.

"I'm sorry, Lauren, I'm not questioning you. This is our biggest fear." John sighed.

"Especially when we don't know what's true and what's not regarding Quinn," Abbie added.

Lauren took another sip of her tea, her hands shaking. The girl was more upset than she let on. "You mean about him following God now?"

"Only God knows if that's true." Abbie shrugged. "But we know Andy Quinn is the king of lies."

John walked over to the kitchen island and leaned against it.

"I'm so worried about him," Lauren said. "He's so excited about this. And I'm afraid to speak my mind. I don't want it to come between us."

Abbie hurt for both Lauren and John. They were fighting the same battle but using different tactics. But she agreed with Lauren. Knowing how Sam had picked Andy over John, he'd most likely pick him over Lauren as well.

"We have to get him to see the truth about Andy somehow." Abbie twisted a long brown curl.

John chuckled without smiling and rubbed the back of his neck. "I don't know how you plan to do that. We've had several conversations along those lines, and every one of them ended badly."

They appeared defeated. "Okay, look, we can't give up. We have to keep trying."

"You know I won't give up on Sam," John whispered. "Not ever."

Until now, Abbie hadn't known that. It seemed John had already given up on him. Tears blurred her vision. Her voice didn't work at the moment. All she could do was nod.

"I'm going to fight for him, Abbie, just like before we adopted him."

This was a huge step in the right direction. Abbie prayed they could hold on to their youngest son.

thirty-three

The drive to Memphis took longer than usual. Sam pulled up to the guard shack and said he was there to see a prisoner, his father. The guard waved him through, and Sam parked his car. He let out a deep breath as he walked through the metal detectors and checked in for the visit. Andy wasn't expecting him, but he didn't think that would be a problem. A guard gave him his pass and he sat and waited. Ten minutes later, a corrections officer came back and got Sam—the same one who'd led him back several times before.

"Hey, good to see you," the young officer said. "You know, I enjoyed when you and your band played here."

Sam's mouth fell open. "Umm, thank you, I appreciate you saying that." He'd never thought about the corrections officers and other prison employees who stood in the background getting anything out of the worship time.

"Yeah, I told my wife, and we visited a church this past weekend." The man blushed a little.

Sam didn't know what to say. "Thank you for telling me. I needed to hear it." *And thank you, God.*

"Of course," the guard said. "Well, here we are. I'll be in the back of the room as usual."

Sam thanked him again and spotted Andy at his usual table by the barred window. He walked toward him.

"This is a surprise." Andy smiled.

"Yeah, I hope it's okay."

"Sure. What else have I got to do?" Andy shrugged.

Sam studied him for a moment. His father seemed small sitting here in prison. Not at all like the intimidating figure he'd been when Sam was younger. He shivered thinking about how his father used to be. Could John be right about him? Out of nowhere, confusion and vulnerability cast a shadow over him. And the Bible verse about guarding one's heart ran through his mind again.

"I need to ask you something." *Please, God, let him tell me the truth.*

"Okay," Andy said.

How was he this laid back in prison? As if he didn't have a care in the world.

"You know when you told me you had nothing to do with trafficking those girls? Is that the truth?" *Please, Lord, give me discernment to recognize the truth.*

Andy didn't hesitate. "Of course it is, son. What reason would I have to lie when I'm already behind bars?"

Sam shivered again. He wasn't ready for Andy to call him son, and for that matter, he might never be ready. It didn't sit right, no matter how far their relationship progressed.

Andy leaned forward and crossed his arms on the table. "What's going on? Why are you asking?"

He studied the man. "Well, let's say that people I'm close to doubt your story. Even my girlfriend. She didn't come right out and say it like others have, but I could tell."

"Since when do you have a girlfriend?" Andy grinned.

Sam didn't know whether to laugh or scream. "That's not the point of this conversation." Sam's voice was louder than intended.

"Okay, okay." Andy squirmed. "Tell me again what this girlfriend thinks I did."

"Well, it's not her, exactly. It's a lot of people." He didn't know why he was protecting John, but he was. "They say you sold those two girls. That you were the mastermind of the whole operation. I have to know the truth."

Andy stared at the barred window and rubbed his chin for a long moment before he looked at Sam again and spoke. "Sam, it happened just like I told you. Once I found out what Blaze was planning, I was out. I stuck to selling drugs only. Then the girls escaped. And if they hadn't escaped, I was gonna find a way to let them go."

"Really?" Sam asked. He'd never heard his father say that before. "You were going to let them leave?"

"Yeah, but they got away before we could let them go."

His father seemed sincere, but Sam still didn't know for sure. "Do you swear to me that's true?"

"Better yet, I swear to God that's true. And if I had my Bible with me now, I would swear on it."

That told Sam everything he needed to know. He believed the man. He was a Christ follower now, and God had changed his life. Andy wouldn't lie to him.

* * *

The cell door clanked behind him. Once the guard walked away, Andy tore into the two-inch thick so-called mattress on his cot and threw it onto the floor. With a sweep of his arms across his desk, he flung all his books to the ground. Including the Bible he just said he'd swear on. He bit back a scream.

"What's up with you, man?" Rio yelled from inside the adjacent cell. "Ain't you supposed to be nice and happy when you come back from your Bible thumpin' meeting?"

"That wasn't a Bible meeting." Andy sneered. "It was my son."

"Good visit, huh?" The man laughed.

Andy ran his hands through his graying hair. "Something I did is about to come to light."

"Yeah," Rio said. "That's how I got five years added to my sentence. I feel ya, man."

"I'm not even worried about extra years right now. I'm more worried about my kid. He's gonna find out I been lyin' to him and may not believe I've changed."

"Have you?"

"Let's just say I'm tryin'. But if my kid finds out about the lies, he'll be outta my life for good."

"What's the chances he'll find out?"

"Pretty good," Andy muttered.

thirty-four

Sam stepped off the stage in Louisville, Kentucky, where he'd played for nearly ten thousand people. The venue was the biggest by far, and the audience, the most people he'd played for so far. Nate and Tara stood by his side, and they were giddy over how the show went.

"Man, can you believe it? Seeing all those people worship together, all singing the words of your songs. How amazing has this night been?" Nate had his arm around Sam's shoulder as they trekked through the tunnel to their green room.

Tara walked a few feet ahead, then skipped.

Sam couldn't stop smiling. The show had been great, and his two new songs had caught on quickly. The radio had only been playing them the last two weeks, but the audience was already familiar with the words. He lifted his eyes to the ceiling, shook his head, and laughed. What an amazing night.

But by the time they reached the green room, it dawned on him that John and Abbie should've been here to share in the excitement. His smile disappeared.

"You okay, Sam?" Tara slowed her pace and fell in line with him and Nate as they stepped into the green room to gather their stuff. They needed to head to the bus in a few minutes.

"Yeah, I was thinking about John and Abbie. They should've been here, you know?" He threw his backpack over his shoulder and exited the room.

"You know we love ya man." Nate followed and slapped him on the back. "We hate that you and John have this riff between you. But I don't know, are you sure about your bio dad? I mean, do you think he's really changed?"

Ugh, not you, too. Sam ignored the question.

"And by the way, since when are you calling them John and Abbie? You've been calling them Mom and Dad since before your adoption."

"I did?" He hadn't even realized it. But come to think of it, they'd been John and Abbie in his mind for several months. He ran his hand through his hair. "It's been tough lately."

Nate nodded toward Tara. "We get it. I guess we hate to see you walk away from this great family who would give you anything in the world, for someone who, well ..."

"So, my best friends doubt me too. You two and Lauren." Sam clenched his teeth. Maybe he was wrong about Andy. But didn't he owe it to himself to find out? The weight of everything washed over him. He wanted to plead to his friends to believe him and help him find his way through this.

"I wish I could get to the truth and find out if he's changed. And I wish I could do that and still have everyone's support." He avoided their eyes.

"We support you no matter what, Sam," Tara whispered. "But that doesn't mean we have to agree with you."

"We love you, bro," Nate said. "You know that."

Sam resisted the urge to roll his eyes. Same conversation, different set of people. He hadn't been this alone in a long, long time. Not since before life with the Grayson family.

He readjusted his backpack and walked ahead. "C'mon, we'll miss our bus."

* * *

John hung up the phone and pinched the bridge of his nose. Abbie laid her head back against the headrest of the black leather sofa in his office and exhaled. She'd heard it all over speaker phone. It'd been a difficult call.

For almost an hour, they talked to Detective Lacey. He planned to contact Sam next, but he wanted the Graysons to know what was coming. Richard Lacey was more than a detective. He'd become a friend—one aware of Sam's struggles and one who understood what this news might do to him.

John rubbed the back of his neck. How could Andy Quinn still take up space in his thoughts, conversations, and fears after all these years?

"I guess my biggest question is what's this going to do to Sam?" John asked. "I mean, he should realize his father is the reason this is happening nearly six years later."

Why would Sam choose to believe the man who'd neglected and abused him for so many years over his parents? How could he willingly go back to that man who'd caused him so much trauma?

Abbie leaned forward with her elbows on her knees. "I've spent so much time wondering the same thing, hon. And I keep going back to that night when he was seventeen, the night we told him his father had signed off on his parental rights, and we could proceed with adopting him. You remember the day."

"I'll never forget, but I still don't understand it. Quinn is such a terrible human being." John scoffed as he paced the floor.

Abbie was silent for a moment. "You remember the family therapist we met with after the adoption? She told us that although adoption is good and Sam is happy, it won't erase his trauma. Do you remember? I keep thinking about it." Abbie's words trailed off.

He considered what she said. He'd thought about it before, but he'd also hoped the love and support this family gave to Sam would prove that untrue.

"I don't want you to take this the wrong way, John. I'm almost afraid to say it."

"You can tell me anything, you know that." He sat back down on the sofa beside her.

"I do." Her smile was weak. "I'm just afraid what's driving Sam is his need to feel wanted by his biological parent. And that need is stronger than his need for us."

John flinched. He hadn't expected her to say that. He certainly didn't want to believe it. "Do you think so?"

"I must confess something. I went back to my therapist last week. I wanted to talk with someone impartial. And that's what she said, reaffirming what I'd been thinking." The tear slid down her cheek, and she wiped it away quickly. "I'm sorry, I didn't even want to tell you that."

He put his arm around her shoulder. He'd prided himself on being strong and able to fix everything, whether it be with his team or family. But like many times in the past concerning Sam, they were in over their heads. Especially with what was on the horizon.

Only one person could fix this, and he and Abbie needed to take this whole situation and give it to Him. John did the only thing he knew to do at the moment. He prayed.

Her eighteenth birthday had come and gone, and *finally*, she was able to tell her story. At last. Her parents weren't in agreement with what she was doing, but who cared. They didn't agree on much these days. So, this was nothing new.

She caught her reflection in the full-length mirror on the back of her bedroom door. Black pants with holes in the knees, a black sweatshirt, and recently dyed black hair. Short and spikey. And when she glanced around her shabby one-bedroom apartment in a seedy part of Lexington, Kentucky, she blended right in. Her parents wouldn't have approved.

That was fine. She groaned, grabbed her bag, and headed to her job at the grocery store down the street. Rain fell from the overcast sky, but she didn't care. The walk was only a few blocks. Not that she could do anything different since she didn't have a car. She could barely afford her tiny apartment, let alone a vehicle.

She'd rather be almost anywhere but here in Lexington. Her parents had sent her here to live with her religious aunt and uncle. The ones who forced her to attend church with them. "Maybe if she comes with us every Sunday, she'll return to her old self." Yeah, she'd heard their whispers.

They belonged to a huge church, one of the biggest in the nation, her uncle had said proudly. Like she cared about God or church. Hardly. She shuddered at the thought of sitting through all those boring sermons every Sunday. What a waste of time.

She'd scrimped and saved from her after school part-time job to move out on her eighteenth birthday last month. She didn't need her parents, and she sure didn't need her aunt and uncle and their church.

Although ... she smirked as she thought about the one reason to be thankful for her aunt and uncle. The music at that church was good as long as you didn't have to focus for long on all those lyrics about God and Jesus. But one Sunday, they had a guest worship leader from the Nashville area. Apparently, he'd recently become some kind of big deal and had a couple of songs on Christian radio. *Whatever*.

But he and his band got her attention when they'd played. The music sounded awesome, way better than anything she'd heard in church before. She wasn't in the worst mood that Sunday, but of course, not the greatest either because, well, she was in church.

She was into the music, trying to ignore the lyrics, when the cameras showed the lead singer close up. Mesmerized, she couldn't turn away. No, it couldn't be him. No way. But when the pastor came out and said, "Let's give another round of applause for Sam Grayson," the confirmation of her thoughts caused her to gasp and nearly pass out.

It was him. The boy named Sam.

Gritting her teeth, she rounded the corner to the grocery store entrance. She reached for her timecard to punch in. Her knuckles were white from clenching her fists.

He would pay for what he did. He would pay for his part.

Ava would make sure of that.

* * *

Sam tossed and turned all night and crawled out of bed at 6:00 a.m. even though it was Saturday. He showered, made a pot of coffee, and reclined on his sofa.

The call last night from Detective Lacey replayed in his head. He'd told Sam one of the girls who'd been held at the motel in Alabama with him had hired an attorney, who'd subpoenaed all the records.

All night he had dream after dream about the two girls, especially Ava. In her yellow tank top and long blonde hair. She'd been so young and seemed sweet and naive. Sam shivered. What had the two girls gone through? He ran through every detail he remembered of his own ordeal. And theirs had to be worse. Much worse.

The knock on the door caused him to jump. He glanced at the clock. 9:00 a.m. He'd been sitting this way for nearly three hours. Was he losing his mind? He walked to the door and remembered the pot of coffee he'd never even poured a cup from. Yeah, he was losing it. His eye to the peephole, he stood back and took a deep breath before opening the door.

"Hi, hon, we would've called first, but we wanted to see how you're doing." Abbie stepped inside and gave him a hug. John was at her side.

"Come on in." He feigned a smile and ushered them inside. John scanned the apartment, and Sam remembered he'd never been there. But if John wanted a tour, Sam was too tired. "Have a seat." He motioned toward the sofa, while he went to pour out the cold pot of coffee and put on a new one.

"Coffee will be ready in a minute." He walked to the armchair by the sofa and took a seat. He blew out a big breath, waiting for "I told you so" to roll off John's tongue.

"Sam, I'm so sorry about all this. Are you okay?" John asked.

Sam's mouth fell open. These weren't the words he expected from John. "Um, yeah, I mean why wouldn't I be okay? He says he didn't do this." Sam chided himself for the sharpness in his tone. John was being nice, but for some reason, the words rubbed Sam the wrong way.

"And you believe that?" John asked with the same edge Sam had spoken with.

"What happened to innocent until proven guilty?" Sam lashed out. But did he even believe in Andy's innocence? He wanted to. He didn't want to believe he'd been born from that kind of evil.

"Look." Abbie breathed out. "Both of you, let's put this aside and talk. Sam, we just want to be here for you, to support you. Did Detective Lacey tell you the whole story?"

"The whole story?" Everything was so jumbled in his mind. Since the girls had been found safe, their families wanted to keep the story out of the media, so the records were sealed. But now, the youngest had turned eighteen, and she told a different story. Why hadn't he asked for more details? He didn't remember if he'd hung up the phone.

Black spots seeped into the sides of his vision. *Oh no, please God, not a panic attack in front of them. Especially not in front of John.* His heart beat way too fast, and he couldn't take in a full breath.

John rushed to his side.

Abbie left the room and returned with a cool wash cloth for his head.

"It's okay, kiddo. We'll get through this," John said.

Sam hadn't been sure he was still part of *we*, but maybe he was.

* * *

Abbie sat with Sam on the sofa while he drank water. He felt better, but obviously, he hadn't obtained many details from the call with the detective. Kyle would help fill in the gaps. He'd also help figure out what this all meant for Sam, if anything.

The doorbell rang, and John jumped up to let Kyle into the apartment.

"How are ya doing, little bro?" Kyle brought a kitchen chair into the living room and sat opposite Sam.

"Better now, thanks." Sam took another sip of water.

John sat on the other side of Sam, which Abbie was grateful for. They had to show they were united with him, no matter what Sam's thoughts about Quinn might be.

"How much did Detective Lacey tell you?" Kyle asked Sam.

"Umm, one girl is telling a different story. But he really didn't say much."

Abbie locked eyes with Kyle, grateful for his role not only as their son and Sam's brother, but as his attorney. Sam would need him.

Kyle cleared his throat. "Okay, first, Amanda, the older one, is twenty now and away at college. She doesn't want her name brought into any of this. She just wants to move on."

Sam's head snapped up. "Wait a minute, this is about Ava? Is she okay?"

"She's okay physically. But she's very angry."

"Yeah, I would imagine so." Sam agreed.

Abbie held her breath. This would be the hard part Sam wouldn't understand.

"Sam," Kyle leaned forward in his chair, hands clenched together. "Ava wants to prosecute everyone involved."

"Meaning my father?"

John winced at Sam's use of the word to describe Andy Quinn.

"Yes. Andy Quinn, the lady who drugged you, Paulette, and their sidekick, Blaze, who was in charge of physically nabbing the girls."

"I get that, even though Andy says he didn't do it. He said that was Blaze's deal."

Abbie didn't understand Sam's thinking. Everyone in the room except him believed Quinn was the true mastermind of the operation. How could Sam not see that? He once did. How had the man blinded him into thinking he hadn't?

"For everything that is hidden will eventually be brought into the open, and every secret will be brought to light." Thank you, God, for reminding me of that verse from Mark.

"Well, there's more." Kyle exhaled. "She's trying to go after you, first and foremost."

"What? What are you talking about?" Sam's eyes widened.

"In her eyes, you were the one who lured her to the coffee shop."

"What? Me? I was also drugged, dragged, and Blaze had a gun on me. And I'm the one who told her to run." Sam sat up, the paleness from earlier gone.

"I know, I know." Kyle held up both hands. "We all know that. So do all the attorneys and the judges. You're going to be okay."

"But what does this mean? Am I going to have to defend myself?"

"No. Since you were a minor, and also a victim, your name is redacted from every document she'll ever be able to see. Your name will never be known to her."

Sam sighed. "Okay, I guess that's good. But how could she think that? I tried to help her get away."

Abbie was a mother first, and that part of her took over. "Honey, it sounds like those two girls were held captive in Miami for more than two years and went through a lot of despicable things. She's going to blame everyone who was around."

"She's right, son." John spoke up. "From what I've heard from Detective Lacey, once she reads all the depositions and court documents, there will be no doubt you were a victim. Just like the girls were."

John's words calmed Sam. Despite their recent arguing and hurt feelings regarding Quinn, he still trusted John. Their bond was somehow still intact.

"And Kyle's going to be working on the case to make sure of it." John nodded toward Kyle.

"Well, actually, Dad, I've handed the case to our senior

criminal attorney." Sam started to object, but Kyle continued. "He's the best one for this. With my transition to entertainment law, I'm not as confident in the criminal side. Dustin Wells is the best, not just in Nashville, but the entire region. But I'll still be briefed and know everything that happens."

"Okay, but do you think I should contact Ava and tell her my side of the story?" Sam's tone was innocent.

"No!" All three shouted in unison, and Sam flinched.

"You can't do that, Sam," Kyle insisted. "Then she'll know your identity, and you don't want that. Let the legal system work. It'll come out in your favor. You can't have any contact with either girl or their families. Promise me."

Sam didn't appear sure at first but slowly came around. "Okay, I get it. I promise I won't contact anyone involved."

Please, God, give Sam the strength to get through this, and please help these two girls who've suffered so much.

thirty-six

John flipped the burgers on the grill. The Grayson family day had been perfect, and that was rare lately. His team had an offseason scrimmage game earlier, and the whole family went. Afterward, they came home for dinner. Even Sam and Lauren.

He salted and peppered the burgers then turned around. The sight of his family on the deck made him smile. Abbie and Cassie sat beside each other, laughing about something. Hannah and Lauren stood in the backyard admiring the lilies in bloom. And Kyle and Sam leaned against the deck rails, chatting. Likely about new songs Sam was publishing since Kyle was his attorney for all his business dealings.

John was surprised Sam even showed up today. Things had been better since the day he found out about Ava going after Sam, and John and Abbie supported him. But all-in-all, the situation was still rocky. John hadn't backed away from his stance of refusing to believe in Quinn's innocence. And Sam accused John of being jealous and Abbie of not seeing his side.

He and Abbie had discussed it at length earlier today. She didn't have any good answers, either, other than to tell him to cool off or he'd lose his youngest son. So that's what John attempted to do, but it sure wasn't easy.

He finished up the burgers and plated them. Hannah and Lauren hurried into the house to get the buns and chips, and afterward, they filled their plates.

"We're ready for you to pray, Dad." Hannah shot Kyle a dirty look because he'd already taken a bite of his burger, and everyone laughed.

Then they settled down and bowed their heads. John prayed for their health and food. He thanked God for his family being together today and prayed for many future occasions.

While they ate, the banter was like it used to be. Easy and fun. The siblings teased each other, then asked about each other's work. Everyone was interested in Sam's upcoming events and new songs. He happily told them everything they wanted to know. And Lauren was by his side. She added her own contributions to the conversations.

He and Abbie found Sam and Lauren's relationship to be a bit of a mystery. The two were boyfriend and girlfriend, but they seemed more like they'd always been—best friends.

Unfortunately, the days of private conversations with Sam about things like this felt as though they were in the past. And that was John's fault. He owned that. He'd made things awkward with Sam. But he couldn't help himself. In his honest, soul-searching moments, he admitted to God he was jealous. Very jealous. He wouldn't lose Sam to Andy Quinn. That's something he couldn't handle.

* * *

Andy pounded on the concrete cell wall until his knuckles bled.

"What's wrong with you?" Rio asked from the adjacent cell. "Meeting with your attorney didn't go so good?"

"You could say that. Those two girls have been found, and one is about to tell her story."

"Oh. But it wasn't you, it was the Blaze dude, right?"

Andy paced his cell. What was he going to do? Things could spin outta control quickly.

"It wasn't you, right? Rio asked again.

"No, of course not," Andy lied. "But what if she tries to pin it on my kid?"

"But I thought you said there's no evidence against him."

"Yeah, right. You're right. I guess I'm bein' paranoid."

"Relax over there, man," Rio said.

Relax? Andy scoffed. That's exactly what his attorney said. He also said the police had no evidence against him. It all pointed to Blaze. The problem was Blaze knew the truth. And he had the evidence. He would cut a deal and turn Andy in. That was for certain. It was only a matter of time. What was he waiting for?

God, if you're there for someone like me, I need to know what to do here. You know I'm sorry for all I done. I just don't want my kid to hate me.

God didn't provide an audible answer, but he never did. His kid had told him he'd heard the voice of God once. Could that be true? He couldn't imagine it, but he didn't think Sam would lie. He must have learned that from his mom.

Sam's mom. When was the last time he'd thought of her? She'd been beautiful in those early days. Always so pure and innocent, like Sam. But then Andy got ahold of her, introduced her to drugs and that whole world, and she'd become more like him every day. That was her downfall. It was his fault, and in the process, Sam was left without a mother.

He wouldn't let himself dwell on those days. What he put her through was too painful. With Sam, he still had a chance. Hard to believe, but true. Further proof Sam was a better person than Andy and his mom combined.

And here he sat in his prison cell. Still a liar.

thirty-seven

"What do you mean I can't press charges?" Ava stood and screamed over the table at the dimwitted old man. Her long, black-lacquered nails dug into the wooden table in the attorney's office.

"Look, I told you when we started, this wouldn't be easy. And now that I've poured through all the files, it appears impossible." The gray-haired attorney explained.

"Well, keep digging!" Ava spat. This guy was supposed to be a great attorney?

The man sighed again, and she was sick of it. Here she was living in a squalid apartment only to throw all her money at this guy. If he couldn't do the job, she didn't know what she'd do. This was it. Her only chance.

"Ava, let me explain, and maybe it'll make sense." The man leaned back in his chair, dropped his pen on the table, and shook his head Where was his fight? Multiple people told her he was the best, but he'd done nothing for her.

"All right." She sat back in her chair, arms folded. "Go ahead. Tell me."

The man opened a thick file. "These are all depositions. From Sam Grayson himself, from the lady who was there,

Paulette, the boy who was thirty at the time, Blaze, and Andy Quinn, whose alias back then was Drew Keller. Quinn is also Sam's father."

"Okay, so what?" She threw up her hands.

"All these depositions say the same thing. Sam was a victim, like you. Every single person says so."

"Well, I say he wasn't!" Ava came out of her chair and leaned far across the table, near the man's face. She was through playing games. "That's a lie. He. Took. Me," she said through clenched teeth. "What part don't you understand?"

The man pushed his chair back and stood. Yep, she'd gone too far, like always. But it didn't help that no one understood. Not even her parents, who'd insinuated if she and Amanda hadn't been somewhere they weren't supposed to be, none of this would've happened. She brushed those thoughts away. She needed to calm down, not become angrier.

"Miss Grant, I need you to sit down and collect yourself. I'll explain the rest, but not if there's another outburst. I won't tolerate it." The man was stern but never raised his voice.

Ava breathed deeply and slowed her pulse. "Fine," she said.

"All right then." The man sat and pulled another set of documents out of his file including x-rays. "These are Sam's medical records. They document his injuries. He was severely dehydrated to the point of kidney damage. He was covered in bruises, had several broken ribs, and was even stabbed in the shoulder. His toxicology indicated he was drugged. And the three who were convicted all admitted to doing this to Sam."

"I don't believe it. They're covering for him." She raked her nails through her spiky, black hair.

The man pressed his lips together and stared at Ava. "Ava, why would they do that? These criminals don't cover for someone else. Especially if there's a kid they can pin it on. Plus, the medical records don't lie."

"If you're telling me he's not responsible, then who is?"

"My guess is the guy who led you to the coffee shop, Blaze."

"No way, that guy's a big lug. Not smart enough." Then it dawned on her. "Okay wait, the guy Drew or Andy or whatever his name was. Did you say he's Sam's father?"

"Yes, that's right."

"Don't you see? He's covering for Sam. And since the Drew/Andy guy is the group leader, they're not going to say Sam did it for fear of that man."

The attorney tilted his head. "That's a huge leap. Nothing here remotely suggests Sam did this. He was only sixteen. There's no way. If I had to guess, I would say you're half right that Paulette and Blaze covered for Andy, the mastermind. But Sam? Impossible."

She'd had it. That was the final straw. "Don't you get it? I don't care about Andy, he's already in prison. I want his son to pay, and if you're too much of an idiot to help, then I'm done here!"

Ava kicked over her chair, grabbed her backpack, and stormed out of the office. All that money down the drain on this complete idiot of an attorney. She walked the twelve blocks home, swiping the hot, angry tears from her face. She'd get Sam Grayson. Whatever she had to do to take him down, she would.

* * *

"Hot story people, everyone in conference room east," the editor-in-chief shouted.

Lauren received the text from her features editor thirty minutes ago. Some big mystery meeting. She wasn't supposed to be in the office, but fortunately, she'd been at the coffee shop around the corner working on a new article and able to get here quickly.

"Any hint of what this is about?" Lauren asked her editor.

Chantal shrugged. "Not really, just something about a local church."

Lauren rolled her eyes. "Oh great, probably another pastor

stepping down for less than honorable reasons." The paper had covered several stories like that lately. Another reason she'd fallen away from church.

As they entered the conference room and took their seats around the massive table, the editor bellowed out more instructions to the dozen or so reporters like herself and editors who settled into their seats.

"We have a scandal brewing at Middle Tennessee Church," Mr. Matthews said.

Lauren gasped, and her hand flew to her mouth.

"What's wrong?" Chantal whispered.

"That's my boyfriend Sam's church. He's a worship leader there."

"Oh, that's right. You know, he probably knows more than we do." Chantel raised one eyebrow.

Mr. Matthews opened his laptop and tapped the keys. "This is a clip from the news that just aired. Everyone watch, please. And take notes."

The clip opened with the news anchorwoman introducing a girl named Ava Grant. Lauren shivered. There had to be a lot of Avas in the world, right? Just because she'd only ever known of one, the one Sam talked about, that didn't mean anything.

Sam had described the girl to her. Pretty, with long, light-blonde hair. The Ava on TV appeared older and had short, black hair. She wore a black jacket and had gauges in her ears. She wasn't the picture of innocence Sam had described.

Lauren squirmed, grabbed her pen, and focused on taking notes. She jotted down the name, Ava Grant, as the young woman spoke about being trafficked at age thirteen. Lauren dropped her pen and grabbed the table. What were the chances—

"—and his name is Sam Grayson. He's the worship leader at one of the biggest churches in the country."

"Are you talking about Sam Grayson, the singer-songwriter?" Candace asked, her mouth gaping. "He has songs on the radio."

"That's the one." Ava smirked. "Singing about how great God is, all the while hiding the big secret about what he did to me."

Lauren knocked her chair over getting away from the table. She sprinted out of the conference room and into the bathroom. Everyone gawked at her when she left the room, but she didn't care. She held onto the sink with both hands and gasped. Surely, her heart couldn't beat any faster without coming out of her chest. No, this couldn't be happening. How could Ava say those things about Sam? She was lying. This would destroy him.

"Lauren, are you okay?" Chantal asked in a breathless whisper.

She couldn't hold back the tears. "It's him, it's Sam she's talking about."

Chantal nodded.

She'd pieced it together already.

"I'm so sorry, Lauren. Did you know about this?"

"Well, sort of." Lauren grabbed a paper towel to wipe the still-falling tears from her face. "But none of what she's saying is true. Sam was a victim, like that girl Ava. All his medical records prove it. He suffered terrible abuse under those captors. They drugged him and used him in their scheme."

"Okay, okay, that's good." Chantal patted her on the back. "And he had to be young, too, right? So, this girl goes on the news and tells this big story that'll turn out to be false. It'll all be okay."

Another friend, Kyra, joined them and stood next to her, handing her more paper towels.

"After you left," Kyra said, "The anchorwoman noted the newsroom told her those records are sealed, but their legal people were trying to find out something."

"See, it'll be fine." Chantel's smile was forced. "Sam was a juvenile, and the records are sealed. We'll go at that angle of the story."

It'll be fine? It would never be fine. Not for Sam. Not only would he be forced to relive the nightmare again, but his name was associated with this now. She'd been around long enough to know people often didn't live down these kinds of allegations. Even after they turned out to be false.

* * *

Abbie stared at the TV, not bothering to stop the tears that ran down her face. On the counter were the coffee and snacks she'd just packed to take on their three-and-a-half-hour trip to surprise Sam at his worship event in Tuscaloosa this evening.

John paced the kitchen floor, but he stopped in his tracks and looked at Abbie. "It's good we're going. He's going to need our support."

"Why is this happening? There's no way that young girl believes the accusations she's making."

"Did you see how angry she was? Absolutely nothing like the sweet, naive girl Sam had described. She's been through it, and she's looking to blame someone."

"But why him? He tried to help her."

Their front door opened, and Kyle walked in. "I thought I'd come over rather than call."

"Oh, thank you, sweetheart." Abbie greeted him with a hug, and John did the same. "What do you think? And have you talked to Sam? Does he know?" They walked to the kitchen, and all three sat around the island.

"I can't get ahold of Sam, and then I remembered he's in Tuscaloosa already. He keeps his phone off on days he's preparing for a show." Kyle looked down at the coffee and snacks. "Y'all are still headed there?"

"That's the plan." John nodded.

"That's good. Once this hits, he'll be devastated. But listen, there's nothing to this. I found out she hired an attorney who's a close colleague of one of our partners. He went through the details of the case and apparently told her a few days ago there's no case against Sam. The courts cleared him long ago, and there's nothing warranting even a reopening of a case against him. But Andy Quinn, probably."

"How did she find out Sam's name though?" This detail bugged both her and John since the report first came on the news. "His records are sealed. His name was redacted from the depositions."

Kyle drew in a breath and exhaled. "From what her attorney said, she'd gone to a church service in Kentucky where Sam played as a guest worship leader, and she recognized him. And of course, the pastor introduced him, so she got his name."

"Wow, of all places." John scratched his head. "But maybe this will open up the investigation, and Quinn will get more time added to his sentence. And his son he supposedly cares about will be off the hook."

Poor John. He'd said all along Andy would hurt Sam again. And now that's exactly what was happening.

But even if police charged Andy, it wouldn't be over for Sam. His name was being dragged through the mud, and the old wounds would be re-opened. That was the last thing Sam needed.

thirty-eight

Sam and Nate sat backstage and tuned their guitars. They chatted while Tara ran though vocals with other members of the band in another room. Sam always loved these quiet moments before a worship event. And tonight was a big one. They were about to lead worship for nearly ten thousand students at the University of Alabama, in the same arena where John had recently led his team to victory in the conference tournament.

Sometimes when he thought about all the ways God had blessed him, he was overwhelmed.

"Did you ever think we'd be here?" he asked.

Nate stopped tuning and turned toward Sam. "This is all you, man. I'm so proud of all you've done. The rest of us are along for the ride."

Sam laughed. "You're the one who introduced me to this genre of music, which I never knew existed. Then John and Abbie got me a guitar, and God did all the rest. Honestly, *we* wouldn't be here without you and Tara. You know that."

"Thanks for saying that. And thanks for staying humble." Nate playfully punched Sam in the shoulder.

"Aw shucks." Sam laughed.

"But seriously, I noticed you're still calling your parents John and Abbie. I thought things had improved."

Sam cringed. "No. Things are weird with them. I don't feel much like I belong these days."

Nate turned and put his guitar on its floor stand and once again turned toward Sam. "What's going on? Is it still the Andy Quinn thing?"

Sam crossed his arms across the top of his guitar and blew a long strand of hair off his face. "It's been tense. I mean, we're talking, but it's not like it was. John is against me having any communication with Andy, and Abbie tries to defend John, which makes everything awkward. To be honest, I hate it. I miss them, and you know, how we used to be."

"Are you sure he's worth it? Andy, I mean."

Few people could get away with asking him that. But Nate had been his trusted friend for a long time. "To be honest, I'm not sure. What I do know is talking to him has helped me heal. That place inside me that's always screamed out, 'no one has ever wanted me,' has quieted some."

Nate sighed. "I get that. Do you think he's really turned to God?"

"Whew, that's a tough one. Sometimes I do, and sometimes I question it. Only God knows. I'd like to believe he is, and this isn't just another con ..."

The knock on the backstage door interrupted his thoughts, and in walked John, Abbie, and Kellen, the minister who would be preaching.

"Oh, I wasn't expecting y'all tonight."

John and Abbie approached him, and he stood. He stiffened at the warm, tight hug he received from them, especially John. But when he stepped back, he realized none of the three were smiling. "Is something wrong? What's going on?"

"Sam, Nate, let's all sit for a moment." Kellen said. He and John dragged three more chairs to where Nate and Sam sat.

"Okay, you're scaring me now." Sam placed his guitar in its case on the floor.

"Yeah, is everything okay with everyone at home?" Nate asked, concern ringing in his voice.

"No, no, it's nothing like that." Kellen held a hand up. "Everyone's fine. We didn't mean to make you think something like that was wrong."

Sam breathed a slight sigh of relief.

Abbie hung her head, hands clasped in her lap, and John had his eyes closed as if he were praying.

"Something's going on," Sam said, "What is it?"

Still nothing. John raised his eyes toward Kellen, and finally, Kellen spoke. "Sam, Nate, we don't know how to tell you this, but the show's been cancelled."

It took a moment for Kellen's words to register. Was this some kind of weird joke?

Nate sat with his mouth open and chuckled. "Mm-hmm, right. The last I checked this morning nearly ten thousand tickets had been sold."

"I guess you haven't been on social media or anything else today." Kellen stated.

Something was definitely wrong. "Well, no, we've been busy getting ready for the show. One of you please tell us what's going on."

"Sam." John jumped into the conversation. "It's about Ava. Well, I'm not sure—"

"What, did something happen to her?"

"No. She went to the media this morning. Big media. Cable network news." John paused and bit his lip. "She told them Sam Grayson, songwriter, minister, and worship leader, was responsible for abducting her into human trafficking."

"What?" Sam stood so fast he knocked his stool over. "No, there's no way she said that. I don't believe it."

"Honey, it's true." Abbie spoke up. "Not only that, her words have spread like wildfire. The university cancelled the show and refunded the tickets."

"No, I don't believe it." Sam paced the floor with his hands clenched behind his head. "This can't be true. Why are we still here then? Why hasn't someone from the university said something?"

Kellen spoke up. "I made the decision an hour ago. I heard your parents were on their way. I asked the university reps if we could wait until they got here to tell you. Sam. It's all true. But listen, it's all going to be okay."

"Ava actually said those things? I have to see it for myself." Sam rummaged through his jacket for his cell phone, pulled it out, and did a search for his name. Various news outlets ran the story. He scrolled past numerous articles containing his name. "*How* is this all going to be okay?"

thirty-nine

Sam replayed the video several times. He found it hard to believe that hate-spewing girl was the naive, sweet Ava he'd briefly known. But there was no mistaking her eyes, though. It was definitely her. Had he been wrong about her?

Each time he watched her video, the truth settled on him a little more. She'd been through something so awful it'd turned her into someone she wouldn't have otherwise been. Obviously tough and street smart. But also filled with hate. And so very broken.

He walked to his coffeepot like a zombie, added coffee grounds, and hit start, then plopped on his sofa. After the long, stressful ride home with his parents, he hadn't slept a wink. He'd opted to ride home with them rather than on the bus. He figured better with them since they were aware of the whole story, rather than with the band who, other than Nate and Tara, knew nothing of his story. Tara and Nate didn't know as much as his parents, but they knew enough they could share with the others so they'd know Sam was innocent.

John wouldn't stop talking about Andy, and how he needed to confess to this. Sam didn't argue. Not because he agreed, but because he was overwhelmed with the situation. Instead, he tuned John out and spent three hours on social media that he wished he hadn't.

When he got home, he put his phone away, but it was time to face reality again. He was sure he'd missed calls and texts. He hadn't talked to Kyle, Hannah, or Lauren yet, though he'd swapped a few texts on the road last night.

He picked up the phone. A text marked urgent got his attention. His senior pastor, Stephan Hayden, asked him to come to his office today.

Ugh ... this couldn't be good. He'd get dressed and go now to get this over with. Stephan would want to know the whole story, but Sam dreaded re-telling it.

He quickly scanned his other texts, mostly from his family and Lauren and all sweet and supportive. Poor Lauren. She had to watch the news interview at work. How must she have felt? Hopefully, she still believed in him.

* * *

Sam sucked in a deep breath and walked into the church office. Under normal circumstances, he would have strolled back to Stephan's office, but something about today felt very formal. Like maybe he shouldn't. At least it was Monday. Most people wouldn't be around today since they'd worked the weekend, including Stephan. Why was he here today?

Sam found the pastor's admin, Liz, in her office and lightly knocked.

"Hi, Liz." He forced a cheerful tone.

"Oh, hi, Sam." She didn't offer a smile.

"Stephan called me in for a meeting. Is he back there?"

"Sure, let me call him."

Sam waited while she punched in numbers then whispered. Liz *always* met him with a smile and a hug. And she never failed to ask about his worship events. Today she was very formal, if not standoffish. He was sure he wasn't imagining it.

"He'll see you now." Liz's eyes went back to her paperwork.

Nope. He definitely wasn't imagining things.

* * *

Stephan's door was open, so Sam walked right in. Jerry Bryce, the lead elder, was there too. Sam's throat became suddenly so dry he could barely swallow.

"Sam, thanks for coming on short notice. And on a Monday." Stephan also acted more formal than usual.

"Yes, thanks Sam." Jerry offered him a handshake.

"Sure, uh, no problem." Sam instantly regretted his clammy palms. He dreaded having to explain the whole story.

Stephan clasped his hands on his desk and leaned forward while Jerry stood and closed the door. Were they trying to freak him out? Because if so, mission accomplished. Sweat beaded on Sam's forehead.

The senior pastor sighed before he even spoke. "I assume you know why you're here."

Was he supposed to answer? "Umm because of the news story, I guess."

"The news story, yes, and the girl, Ava Grant." Stephan propped his elbows on his desk. "We want to get your side, and we will when we can get the rest of the elders together. But for now, I'm sorry, but we have to place you on a leave of absence."

Sam's mouth fell open, and he stared at them. Surely, he hadn't heard him correctly. "Leave of absence, sir?"

"Yes, unfortunately there's no way around it. We've had scores of people call the church today asking for your resignation—"

"My resignation?" The words came out louder than intended. "For something I'm accused of doing that I didn't do?" His head spun. *How is this happening, God? Isn't this the dream you gave me? Or was this another dream that wasn't meant to be?*

Stephan raised his hand to speak. "I know it doesn't seem

fair. And like I said, we'll get your side of the story. But for now, we have to appease the church donors, which is why the leave of absence. We'll continue to pay you until the church completes the investigation."

He didn't care about the money. What he made here was a small portion of his earnings. But what if he couldn't tour, and what if the radio stations stopped playing his songs? Then his finances would dwindle. His thoughts spun out of control.

"Sam, are you all right?"

Pastor Stephan's voice put a stop to his mind's tailspin. "Yes, sir. Is that all?"

"Yes, for today." Again, way too formal.

"Thank you both." Sam swallowed hard and left.

Thank you? Did he just thank them for not hearing his story and for basically firing him? Sure, they didn't exactly fire him, but their demeanor told him they weren't on his side of this. In fact, they didn't even want to hear his side.

God, I need you now more than ever. I thought this was always your dream for me. Please show me where to turn.

Isaiah 41:10 popped into his head. *So do not fear, for I am with you; do not be dismayed for I am your God. I will strengthen you and help you; I will uphold you with my righteous right hand.*

Peace settled over him for the first time in the past twenty-four hours. The first time he'd heard that verse he'd been at an all-time low, but then the Graysons told him their plans to adopt him.

He'd be okay. God would take care of him, even if it would be a bumpy ride to get there.

forty

"Another surprise visit." Andy said over the metal table to Sam. "I like these."

Sam fidgeted and found it hard to smile back. "Yeah, I guess you don't watch or hear much news in this place?" His father didn't seem to know why he was here.

"Nah, there's a TV in the common room, but it's not on the news much. Mostly sports and stuff. Why you ask?"

Sam licked his dry lips and figured out how to start this conversation. "The girl, Ava, went on national news a few days ago and told her story." Diving right into the conversation was certainly one way.

His father's face paled a couple of shades.

"What do you mean?" His voice was shaky.

"She told the story of how she was taken and sold into trafficking in Miami, and she's blaming me for the whole thing." He leaned forward toward his father, watching his face carefully.

"Well, that's a total lie!" Andy exclaimed, his face turned from pale to maroon.

"I know, but what is the truth? You have to tell me. I deserve to know. Was it Blaze, like you said? Or was it ... someone else?"

He needed the truth now. If it was his father, he'd tell him. Especially knowing Sam was being blamed for this.

His father bit his lower lip and avoided Sam's eyes altogether. He focused his gaze on the table instead. "It was Blaze. I swear to you. I didn't know they planned to steal any girls. I never woulda done that."

Sam sat back in his chair. His memories from that time in Alabama were hazy due to the drugs he'd been forced. But he remembered bits and pieces. One specific memory stood out of his father telling him it was show time, and he had to go out and bring in the girls. But could he even trust his memories from then? He had to get the truth out of him.

"Because of this, my worship events have been cancelled. And the church I work for has put me on leave of absence pending an investigation." Surely, if his father were involved, he'd speak up now that the lies were ruining Sam's life.

"No way, they can't do that to you. Can't they see you'd never do something like that?" Andy shifted in his seat.

"The police don't have evidence against anyone else, so all they have is her word against mine. And she says it was me. Until Blaze or ... someone else comes forward, I'm all they have."

Andy ran his hand over his scruffy beard. "I'm sorry, kid. I'll always hate myself for the position I put you in."

Sam studied him long and hard. "Look, I have to know." Sam leaned over the table again and looked into his father's eyes—dark and hollow. Weird he hadn't noticed that before. "Have you really given your life to God? And do you swear you aren't lying?"

Andy stared at Sam and then the ceiling. It took forever for him to answer, but when he did, Sam could've sworn a tear formed in the corner of the man's eye. "I swear to you on both, Sam."

Sam jumped to his feet. He motioned for the guard and walked away. "That's all I needed to know. Please pray for me," he said over his shoulder.

* * *

Rio lay on his cot. Quinn walked past his cell on the way to his own, his head hung low. His cell door clanked as it locked.

Rio moved as close to the shared wall between him and Quinn as possible. "What happened man, something with your kid?"

The man let out a long sigh. "You ever lied to someone, and it hurt them? I mean, hurt them really bad?"

Rio laughed. "Nah, man. What's a lie anyway? You do what you gotta due to cover yourself."

"Yeah, it used to be that easy until my kid started believing in me."

"Not following you, man." This Quinn dude used to be hard-core, what happened? "Since when are you bothered by lyin' anyway?" Rio laughed.

"Since my kid is taking the blame for something I did. It's gonna ruin his life. I coulda put a stop to it just now, and he'd be off the hook. But I didn't."

"Ah. I'm with ya now. You talking about that whole trafficking thing?" Mm-hmm, would Quinn confess? A confession from Quinn would open up all kinds of possibilities for himself. "It was you who was in charge of the whole scheme, right?" It was worth a shot, but surely the guy wouldn't be stupid enough to—

"It was me," Quinn blurted out.

Rio laughed. Quinn wasn't nearly as bright as he gave him credit for.

"How old were the girls, man?" Rio pushed. The younger the better for Rio's bargaining concerns.

"Thirteen and fifteen." Quinn admitted.

"Whew." Rio whistled through his teeth. "Your kid's gonna get jail time for that, you know."

"No, that can't happen." Quinn's voice was stern.

"Maybe it won't," Rio said. He didn't want the guy to confess to the authorities before he could get his own lawyer to go to the DA on his behalf. Turning Quinn in would he his ticket for an earlier release. "Let it go for a while. You know, see how it plays out."

Rio needed to buy a little time. Enough time to talk with his lawyer who could meet with the DA and make a deal to trade his knowledge of Quinn's crimes for a reduction in his own sentence. And maybe, with any luck, he'd be outta here in time to see his kid graduate from high school.

forty-one

The past few weeks had been long and hard. Lauren had kept in touch with the newsroom at the *Tennessean* to keep tabs on Sam's story, but she'd asked the editor-in-chief not to assign her any pieces regarding Sam due to their relationship.

The rain fell harder, and she turned on her windshield wipers on her way to Sam's apartment. She'd stopped at Newk's and picked up lunch. He'd been hiding out in his apartment for the past few days.

She made a left turn onto Columbia Avenue, and her thoughts drifted. What was their relationship these days? Since they'd been boyfriend and girlfriend, their relationship had gone nowhere.

Sam was consumed with all the drama in his life. She chastised herself. He had a right to be. This whole story destroyed his career and his relationship with the Graysons. She had no right to feel sorry for herself just because he hadn't taken her out to dinner or bought her flowers lately.

She sighed and got out of the car with the sack of food and climbed the steps to his second-floor apartment. Sam opened the door before she even knocked.

"I saw you pull up." He smiled.

Lauren handed him the bag, and her heart skipped a beat. He seemed better than he had been in a couple of weeks. He'd shaved and wore khaki shorts and a navy-blue shirt. Maybe he was coming out of this spiral.

"Thanks for the food." He led her to the kitchen.

"You're welcome. It looks like you're feeling better today. I'm so glad." She opened his kitchen cabinet, grabbed two plates, and set them on the counter.

"Hey." He put his hands on her waist, she turned toward him, and they kissed. "I'm sorry. I've been completely pre-occupied. I know I've been neglecting you."

She studied him. "It's okay. You're going through a lot."

"It's not okay. I'm gonna do better, promise," he whispered.

Her eyes burned, and the lump in her throat wouldn't allow her to speak. This was the most real moment they'd had together in weeks. She thanked God for the good sign.

They carried their sandwiches and chips to the table. Between bites, they discussed Daisy and the toys she destroyed this week, today's rain, and a reality show they both watched. When there was nothing else to discuss, she forced the question she was afraid to ask. "Have you heard anything new from church?"

His expression darkened, and he shook his head. "Not a thing. I left a message for Pastor Stephan two days ago and haven't heard a word."

"He hasn't returned your call?" How could they treat him that way?

"Nope. And they've yet to ask my side of the story. So, do you know what I did? I typed up an email. I mean, how can they not even want to know my side?" Sam walked to the fridge, grabbed two diet colas, and set one in front of her.

"I don't know, that doesn't even make sense. Has anyone else from church called you?" She popped the top of the can.

"No, just Nate and Tara. They're amazing friends. They believe I'm innocent."

"Of course they do. Anyone who knows you believes you're innocent."

Sam ate the last of his sandwich and crumbled the wrapper. "But Pastor Rob from John and Abbie's church has called me a few times. He even prayed with me over the phone. He believes me too."

"I'm so glad." She hesitated. Should she bring this up again? "Umm, you're still referring to your mom and dad as John and Abbie? Things aren't any better?"

Sam pushed his unopened bag of chips aside. "You're the second person whose mentioned it. I guess more and more I've been thinking of Andy as my father."

A cold chill ran down her neck, and she shivered. Thankfully, he didn't seem to notice. How could he believe anything that man said? She'd never understand how much Sam wanted to believe him. And believe in him. But she didn't want him to know she didn't understand.

"What about John and Abbie? They've been supportive lately." She shrugged. She wasn't about to comment on Andy Quinn.

"Yeah, sort of. But they constantly bring him up. I'm going to tell them tonight that I confronted him and what he said."

Lauren slowly nodded her head and finished the last of her sandwich. She swallowed, took a small sip of her drink, and said what she'd promised herself she wouldn't. "Do you really believe him? I mean, after all he's put you through?"

Sam's head snapped up, and he looked at her. He didn't speak for a few long seconds. "You too, Lauren? You don't believe it either?"

"I'm sorry, Sam. I want to. You don't know how much I want to believe he had nothing to do with trafficking those girls. But he's been a con man all his life ..."

Her thoughts were interrupted by the ringing of Sam's phone.

He walked out on the deck to take the call without saying anything else.

She deserved that. *Why can't I be supportive?* If only she didn't know as much about Andy Quinn as she did. The crimes he'd committed, the reasons the authorities had removed Sam from the man's home over and over as a child. She'd never be able to trust that man.

The sliding glass doors opened, and Sam trudged back in, his head hung as he flung his phone onto the sofa.

"What's wrong?" Lauren rose and trekked to the living room area where he stood, running his hands through his shoulder-length hair. The flashes of anger in his eyes from a few minutes ago were gone and replaced with a look of defeat.

He blew out a long breath. "That was Kyle. He said the two top Christian radio stations dropped my songs." He flopped on the sofa. "What am I supposed to do now?"

"Oh, Sam, I don't know what to say. I'm so sorry. Once they hear your story, this is bound to blow over."

"But when am I ever going to get a chance to tell my story? The church doesn't want to hear it. Radio doesn't want to hear it. And even if they did, Kyle and the criminal attorney don't want me to tell my side to the media until they can crack the Blaze guy and get him to confess. So far, he's refused."

Sam slumped over, head in his hands. "Talk about cancel culture. This is my career. Everything I've worked for. Everything I thought God wanted me to do. Gone."

She wanted to say, "all because of Andy Quinn," but she didn't dare.

forty-two

Dinner with the Graysons was the last thing Sam wanted to do tonight. The whole clan would be there. He still loved his family, but right now, none of them, not even Kyle who was closest to the situation, understood what he was going through. And John couldn't hold back his feelings toward Andy.

During dinner, everyone avoided mentioning the things he dealt with. John told funny basketball stories, and even Sam laughed. But John saw him differently now because of his relationship with Andy. Sam longed for the relationship he and John had the past few years. It was severely strained now, and Sam didn't know what to do about that. Avoiding Andy Quinn wasn't an option.

"Who wants dessert?' Hannah asked.

"We'd love to, but we have to get home." Kyle glanced at Cassie.

"The dog hasn't been let out since this afternoon." Cassie grimaced.

They said their goodbyes, and John, Abbie, Hannah, and Sam took their strawberry shortcake to the family room. "I forgot how much I love in-season strawberries." Sam scraped the bottom of his bowl.

"I'm just glad to see you eat," Abbie said.

He had picked at his dinner, even though she fixed one of his favorite dishes. His appetite hadn't been huge lately.

"I didn't want to ask during dinner, but anything new with church or your worship tour?" John scraped the last of his dessert with his spoon.

Sam set his empty bowl on the coffee table. "No, nothing. The church won't even give me a chance to tell my side."

John's eyes widened. "That doesn't seem right, son. What's the pastor saying?'

"That's just it, he's not saying anything. They won't even return my calls. Kyle is looking over an email I want to send, telling my story."

"I'm sorry, honey," Abbie added. "This is awful. Pastor Rob would love to have you back at our church, you know."

"Yeah, he's been super nice. He said he'd like me to fill in as needed, but I don't want to be a distraction. And I would be."

"I'm sorry," John said. "I know you don't want to hear this, but Andy Quinn needs to confess."

Here we go again. Sam gritted his teeth.

"John." Abbie shook her head at John.

"Daddy, *please* don't go there." Even Hannah was done with these conversations.

Sam was in no mood to debate Andy Quinn for the hundredth time. "Don't. Just don't." He stared at John. "I didn't tell you, but I confronted him last week, and he denied everything. He said it was all Blaze, just like I thought."

"Sam." John placed his head in his hands before looking back up. "You can't believe him. Surely not. Not after all he's done to you over the years."

This conversation played like a broken record, and Sam refused to continue. He stood up and directed his words at John. "I'm done discussing this with you. And until you can stop bringing my father into everything, I'm done with you too."

He hated to be that way, but John gave him no choice. The

man just couldn't drop it. He left the room with Abbie right behind him.

"Sam, please don't go. Let's sit and talk about this."

"Are you serious, Mom? How many times have we had this exact same conversation? He's not capable of talking to me without blaming all of life's problems on Andy Quinn."

"Sam—"

"I'm sorry, Mom. I love you. I can't deal with him on top of everything else. You're welcome to come over anytime, like always."

Sam closed the door and stood on the front steps. The same place he stood when he came to the Graysons for the first time nearly eight years ago. So much had happened in those eight years.

And now nothing would ever be the same.

* * *

"I'm sorry, Hannah." John had pushed too hard, once again. "I can't stand to see what Quinn's doing to him. And it makes me crazy he can't see it."

"How can you be so sure Andy Quinn hasn't changed, Dad? I mean, its possible right?" Hannah asked.

John shrugged. "Even if he has changed, he's still lying about the trafficking of those girls. And that forces the blame on Sam."

Abbie stood in the doorway, and she and John locked eyes. "I'm sorry, Abbie. I know I shouldn't have brought it up. I'll text Sam later and apologize."

His wife nodded. "We need more than apologies. We need the truth from Andy Quinn before Sam's life is ruined."

John bowed his head and prayed God would shine light into the darkness of this situation like only He could.

forty-three

Lauren couldn't stop checking the time on her cell phone. Sam was supposed to be here almost an hour ago. He'd texted her twenty minutes ago, only saying he was running late. They were supposed to order a pizza, but he'd told her earlier he didn't think he'd stay that long and for her to go ahead and eat.

What's happening with us, Lord? If there even still is an us.

Her faith gradually grew stronger. She'd been praying more lately. For Sam, especially, but also for their relationship, which hung by a thread. She didn't know where Sam's head even was these days, and their relationship hadn't advanced at all. In fact, they'd gone backward.

She peered at the time again, but this time, her eyes focused on her lock screen picture. Her and Sam at the American Christian Music Awards. Sam in his black suit and her in her blue sparkly dress. Both with huge smiles on their faces.

That'd been such a happy night. He'd declared to the world she was his girlfriend. It'd been news to a lot of people, including her, but she'd loved it. And she was so proud of him, and what God was doing through him. On top of that, they'd shared their first kiss.

Why was all that crumbling away now? She wiped a tear from

her face with her sleeve. She grew weary of asking God the same questions over the past couple of months. Was God tired of her questions too? Sam had suffered so much as a child, and now his dreams of pointing people toward God were shattered. Why would God allow that? She'd asked her mother that exact question last night. At least Mom was sympathetic. She loved Sam too. But she said God doesn't guarantee a perfect, pain free life to even his closest followers. Mom told her to read John 16:33.

She pulled that verse up on her phone for the third time today. Jesus' words to his followers were in red: *Here on earth you will have many trials and sorrows. But take heart, because I have overcome the world.*

Indeed.

The knock on her door and Daisy's ferocious barking interrupted her thoughts. Sam was going through trials and sorrows right now, but she would be there for him.

* * *

Even the sound of Daisy barking at his knock didn't make him smile like it always did. It only made him sadder about what was to come.

"Hey." Lauren grinned as she opened the door.

"Hi." He leaned over to pet Daisy and to keep her from running past him. But as hard as he tried, he couldn't muster a smile.

"Do you want some water? Or I could make hot tea or coffee."

He'd prayed about this, and he'd told God this is what he thought he should do. But he hadn't felt any particular answer from God. When he had a major decision to make, more times than not, God put a Bible verse on his heart. But there was none today.

"Umm, no thanks. Could we sit for a minute?" He couldn't do this on his feet.

"Yeah, sure." Lauren ushered him to the sofa in her living room area. She sat beside him and twisted a piece of her long, blonde hair around her finger.

He gulped. *Please help me get the words out, Lord.* "You know you're my best friend, right? I mean you've always been my best friend, and I hope we can always be that for each other."

The color drained from her face, and the hair twisting stopped. She sat up straighter than before. "What do you mean? Of course I'll always be your best friend. But ... I thought we were more. I know you're going through a hard time now, but we can get through it together. In fact, my mom gave me a verse—"

"Lauren." He reached for her hand as her eyes filled with tears. "I'm no good for you. You deserve better."

"Don't even say that. It's not true. I love you, Sam." She took a deep breath. "There, I said something neither of us has had the courage to say to each other. I've always loved you. You have to know that." Tears streamed down her cheeks now.

"No, you can't love me. You deserve someone who can love you the way you deserve to be loved. Not someone like me who doesn't even know what that kind of love is." His eyes blurred with tears, but he quickly swiped them away.

"You're the only one I want, Sam." Her whisper pierced his soul.

"It's too much. I've been through too much trauma, and it just keeps coming. I don't even have a job or career anymore. You need to forget about me and move on." He turned his head. He couldn't stand to see her tears. They weakened his resolve.

She grabbed his other hand. "I'm not giving up. We'll get through this as a couple."

His heart wanted to give in, but his mind knew better. No, he couldn't let her pull him back in. She deserved so much better. With him, she'd never have the peaceful, perfect life she dreamed of. He was too broken, had too many scars, and didn't know how to love anyone. He dropped her hand and stood. *I love you too. Please forgive me for this.* "You're not understanding me. You don't have a choice in the matter, Lauren. I'm breaking up with you."

She stood too, shock and anger passing over her face before the tears came again. "What? How could you do this? I want to be with you. Can you honestly tell me you don't want to be with me?"

Her stare bore through him. He'd never lied to her. Not once. But this was for her own good. His hope was they'd remain close friends. But seeing her now, like this, that might not be possible. What he was about to say would change things between them permanently.

"I'm sorry, Lauren. I don't want to be with you." His words not only shattered her heart, but his own as well.

Unable to wait for her reply, he turned and left her apartment and barely made it to the other side of her doorway before his own tears poured down. Somehow, he dashed to his car where he sat for a long time, crying, asking God's forgiveness for both lying and tearing her apart like that.

Even if it was for her own good.

forty-four

Andy sat at the cold metal table by the barred window and waited. He couldn't believe Sam was coming back since he was here yesterday, although he wasn't complaining. He'd be happy to see his son every day.

The heavy metal door clanked, and he looked toward it. Not Sam. Must be a visitor for somebody else. He turned his head but out of the corner of his eye, he noticed the man walking straight toward his table. Then it hit him. His heart hammered against his ribcage. The man's hair was grayer than before, but otherwise, his appearance wasn't much different. There was no doubt who it was—his old coach, John Grayson.

What was he doing here? Andy couldn't meet his eyes. Instead, he focused on the metal table.

John sat opposite him without saying a word.

Andy squirmed. Could John hear his heartbeat? He finally got up the nerve to look at him.

"It's been a long time, Andy." John's voice was soft, but he glared into his eyes.

He'd expected the man to yell and scream. That was probably coming.

"Um, yeah, a long time." Andy clenched his handcuffed hands in front of him until his knuckles were white.

"I guess you're wondering why I'm here?"

Andy could probably guess. Surely, John would scream and cuss him out at some point. "I'm guessin' you're here about Sam."

His old coach nodded.

Andy wished John would yell and scream. It'd be more comfortable than this.

Finally, John cleared his throat.

That was something at least.

"You know, Andy, back when you played for me, I tried everything I could to get you on the right path. To stay away from drugs, play basketball, and get a college education. I really did."

John's sadness caught him by surprise. He hardly knew what to say. But John was clearly waiting for a reply. And he wasn't in any hurry for this conversation to end, unlike Andy. "You did, I know. But I was on a bad path. There was nothin' you could've done."

"Do you know I lost sleep over you for years? Wondering what happened to you, and figuring you were probably dead."

Andy's mouth hung open, and he quickly shut it. "No, I didn't."

"And when Sam became our foster child, I had no idea you were his father. It hurt when we couldn't help Sam at first. I relived the whole situation with you again. It's ironic, don't you think?"

"Umm, I guess so." Andy had no clue where this was going. The sadness in Coach Grayson's eyes was a lot to take. Now he really wished the man would yell and cuss him out instead.

"My wife, Abbie, you remember her," John continued. "She and I love Sam with all our hearts. And so do our kids. He's been part of our family for about seven years now, even before we adopted him. You hurt him very badly back then. When you signed your rights over instantly, like you were selling a car."

"Yeah." Andy hung his head again. "If I had it to do over, I wouldn't have done it that way."

"You're hurting him again now. You can't fool me, Quinn. I know it was you behind the scheme to take and sell those girls. You were behind every single part of it. But Sam doesn't see it. You really have him fooled."

He wasn't about to admit anything to John Grayson. "You won't believe this, but I'm a different person now. All I want is a relationship with my son."

John laughed, but anger flashed in the man's eyes. "He's *not* your son. We already discussed how you severed that relationship. And you were never a father to him in the first place. I know way more than you think, Quinn."

He raised his voice. "I've read every file. Everything from social services to hospitals. I know all the things you were accused of and suspected of. That boy was *never* a son to you. Only a pawn in your schemes."

Throughout the years, Andy pictured meeting with John Grayson. In those scenarios, Andy was the one yelling. Telling John Grayson he was a fool, and a loser, and he deserved his loser son. But that's not who Andy was anymore. He'd been saved by Jesus, confessed his wrong doings, or at least most of them, and he'd read in his Bible about right and wrong.

"I can't deny anything you've said. But I have a relationship with Jesus now. I realize I can never change the past, but I want a relationship with Sam. I want him to see I've changed. I don't want to take him from your family. I just want to be a piece of his life." That was the truth, although he didn't expect Coach Grayson to believe it.

Coach stared at him for an uncomfortable amount of time, but when he spoke, his voice was quiet again. "I'm not here to judge you, only God can do that. If you've truly accepted Christ and want to do what's best for Sam, then there's only one thing to do. Confess your crimes and let Sam off the hook. And let your son get on with his life."

Andy flinched. "He wouldn't want anything to do with me ever again if I did."

John shrugged. "You don't know that for certain, and neither do I. But if you're truthful, and he still wants a relationship with you, well, I won't stand in the way. But as it is now, your lies have divided our family, and they're destroying Sam. We only want what's best for him. I know you can't say that's always been the case with you."

He was right. But things were different now. He did want the best for Sam.

Coach opened his mouth to say something else, but instead, he got up and left.

Andy let out a breath he hadn't realized he was holding. He had a lot to think about.

* * *

John struggled to catch his breath as he walked to his car. He'd wanted to say more, wanted to tell Andy how hard he and Abbie had worked to regain Sam's trust after Andy had stripped it all away. How hard they'd worked to alleviate his fear, his abandonment issues, and his trauma. So much. A lifetime full.

But John couldn't. He suddenly couldn't breathe. A panic attack maybe? He'd seen Sam have them, but he'd never had one in all his sixty years.

He climbed in his car and turned the air conditioning on high. His skin grew suddenly hot and clammy. It was warm and humid for early May. The cold air coming from the vents helped a little. He grabbed a half-empty water bottle from his console and took a swig. It wasn't cold, but the warm liquid still made him feel better.

Until the pain shot up his left arm. John panicked again. Wasn't that a sign of a heart attack? He grabbed his phone to call

Abbie but remembered he hadn't taken his blood pressure pill this morning. That's what this was. It had to be. He'd put the pill in his pocket and meant to take it earlier but forgot. He dug the pill out and popped it in his mouth, chasing it with the warmish water.

He took some deep breaths, and the pain subsided. Five more minutes with the cool air blowing on him, and he felt like himself again.

Just his blood pressure. No wonder, considering the twenty-three-year-in-the making conversation he'd just had with Quinn. He was okay. Abbie didn't need to know about this. In fact, she didn't need to know about the prison visit at all.

forty-five

Ava cleared the pile of dirty clothes off her thrift store sofa and plopped down with her bowl of ramen noodles. Work at the grocery store had been a real drag. Customers in her line were always on their cell phones or had bratty, screaming kids. She was sick of it. But unfortunately, she couldn't find anything better, especially without a car. Wherever she worked needed to be within walking distance.

She wound the noodles around her fork but froze in place. Who was knocking on the door? Oh no, surely, her parents wouldn't show up unannounced. They'd never seen her place and would hate it. She set her bowl on the sofa and hurried to the door. She closed one eye and peeked through the peephole. Her stomach fell to her knees.

She spun around and leaned against the door, eyes closed. *What is she doing here? We haven't seen each other since—*

"Ava, I know you're in there. I can hear the TV. Please let me in. I need to talk."

Ava steadied her breathing. She didn't want to talk, especially to *her*. But she wasn't likely to go away. She needed to do it and quick. Like ripping off a bandage. Just get it over with.

She turned around, faced the door, and opened it. There she

was, looking stunning and put together. And normal. All of the things Ava wasn't. That's how Amanda had always been. Even during the worst of times.

"Ava." Amanda said her name as if it were her last breath.

Tears formed in Ava's eyes, and she couldn't stop them from flowing.

"Can I come in?" Amanda asked.

All she could do was nod. Once inside, Amanda closed the gap between them and hugged Ava. Gingerly at first, but Ava sobbed as if releasing all the trauma she and Amanda had been through. They held onto each other tightly.

They stayed that way for a long time, until Ava pulled herself together and moved away. "I'm sorry, its just—"

"I know," Amanda whispered. She was crying too. "The last time we saw each other was in the safehouse after, well, you know."

"Yeah." Ava wiped her tears with the back of her sleeve. "Umm, how are you? And how in the world did you find me?"

Ava led her to her thread-bare, ugly brown sofa. Why hadn't she bought something at the thrift shop that wasn't so ugly? Amanda always made her want to be better.

"I called your mom, and she gave me your address." Amanda shrugged. "And I'm good. I finished my second year of college."

"Wow, that's great." She couldn't imagine having her life together enough to go to college. She hadn't even finished high school.

"How about you?" Amanda peered around the room.

Ava never cared what anyone thought. But with Amanda, it was different. After all, they'd been through some real tough stuff together. "I'm okay. Just working at the grocery store a few blocks away."

Amanda swallowed hard. An uncomfortable silence hung over them. "Can I tell you why I'm here?"

"Umm, okay." She wasn't so sure she wanted to know.

"Ava, I can't stand to see what you're doing to Sam Grayson." Amanda blurted out.

"What?" Ava jerked her head back. If anyone should see her side, it'd be Amanda. "What are you talking about? He did that to us!"

Amanda shook her head. "No, Ava, he didn't. He didn't do anything. He was a victim, like us. He's out there trying to do good things with his life in spite of everything, and you're destroying him. Why?"

Ava's stomach felt like she'd been punched. Had everyone gone mad? Was she the only one who knew the truth? "He lured us in, Amanda. You were there. You know this!" How could her cousin turn on her like this?

"No, he didn't." Amanda closed her eyes as if replaying it in her mind. "Don't you remember? He was so drugged up he couldn't even walk. The other guy, Blaze, practically dragged him. I remember it like yesterday." Amanda's eyes opened wide as she made her case.

Ava took a step back and stared at Amanda. "No. That can't be right."

"It's what happened. It wasn't Sam, Ava. It wasn't. I swear to you. You know I'd never lie to you."

Tears rolled down her face again at her cousin's words. How was Amanda so strong? So unlike herself. She was weak, putting the blame on someone else. "My memories are hazy," she admitted.

"I know. You were so young. Barely thirteen." Amanda's voice was gentle. "But I know what happened. Sam even told us to run, do you remember that?"

She did, and that part Ava was never able to make sense of. Why would he have done that? She'd tried hard to forget that part. She needed to blame him so badly.

"And he kept yelling through the wall, asking if we were all right. Do you remember? I was gagged and couldn't answer, but you talked to him. He was being held against his will, the same as we were."

"I don't know now. I'm so confused." Ava paced the floor, and everything she'd been so sure of was a huge question mark. Could Amanda be right? Her stomach dropped. Could she have been wrong all along? Had she been so bent on making someone pay she didn't look at the situation hard enough?

Amanda got up off the sofa and stopped Ava from pacing. She grabbed her by the shoulders and gazed straight into her eyes. Suddenly, tears poured from Amanda's eyes. "I steered you wrong in a big way when I thought we'd met two cute guys. But I swear I will never steer you wrong again. I'm so sorry. If you're going to blame someone, blame me. I was fifteen and boy crazy. I am more guilty of putting us in that situation than Sam Grayson ever was. He was innocent, Ava."

"I *never* blamed you." She hoped Amanda believed that. "Like you said, we thought we were meeting two cute guys. We were just naive, and it cost us."

Amanda hung her head. "Yeah. It cost us plenty. Please drop all this against Sam Grayson."

Ava sniffed hard. "I'll think about it."

"Will you think about something else too?" Amanda grabbed Ava's hands and studied her through her tears.

"What?"

"Will you come back home? You don't need to live like this. Your parents want you home. You can live with them, get your GED, and go to college. We can still have a good life, Ava." Amanda insisted. "I promise you, we can."

She didn't know about that. She'd never once considered the possibility. But she'd always admired Amanda, and she'd pulled her life together. Maybe Ava could put her life back together too.

She'd definitely think about what Amanda said.

forty-six

Wendy waved and grinned when Abbie walked through the door of the clothes closet.

Abbie flipped the sign on the door to Open and rushed to her friend. They shared a quick hug.

"I'm so happy we're both here today. I need a friendly face." Abbie ran her purse back to their office and joined Wendy at the front counter.

"That bad?" Wendy frowned.

"Yeah. Let's just say we're losing Sam more every day. And this whole mess with the girl, Ava. It's ruining Sam's career. I'm giving my worry to God, but some days, it's so hard." Abbie forced a weak smile. She refused to allow the tears to escape.

Wendy sighed. "Roger told me about the radio stations. He's doing everything he can to fix things, but you know how today's cancel culture is. It's beyond sad no one wants to even hear Sam's side of the story."

Abbie nodded. "I know Roger is doing everything he can. Please let him know we appreciate that. But part of this is Sam's reluctance to go public with his story. He's willing to talk to the leadership at Middle Tennessee Church, but so far, they don't want to hear it. He doesn't want to relive all this publicly. And I can understand."

The bell on the door signaled their first customers of the day. A pretty red-head who looked to be in her forties, accompanied by a teenage boy with stringy hair hanging in his cast-down eyes. *I've seen that look before.* "Welcome to Sam's Closet." Abbie walked over to greet the two. "I'm Abbie, and that's Wendy. We're the owners."

"Hi, I'm Renee." The woman said and then waved at Wendy. "And this is Max."

"Hi, Max." Abbie quickly moved on when the boy didn't look up. "Are you shopping for Max?"

"Yes." Renee clasped her hands together and bit her lower lip. "Max, do you want to look around, and I'll join you in a moment?"

The boy nodded and headed deeper into the store.

Oh, my heart, this is like watching a scene from my past.

The woman's perfect posture now slouched. "We're new in town. I got your name from Pastor Rob at Franklin Community Church. He told me about your shop and a little about your background. He also thought maybe you could offer some advice to this newbie foster mom." Renee's eyes glistened with unshed tears.

"C'mon over here, and we'll chat." Abbie directed Renee to the checkout counter where Wendy stood. "Max is out of earshot here. Your first teenager?"

Renee sighed. "Our first placement ever."

"Whew," Wendy said. "You moved to a new town *and* began fostering at the same time. That's a lot."

"It is, but so far, we love Franklin. It's just—"

"You're wondering what you've gotten yourself into," Abbie said.

"Yes! Pastor Rob said you'd understand."

Abbie ached for this woman. This was she and John when Sam came to them as their first foster child. "Is he an emergency placement?"

Renee shook her head. "No, but short-term. Whatever that means."

"Abbie knows all about 'short-term'," Wendy tilted her head.

"Wendy's right about that," Abbie sighed. "Our first foster was a sixteen-year-old emergency placement. When you walked in, I flashed back to when Sam came to us. The hair, the facial expression that says 'I'd rather be anywhere but here' and of course, the mumbling. Or not talking at all."

The three chuckled.

"You *do* understand. Please tell me it gets better."

Abbie wanted to hug this new friend and assure her everything would be fine. But she couldn't promise that. She and John had gone through a lot to get where they were today with Sam. But where were now? She shivered.

"Renee, I have to be honest. Things were hard for a while. It took time to gain trust, and even then, it was always one step forward and two steps back. My best advice is to be patient but firm. Set rules and guidelines and be true to those. It's hard, but it's worth it when you see him making progress. You have to take it one day at a time." Abbie brushed away a tear of her own that caught her by surprise.

"Thank you for being honest. My husband and I agree we're in this together."

Abbie laughed. "That's good, because it took my husband and me a few days to get on the same page." She didn't want to get into the whole story about how John never even wanted a teenager. Until he fell in love with Sam.

"How did things end up with your son?"

Abbie inhaled. "We ended up adopting him at age eighteen. He's twenty-three now, and we're so proud of him." No need to tell this sweet woman any more. Maybe another time. "By the way, if you could slip out of the house sometime, would you like to meet Wendy and me for coffee?"

Renee laughed through a tear that escaped. "Oh, I would love that. You two have been so nice. And I still have so many questions."

They made a plan to meet for coffee next Saturday after the shop closed, and Renee went to help Max find clothes.

Wendy laughed and grabbed Abbie's arm, her eyes dancing. "Now *this* is what this shop is supposed to be all about. More than clothes or books, but a community of people helping each other and these kids."

"Thank you, Lord." Abbie lifted her eyes to the ceiling.

She only hoped by next Saturday she would have a new story of God's grace and goodness to share with Renee.

forty-seven

The weather was nearly perfect for Franklin in May. But the cloudless blue sky and seventy-two-degree temperature didn't help Sam's mood any. Neither did the sight of his brother sitting on the park bench holding two coffees while Sam pulled into a parking spot. He wasn't up for this at all today. But Kyle convinced him coffee and a walk at Franklin Park would make him feel better.

Right.

"Hey little brother." Kyle addressed him by his nickname. Sam had always liked it when he called him that, but today, it struck a nerve.

"I'm not a little kid, you know," Sam bristled.

Kyle handed him a coffee cup and then held up a hand. "Sorry, I didn't think you minded me calling you that."

Sam shrugged and sipped his coffee. "I don't. I'm sorry. I'm in a bad mood this morning. Just warning ya."

"C'mon, let's walk. I think you could use some fresh air. I know I could."

They walked slowly on the paved trail around the outside edge of the park. They passed by a pre-teen basketball game, and Kyle laughed. "I'm surprised Dad's not here recruiting."

Sam had to laugh at that. "Yeah, I'm surprised too. He loves his recruiting trips. And he's good at it."

"Yeah, he is. Speaking of Dad ..."

So that's what this is about.

"He means well, Sam. He loves you. And no matter how many disagreements you two have had, and no matter what's been said, that'll never change. He'll always be here for you."

"Right. Even if I keep seeing Andy Quinn."

"Yes."

Sam shot him a quick look.

"You don't believe it? He told me that yesterday. He wants our family back together, and it's not together without you. Even if it means Andy Quinn is on the outer fringe of our family."

They stopped walking, and Sam focused out past the tennis courts, toward the tree line, and remembered all the times he'd come here with John. Shooting hoops, hitting tennis balls, or walking the park like he and Kyle were doing now. He missed his relationship with John a lot. And he still doubted Andy was telling him the complete truth. But he couldn't admit that to anyone. Especially his family.

"Lauren and I broke up." He blurted it out but wasn't sure why. He hadn't told anyone that either. But his chest felt like a weight had been lifted as soon as he said it.

"What? Sam, why? Who broke up with who?"

"Wow, all the questions." Sam turned and walked on. "I broke up with her."

"What happened?"

His eyes straight ahead, he took a deep breath. "I'm no good for her, man. She deserves so much better. My life is a complete mess. I don't have a job. I'm not speaking to my family. I'm hated by the Christian media right now. And come to think of it, hated by other Christians too."

Kyle grabbed his arm, pulling him to an abrupt stop. "Okay, for one thing, you're a good person, Sam. When I think of striving to do God's will, you're the example that comes to mind. Everything you do, you do for God. So much of what's going on has nothing to do with you. It has to do with what's been done to you. There's a difference."

"I don't know." Sam looked at the ground. "Everything was going so well, and I thought if I followed God, He'd take care of me. And He hasn't.

"And you think that makes you a bad person?"

Sam exhaled and attempted to walk on, but Kyle caught his arm again. "Pull out your phone. I want you to read John 16:33."

"Right now?"

A woman walked by trying to wrangle her three dogs, but they tugged her in three different directions. One was a dachshund, and he thought of Lauren. She had tried to tell him about a Bible verse, too, but he'd shut her down.

"Yes, right now."

Sam pulled up his Bible app and opened it to John 16:33. *Here on earth you will have many trials and sorrows. But take heart, because I have overcome the world.*

He'd read that verse a hundred times. He'd even done a paper in college about it. So why hadn't he thought of it during his own trials? Jesus was speaking to his disciples.

"I know this verse well. I don't know why I haven't thought of it." He re-read it again. "Maybe I've been too busy feeling sorry for myself."

Kyle motioned for Sam and walked ahead. "Things have been hard, for sure. But I have no doubt you'll get your career back. You'll point people to God again. It may take a while, and it might look a little different from what you thought it would."

"God's good at that. Taking you somewhere you thought you'd never be."

"And it always ends up better than what we could have done on our own. Right?"

"True." Sam had seen it in his life. He began college intending to be a social worker like Jamie, his case manager from the foster care system. But he quickly realized he wasn't healed enough from his own trauma to do that. So instead, God used his love of writing and music to create something better than anything he could've dreamed for himself.

Becoming a social worker had been just another dream, but God had given him his ultimate dream, the one he never knew he wanted.

"You'll get it back." His brother read his mind.

"You know what? Even if I don't, God gave me something great for a while. And I'll do whatever it is he wants me to do next. Thanks for reminding me."

Whatever you want, God. I'm so sorry I forgot that promise I made to you all those years ago. You're in control, not me.

* * *

"Oh, they've moved things around a bit since I was here last," Hannah said as they entered Landmark Bookstore.

What a great mother-daughter outing this had been so far. It was Abbie's day off at the clothes closet, but she and Hannah had stopped by to check on things and say hi to Wendy. They had lunch at Gray's and then hit a few shops, including the bookstore. Their last stop before they went home would be the coffee shop.

"There's the owner. I'll ask if Lauren's working today." Abbie walked over to the classics section where a woman stood with a clipboard and her pen.

The woman peered over her purple frames with a smile. "Well, hello, ladies. How can I help you today?"

"Hi, we were wondering if Lauren is working. We're friends of hers."

"She certainly is. I believe she's in the back, in the children's section."

Abbie thanked the woman, and she and Hannah made their way back to the children's section, stopping to browse along the way. They rounded the corner and spotted Lauren, surrounded by an empty shelf and stacks of books.

"Hi, Lauren," Hannah said first.

Lauren turned around. "Oh sorry, I was in my own little world." She rose from the floor and brushed her jeans off.

"It's so good to see you." Abbie gushed.

Lauren stood with her hands in her pockets and gazed at the floor. "Good to see you too," she whispered.

Abbie caught Hannah's eye, and Hannah shrugged. Lauren was always smiling and bubbly. A few months ago, when Lauren had come into the clothes closet, she had rushed up to Abbie, greeted her with a smile, and the two had hugged. Today, she made no attempt to approach Abbie or Hannah and didn't even smile.

"We haven't seen Sam much lately," Hannah offered. "How's he doing?"

Lauren hesitated for a moment before looking up at Hannah, then at Abbie. "Umm, so you don't know about Sam and me?"

Abbie looked to Hannah, but Hannah shook her head.

"No, honestly our communication with Sam has been limited lately. What's going on, honey?" Abbie asked in a gentle voice.

Lauren sniffed, and her eyes brimmed with tears. "He broke up with me. I haven't seen him for a few weeks."

Hannah gasped. "Are you serious? What happened? I've always thought you two were perfect together."

Abbie shot her daughter a look. "Hannah, it's not our business. It's okay if you don't want to tell us, Lauren."

"No, actually, maybe you can help me figure it out." Lauren pulled a chair out from the table and sat, and Hannah and Abbie followed.

Lauren exhaled and finally made eye contact with them. "Like I said, he broke up with me. Said he's no good for me.

That I deserve better. That was it. But honestly, it's been downhill ever since he began talking to Andy Quinn months ago. But all this stuff with Ava and Amanda, and everything he's been through, he just thinks he's no good for anyone and needs to stay single."

Abbie reached across the table for Lauren's hand. She was thankful the girl didn't pull away. "I'm so sorry, Lauren. That's not Sam. He's always been crazy over you. Ever since we've known him. Even if he didn't know it yet back then." Abbie half-smiled.

Lauren wiped away a tear and sniffed.

"Mom's right. The first time I met you, back when you two were sixteen, I knew you and Sam would be together someday." Hannah grabbed Lauren's other hand. "Did you know that he wanted to ask you to your senior prom?" Hannah smiled.

Lauren sniffed again. "No, I never knew that."

"He did, he just couldn't get up the courage. I think he loved you, even back then, but he's never thought he was good enough for you."

"I don't know why he's always thought that." Lauren sighed. "But the truth is, things have been off between us for months. And to be honest, there are things in my past that may have spooked him too."

Abbie wondered what would make Lauren say that, but she wasn't going to pry. "You know, with all Sam's been through, I doubt whatever you could've done would bother him."

"Well, he said it didn't, but I don't know now."

"I'm sorry, we had no idea this happened. I sure didn't mean for us to come in here and bring it all to the surface." She hurt for Lauren.

"It's okay." Lauren mustered a slight smile and wiped away a tear. "I am glad to see you two. I miss your family."

"You know you're welcome to our home anytime." Abbie and Hannah rose to leave.

"And I'd love to grab coffee with you sometime," Hannah added.

Lauren came around to their side of the table and hugged them both. "It's helped me so much just talking to you too today. I'm praying for Sam. He's so lost, and I hope we can be friends again someday."

"We'll pray for that too," Abbie said.

forty-eight

Sam waited at the metal table in the visitation room. The guard told him Andy was in a meeting with his attorney but would be brought in to see him any minute now. What could the meeting with the attorney be about, and why had Andy summoned him here? Were the two related?

Calm down. Andy probably met with his attorney all the time, so maybe it didn't mean anything. Or perhaps it was news about his early release.

The door opened, and a guard brought his father in. Andy nodded at Sam but otherwise remained expressionless. "Hey, kid, how you doin'?" He sat at the table opposite Sam.

"I'm okay. Everything okay with you? I heard you met with your attorney."

"Yeah, I'm good, yeah," Andy said quickly. "But you go first. I've been reading about all the stuff you've been accused of. I'm so sorry. You don't deserve this."

Sam struggled with why God would allow this to happen. Hadn't he already been through enough? And just when he thought his life might be making a difference for God ... no, enough. He couldn't let himself go down that hole again. "Yeah, it's been rough."

Andy didn't reply. Instead, he stared at his hands for the longest time. Something wasn't right. His father's eyes were sadder than he'd ever seen.

He cleared his throat. "About that meeting with the lawyer. Sam, umm, I don't even know how to say this."

Maybe he wasn't getting early release after all. "Oh no. Did you get bad news about your early release?"

His father chuckled lightly, then sniffed hard. "Early release, yeah." He chuckled without smiling. "There won't be any early release for me. Listen, I've lied to you about everything. It was me who cooked up the plan with those girls. And umm, the rest is even harder to say."

Sam couldn't form any words. The air left his lungs. All he could do was wait for the man to continue. He forced himself to inhale in the meantime.

"It was my plan to use you to lure those girls in. I gave the order to have you drugged. And I took the girls to Miami and sold them. It was all me. My idea. I planned it all. I'm the one who made every bit of it happen." He exhaled.

Sam reached out to grasp the cold metal table to keep from falling. The room spun around him. His father's words couldn't be true. Then it dawned on him. "Don't make this up just to get me off the hook. We both know it was Blaze."

Andy shook his head. "No, Sam, it was me. All of it. Yeah, he helped, and he isn't innocent, but it was my plan. I hired Blaze and Paulette to help, along with a few other people. Honest. For once in my life, I've told you the truth."

Sam stood and paced the room. The guard had his eyes on him, so he took his place back at the table but didn't sit. "You let *me* take the fall for this?" He said through clenched teeth as his heart hammered inside his chest.

"I know, I know, I'm sorry. I don't expect you to believe that. But when I realized how bad things were for you, I called my attorney, and that's where I just came from. I confessed everything. I won't receive early release now. I'm sure I'll get time added. But that's okay, I need to pay for what I did."

Sam's mind was unable to process everything. The all-too-familiar dizziness set in. "So, all this was a lie. You wanting to have a relationship with me. Following God. Was that a lie too?"

"No, absolutely not. I wanted to make things right. That's why I had to come clean. The old me wouldn't have cared if you were blamed for things I did. But I owe it to you and God to tell the truth and confess."

Sam's mouth fell open. How could he trust anything out of this man's mouth ever again? Had he really sacrificed his relationship with the Graysons for this man? This liar. This criminal.

He leaned over the table. "You won't ever see me again." Sam hissed, then turned and motioned for the guard to let him out. And he didn't look back.

* * *

Rio paced his cell, stopped, and punched the concrete wall. That was a mistake. His throbbing fist made him want to scream. He couldn't remember when he'd been this angry.

If that jerk Quinn hadn't confessed to his attorney, Rio would've been able to see his own lawyer this evening to tell him everything Quinn had done. That information would've helped Rio make a deal to shorten his sentence.

This had been the best shot he'd ever had to get out early. He'd probably never get a chance like this again. And Quinn had blown it all by confessing. What kind of idiot confesses anyway? All because he was some kind of born-again Christian? It didn't make any sense.

The more he thought, the angrier he became. He continued pacing and tried to lift his desk chair to throw it, forgetting as always that it was bolted down. Instead, he plopped himself onto his cot and clenched his teeth.

Revenge would be sweet. But not at all merciful.

forty-nine

John and Abbie walked in through the garage, hung their jackets in the foyer closet, and headed to the kitchen. "How about some popcorn and a movie?" John rummaged through the pantry and pulled out the microwave popcorn.

"Sounds good to me." Abbie took a diet cola out of the fridge and poured John a glass of sweet tea while he punched in the time on the microwave. "It was a nice evening at Kyle and Cassie's, don't you think?"

"It was a great night. Good food, fun conversation, and everyone there. Well, except for Sam." He exhaled.

His words stung. She'd had a great time tonight with him and the kids. But she missed Sam being there. "We all missed him tonight."

The microwave beeped. John grabbed the popcorn bag and poured it into a bowl. "I missed him being there too. More than you know." John carried the bowl to the family room, and she followed with the drinks.

"You know, I keep thinking about all we've been through." John set the popcorn bowl on the coffee table in front of the sofa. "Sam and me, that is. I love that boy. You know I do, Abbie."

"Of course. That's what hurts so much about this. You and he were so close, and now ..."

"I've been praying hard, Abbie." He massaged his left arm.

"What's wrong, hon?"

"Oh, nothing, probably just a pulled muscle." He stopped rubbing his arm. "Anyway, I see now I need to back off. I need to let Sam make these decisions. And whatever decision he makes, I'm going to have a good, long talk with him..

"John." Abbie cringed.

"No, I don't mean like the conversations we've been having. I've come to a decision. I have to accept Quinn may always be in Sam's life. And I have to let that happen if it's what Sam wants."

"I agree completely." She scrunched her eyebrows when her husband rubbed his upper left arm again. "Are you sure that's just a pulled muscle?"

"Oh, yeah." John pulled his hand away from his arm. "You were saying you agree with me?"

She laughed at her husband's smirk. "Yes, I agree. We need to talk to Sam sooner rather than later, though. He keeps getting farther and farther away from us. I don't want to lose him."

"We won't lose him. I'll make sure."

Those were the most reassuring words he could've said to her. She'd sleep better tonight for sure. "Thank you, hon. Now pass the popcorn and let's find a movie to watch. A comedy, please. No drama."

"Right. I've had enough drama to last until the day I die."

* * *

"You guys hear about Quinn?" Rio directed the question to the four guys he ate with in the chow hall.

"That guy?" The big man next to him tilted his head in Quinn's direction. "What about him?"

"His cell's next to mine. Pedophile, man. He confessed and everything." So he stretched the truth a little. Quinn deserved it.

"No way, man," the man across from him insisted. "That guy's a big time Bible thumper. I went to one of them meetings once just to get time out and ice cream. Quinn even spoke to the room."

"Yeah, well, believe it. Quinn told me himself. He ran a trafficking ring of twelve- to fourteen-year-old girls. He admitted what he did. Even tried to put the blame on his own kid."

"He's one of them fake Christians, huh." The big man pointed with his fork. "I know a lot of 'em. What are we gonna do about it? About Quinn, I mean?"

Rio smirked. It was no coincidence he sat for chow with these guys. They'd roughed up other pedophiles before. And he was sure they'd do even more than that. They were in for life anyway. They had nothing to lose.

Quinn may or may not have been a pedophile, but he confessed and messed up Rio's chance at a deal. He got in the way of him getting out early. This was personal, and he would pay.

"So let me tell you what I'm thinkin' we should do." Rio smirked.

fifty

Sam sat on his deck and drank his second glass of water since he'd been back from his run. Eighty degrees at 9:00 a.m. He hated the heat and humidity so early in the season. It was still May.

Only three and a half months ago, he received two prestigious music awards. Now the Christian music scene wanted nothing to do with him, and neither did the church that had hired him.

And what about Lauren? The night of the awards had been magical in several ways. Not just the awards, but Lauren had been his date. He'd asked her to be his girlfriend, and she'd said yes. How could everything have changed so much in such a short period of time?

He sighed, walked to the balcony railing, and admired his view. It was nice enough, but nothing like the view at John and Abbie's home. Yeah, he'd messed that up too. And to make it all worse, his biological dad had done all this to him. All of it. The sound of the doorbell halted his spiraling thoughts.

He gazed through the peephole and his pulse raced. Kyle and Roger Nelson. What kind of bad news would they pile on today? He held his breath and opened the door.

"Hey, I'm surprised to see you here this morning. More bad news?"

"Can we come in, Sam?" His brother asked.

"Of course, I'm sorry, come on in. You caught me in the middle of a pity party. Can I get you coffee or water?"

Roger Nelson shook Sam's hand like always. "No thanks, Sam. I wanted to talk for a few minutes. Kyle told me about your biological father, and how he'd confessed. He let me in on all the background too."

"Oh, okay. Let's sit down." The three men sat at the kitchen table. Sam swallowed hard. He hated Roger knew things he never intended for him to know. He attempted to make eye contact with Kyle, but his brother's eyes were focused on the table in front of him. Yep, Kyle had told him. At least everything was out in the open whether Sam wanted that or not.

"I'm so sorry for what you've been through." Roger spoke in a soft tone. If Sam didn't know better, he could've sworn a tear formed in the man's eye. He couldn't imagine a man like Roger Nelson crying. He paused a moment to compose himself. "I want to assure you, we're going to get you back on your feet. Because there's a confession from him on record now, I want our publicity team to release a statement about what you've been through. And how this Quinn guy was responsible for it all."

Sam's stomach flip-flopped. "With all due respect sir, I don't know if I want all that put out there publicly."

"I understand," the man said in a gentle tone. "It would only be what you're comfortable with. My team would get your input. They won't publish anything until you approve it. And it doesn't have to get into your whole life story."

"Oh, good. Okay then, I guess." He wasn't entirely convinced.

"This will be a good thing, Sam." Kyle finally spoke up. "We're convinced this will get you back on the radio, and more importantly, back into the churches."

As long as he didn't have to tell everything he'd been through. He couldn't do that. But if he had the final say on the statement, what could it hurt at this point? He glanced from Mr. Nelson to Kyle and slowly nodded his head. "Okay, I'll do it."

* * *

Sam stood on the front porch of the only home that had ever mattered to him. John and Abbie's house. His home.

But he didn't live here anymore, and other than a couple of texts, he hadn't talked to his mom and dad for some time. He wasn't comfortable just walking in the house, even though he had a key. It seemed weird to ring the doorbell too. He lifted his hand to ring the bell and heard laughter. It was Abbie, and the sound came from the back deck. He breathed a sigh of relief. For some reason, it seemed easier to approach them outside.

He walked around the house to the back yard and up the steps to the deck. As he reached the gate at the top, John spotted him and froze for a second, then flashed him a smile. "Hey, Sam, it's good to see you." John rose from the table where he and Abbie sat and walked toward him. His smile remained in place as he approached, and he seemed more relaxed than he had in a while.

John closed the space between him and hugged him. "Come sit."

Abbie was a few steps behind, and she hugged him and gave him a kiss on the cheek. "We're so happy to see you, honey."

Of course. It dawned on him. John was playing nice because he'd been right all along. He'd heard about the confession. They were right. Sam was wrong. Andy Quinn would be behind bars for a long time now, and they were gloating.

He'd been wrong to come here. It was a mistake.

"So, you all know." Sam said. He stood, rather than sit. He wouldn't be here long after all.

John and Abbie glanced at each other, and then back to Sam. "Know what, Sam?" John asked.

"I know Kyle told you, so you don't need to pretend you don't know what's going on." Sam had never realized his parents were such good liars. The confused looks they gave each other were pretty convincing.

"We haven't talked to Kyle since Wednesday." Abbie shrugged.

Wednesday? Andy's confession had taken place on Thursday, and today was Friday. Was it possible they didn't know? "So, you don't know the latest with Andy?" Their reactions gave nothing away. If they were aware, they sure were good at hiding it.

"No, we haven't heard anything about Andy. What's going on with him?" John's eyes were wide.

John reached out and put his hand on Sam's shoulder. "Wait, Sam, before you say anything, I want you to know I'm so very sorry for all the things I've said about Andy." He stopped and bit his lip. "I was jealous, plain and simple. And I had no right to be. I was also afraid of you getting hurt again. But Abbie helped me realize something. You're nearly twenty-four years old now, and I have to trust you know what's best for you. If you think Andy has changed, then that's good enough for me."

"Well, uh, I don't think—"

"No." John held both hands up. "You don't owe me any explanation. I've accepted Andy will be in your life. But I can't lose you. I miss our relationship, and I want it back." John brushed away a rogue tear.

"We promise you, Sam," Abbie said. "You can continue your relationship with him without our interference. We just want to get back to the way we all were before."

He couldn't speak. They actually didn't know about the confession. John wanted him back and was willing to let him have a relationship with Andy. He wouldn't interfere. Sam didn't know what to say.

It made sense John would've been jealous. There had been

times when Sam had been jealous of John's relationship with Kyle until he realized John loved both him and Kyle as sons. His eyes locked with John's. "That's what I want, more than anything. I've missed you so much." He hugged John. "You have no idea."

He didn't bother to brush his own tears away, and he hugged Abbie too. He had his mom and dad back, and he couldn't stop smiling.

But he had to tell them the truth. He sat with them, inhaled, and prayed. "Well, I came over here today because I thought you knew, but evidently you don't." Again, their looks of confusion. "He confessed to everything."

"Quinn? He confessed?" John's eyes widened, but he didn't smile.

"Yeah. I thought maybe Kyle told you."

"No, like Abbie said, we haven't talked to Kyle in a couple days. I'm sorry, Sam," John said.

"It's okay." Sam stared at the deck floor. "You can tell me you told me so."

"I would never say that." John paused until Sam met his gaze. "You probably won't believe this, but I'm sorry it turned out this way. But I'm glad for your sake he claimed responsibility for what he did. Now you can get your life back."

"This doesn't change anything about what we said. We won't speak out or hold you back if you want to continue the relationship with him," Abbie said.

John nodded along.

They both seemed sincere. "I don't think I want that anymore. After the way he lied to me over and over and let me take the fall. I just don't know." He was so confused.

At first he'd thought he never wanted to see the man again, but there was some kind of pull there. Like he needed for the man to like him. "I think I need time away from him to sort things out. I want to spend time with you and also try to get my career back on track. Maybe after all that, I'll decide whether I want to see him again."

"We're happy to have you home, kiddo." John's eyes were sincere.

Their kindness overwhelmed him. No matter the shock and confusion, he was happy to be home with the only two people who truly were his parents.

fifty-one

Sam had never been so happy in all his life to turn his calendar to a new month. May had been brutal, but June started off much better. Even the weather was cooperating. The temperatures had cooled into the eighties, everything was in full bloom, and he could spend time outside without feeling like he'd been in a sauna.

He turned off his car air conditioning and opened the sun roof. As he pulled out onto his street, his newest song, "My Father Above," played on the radio. He laughed and couldn't stop. Roger Nelson had done it! He'd gotten his songs back on the air.

He hit the Call button on his phone.

"Hey, kiddo, what's up?" John asked.

"Are you near a radio?"

"Yeah, I'm in my car."

"Turn it to 88.9. And hurry." Sam laughed again while he waited.

"You're back on the air! That's the best news ever. Congratulations. I'm so happy for you."

Sam could practically see the grin in the man's voice.

"Roger did exactly what he said he would." Sam couldn't

believe how fortunate he was to have a godly man like Roger on his side. For that matter, all the godly men in his life, which included John and Kyle.

"Your statement sure helped. Who couldn't read that and not have compassion for what you've been through."

"I can't tell you how relieved I am." Sam pulled into the middle lane and turned his left turn signal on. "And now I'm on my way to try to get my job back at Middle Tennessee Church."

"They finally called you." Even more excitement rang out in John's voice.

"Nope, they still haven't called. And they've never once asked for my side of the story. But I'm going to talk to them to see where I stand. I'm meeting with Pastor Stephan, and Jerry, the head of the elders. Please pray."

"I will son. I will."

* * *

Sam sat in the waiting room outside Liz's office. She was as cool to him as last time, but this time, she didn't even tell him to go on back. She made him sit and wait. This couldn't be good.

"Sam." Pastor Stephan came from around the corner. "Come on back."

The man didn't offer a handshake, not even a welcome. He didn't even turn around to look at him.

"Thanks for seeing me today."

"No problem." Stephan still didn't turn around. "So, how have you been?"

How have I been? "Better now, sir. Now that this is resolved."

"Mm-hmm," the man said as he closed his office door behind them.

"Good to see you, Sam." The elder, Jerry, offered a handshake.

"Have a seat." The pastor pointed to a chair. "What can we do for you?"

How could they not know? "Well, I, uh, sir." Their supposed cluelessness threw him off. "I was wondering if you've seen the news about my birth father's confession and how he was responsible for all the things I was accused of?"

Both men were without expression. "We did, and we're happy it worked out for you." Pastor Stephan sat stoically.

He waited for them to say more, but they didn't. *Happy it all worked out for me* ... "Umm, well, thank you. I guess the reason I'm here is I wondered if I can have my job back." There, he said it.

Jerry stared at his clasped hands. Pastor Stephan removed his glasses, rubbed his eyes, and sighed. "Sam, I have to be straight with you. We've replaced you. We just can't bring you back."

Even though Sam thought there was a chance they may do that, the words still stunned him. "Can I ask why, sir?"

"You come with too much baggage. I'm afraid even though this man confessed, a cloud of suspicion will always be over you. People don't forget things like this."

The man's words pierced his soul. All he'd ever tried to do was obey the rules, not get into trouble, and not make trouble for anyone else. Other than a few teenage mistakes, he'd done pretty well. But these men were going to hold his father's mistakes and crimes against him.

Sam hung his head for a brief moment and then looked up at the pastor. "I don't want to speak out of line, Pastor Stephan, but didn't Jesus befriend those with baggage? He called tax collectors and sinners to follow him. But you're telling me I can't be a part of this church?"

"Oh, you can be a part of the congregation, Sam. But not on staff and certainly not in a leadership position." The man leaned forward and crossed his arms as he smirked.

How had Sam thought this was the church for him? Had they always been like this, and he'd never seen it?

"We're sorry. This doesn't change the fact you're incredibly talented. You'll land on your feet somewhere. Probably in a smaller church," Stephan continued. "Oh, I have to ask you. This won't turn you away from Christ, will it?" The man asked.

Anger brewed in Sam's heart, but he wouldn't let these men do that to him. On the other hand, he wanted to laugh. *Turn me away from Christ?* "Absolutely not, sir. I know He still loves me despite anything I've done, and He knows I'm innocent of things I've been accused of. Thank you for your time today."

He walked out of the office and out of the church, shaking. How could he have been so deceived by these so-called men of God? And for them to ask if this would turn him away from Christ? When he thought about that question, he quit shaking, and peace washed over him. He didn't want to be part of a church where they couldn't even try to understand. They couldn't be bothered to ask his side of the story.

God knew his heart, and He would have something better for him. He always did.

fifty-two

"You know Mom and Dad will help you." Kyle sat at Sam's kitchen table beside him, thumbing through a file he'd brought.

Sam groaned. He'd lost his place adding up numbers. "I know they will, but I don't want them to. C'mon, you're supposed to be helping me."

"All right, grumpy. I've got all your financials and your royalty statements right here. Did you list all your bills on this paper?"

"Everything but my cell phone bill. Here let me add it." He reached over and added the number to the total at the bottom of the sheet and pushed the paper toward his brother.

Kyle opened an envelope and whistled through his teeth. "Here's your new royalty statement. It's pretty good, and it's only going to go up now that radio and streaming services are playing your songs again."

Sam tapped his fingers on the table. His brother swiped the calculator from him and punched in some numbers.

He'd been tracking which of his songs were being played on radio and streaming. Four songs for now. Plus, he received songwriter royalties from Caleb Hartley's songs, and from the song Evan Cross recorded. The problem was those numbers fluctuated monthly. He needed a stable monthly income.

"Here's what I think." Kyle leaned in his chair and held the paper full of handwritten numbers in front of his face. "You can make it here in this apartment off your royalties alone. It would be tight. And when you have a good month, you'd have to put everything extra in your savings to put toward next month's bills. But you could do it."

"Really? Let me see." He snatched the paper from Kyle's hands.

"I wasn't quite done." He huffed.

"Now who's grumpy?" Sam studied the paper and frowned. "Yeah, but like you said, it'd be tight. Real tight."

"I'll say it again. You can always ask Mom and Dad for help if you get into a jam or have unexpected bills or something. For that matter, I can help you too."

Sam shook his head. "I don't want to ask them for anything. Or you. Y'all have helped me enough as it is. I want to prove I can stand on my own two feet."

His cell phone caught his eye. It was on silent mode, but a number flashed on the screen. Pastor Rob from his mom and dad's church, Franklin Community. He got up and took the call out on the deck and left Kyle to the calculating. "This is Sam."

"Hey, Sam, Rob Nichols here. How are you doing?"

The sound of the man's voice brought him joy. Pastor Rob had always been kind to him. "Hi, Pastor Rob, I'm doing well. How are you?"

The man chuckled. "I'm doing well too. Do you have a minute to chat?"

Sam pulled the chair out from the deck table and sat. "I've got all the time in the world right now." He laughed lightly while he ran his free hand through his longish-again hair.

"I heard you're not working now."

"Mm-hmm, good news travels fast, huh."

"I'm sorry, Sam. That was tough. But I wanted to ask again if maybe you'd consider coming back to Franklin Community Church? And not as a fill-in. We'd absolutely love to have you on staff. We've put together an offer for you."

Sam pulled the phone away from his ear and glanced at it. Did he hear the man right? Was the pastor offering him his old job back in student ministry? "Um, wow, I don't know what to say. My old job as worship leader for student ministry?"

"Well, no," Pastor Rob said. "The young man we hired to replace you is working out great."

Sam's heart sank. But whatever job was open, he'd take it. He'd answer phones if they wanted. He needed a job, and he'd make it work.

"We have something bigger in mind. Our main service worship leader has given notice. He and his wife have decided to become overseas missionaries. We'd like to offer you the lead worship pastor position."

Sam bolted from his chair and paced the deck. "Me? You want me to be your main worship pastor?"

"We would absolutely love it, Sam."

He stopped pacing and remembered the words of Pastor Stephan that had stung so deeply. "Aren't you worried about people connecting me to my biological father and the baggage I'd be carrying with me? Will donors walk away from the church?"

Pastor Stephan laughed. "Oh, I'm sorry, Sam, I'm not laughing at you at all. It's just, we all have baggage. We're all human. You were innocent in all that. You were a victim. People will realize that, Sam. And if they don't, well, we'll pray for them."

Sam sat down again. He could've cried, but he didn't. "You don't know how much this means. The other church let me go because of my so-called baggage."

Pastor Rob sighed and was silent for a moment. "I heard that. The church community is small, and word gets around. I'm sorry that happened to you. You didn't deserve that."

Sam swallowed the lump in his throat and didn't quite know what to say. "Thank you for saying that."

"It's the truth. And like I said, we want to make you a formal offer. I'm sure it's not nearly what you made at Middle Tennessee, but we'll give you the freedom you need to write your own songs, and even tour when the time comes. And we'd like to send you out to do worship events at other churches like you did there. If you want to. And of course, you could bring Nate Martin back also."

Pastor Rob's words left him breathless. "I don't know what to say. This all sounds amazing. Honestly, I thought my ministry career was over. I'd love to do it."

"I'd say your career is just beginning. You have no idea how happy we'd be to have you back. I'm going to email our offer. Read through it and let me know what you think."

"I will, but I can't imagine there'd be anything there that would make me turn it down. Pastor Rob, I can't tell you enough how grateful I am for the opportunity."

"We're grateful for you, Sam."

They ended the call, and Sam walked to the balcony rail and lifted his eyes to the sky. *Thank you, God, for once again working things out for my good. And thank you, Jesus, for overcoming the world.*

fifty-three

John closed his phone and couldn't stop smiling. How great was God to put Sam's life back together again. His youngest son had called and read him the offer from Franklin Community Church. The job was perfect for him and gave him room to grow. Once again, God brought Sam up from the ashes. *Thank you, Lord.*

He walked back to the bleachers and sat next to his assistant coach and best friend, Wes, and told him about Sam's offer.

"Praise God, John. That's amazing. I'm so happy for him." Wes patted him on the back. "God always works it all out somehow."

"He certainly does. Everything's coming together for Sam like he deserves."

The summer pickup games were going on, but today, John and Wes were spectators. This was such a fun time of year for John when players from the past, some who even played professionally now, all came back on campus and played pickup games with the new recruits and current roster of players. He and Wes weren't allowed to coach in the off season, but they took notes on what each of the players should work on.

"Hey, you're rubbing your arm again, John. Did you ever get that checked out?"

He hadn't realized it and stopped. "Oh, it's just a pinched nerve or something." But to be honest, lately, he was having chest pain too. He'd get checked out, and soon, but he didn't need to worry Wes. Or Abbie. Especially Abbie.

"Okay, well keep an eye on it."

"I will," he said. But out of nowhere, dizziness overtook him. "Is it really hot in here?"

Wes sat back and looked at John. "Not really. You sure you're feeling okay? You're pale all of a sudden."

John breathed in deeply and panicked. Something wasn't right. Excruciating pain shot through his upper left arm, and the sensation of someone sitting on his chest took his breath away.

"John, answer me." Wes shouted, wide-eyed.

He couldn't answer. And he wasn't okay. Suddenly, sweat poured from his forehead. He breathed but couldn't take in oxygen. He clutched Wes's arm.

Wes's lips moved, but John couldn't hear his friend's voice. A black circle rimmed his vision, and it grew until he could see nothing but black. The last thing he remembered was Wes's voice call out from a faraway place, "Call nine-one-one!"

* * *

The cell doors opened, and the prisoners stepped out one by one and waited to line up. Andy didn't care whether he got yard time or not. He'd as soon sit in his cell and mope. Since the day he'd told Sam he'd confessed, he hadn't communicated with his son.

The visits completely stopped. Andy had resorted to mailing letters like before. But he hadn't bothered to get Sam's address. He'd told him he had an apartment in Franklin, but Andy didn't know where. Now he was right back where he started. Sending letters in care of John Grayson. Sam probably would never get them.

"Line up," the big guard yelled.

Andy stepped out behind Rio, but his cell neighbor never turned around. He'd quit talking to Andy since he confessed. What was that all about? That didn't even concern him. *Whatever.* The last thing he wanted was a prison friend anyway.

The line moved. The prisoners walked slowly in a single-file line until they reached the main hallway leading to the outside yard, and then the line stopped. Another line of prisoners came inside and ambled toward them, also single file. This was the daily routine.

Andy sighed. This was for the best. He had to take accountability for what he'd done. He couldn't let Sam take the fall. He told the truth, and it cost him Sam, but at least his son could get on with his life and career now.

"Keep it moving," the guard yelled, louder this time. They meandered along the right side of the hallway as they passed the prisoners coming in from the yard.

The idea was to be far enough away that one couldn't touch another prisoner coming toward him. Why didn't they just wait until the ones coming in were back in their cells before taking Andy's group outside? He chuckled. That would make too much sense.

His thoughts turned back to Sam. Even if he never talked to him again in this life, he wanted him to know he was telling the truth about giving his life to God. He'd finally confessed everything to God. Everything. He had no doubt that even if he couldn't be with his son in this life, God would give him a chance to make it up to him in eternity. And not just Sam, everyone he'd hurt over the years. Those girls. Sam's mom. Everyone he'd hurt. It was a long list.

He didn't know whether heaven worked like that or not, but he hoped so.

The line slowed again, and oddly, both his outgoing line and the incoming line merged ahead. This wasn't normal at all. Andy moved his head to the left to see past Rio, but everyone was bunched together. He couldn't even see the space in the middle. *This is weird.* Something definitely wasn't right.

He yelled at Rio, who was a couple inches taller, making it hard to see ahead. "Hey man, what's going on?"

Rio didn't answer, but a big man coming toward them bumped into Rio, handed him something, then smirked at Andy as he passed.

"What's his deal?" Andy said to whoever would listen.

At last, Rio turned around and faced him. "Sorry, man." Rio stared blankly. There was nothing in the man's eyes, only darkness. He stepped towards Andy and plunged the object he held into Andy's stomach, then pulled it out.

Andy wanted to say, "Sorry about what," but the pain in his stomach made him double over. It was hard to breathe let alone talk. What happened? Flames shot through his stomach. He mouthed the word "Help," but Rio smirked like the big guy had.

Rio stooped near and whispered in his ear, "You confessed, man. You confessed and took my future away. I was *hours* from turnin' you in and cuttin' a deal."

None of it made sense. Andy couldn't think due to the fire in his stomach. After he dropped to the floor, he rolled to his side, then forced his eyes open and focused on his stomach. He expected to see flames, but instead, he saw blood. Lots and lots of it. And he couldn't keep his eyes open any longer.

fifty-four

Abbie rolled their chalkboard sign out to the sidewalk. "Hannah, this sign is amazing. I'm glad you have artistic talent because I sure don't."

Hannah laughed and helped her place the sign in front of the shop. "We should leave the doors open today. The weather is perfect."

"You're right, it is." She tucked a long brown curl behind her ear. Perfect in every way. Not just the weather, but school was out for the summer. That meant Hannah and Wendy's daughter, Isabella, were helping in the shop. And their relationship with Sam had been restored. Everything was right in their world. *Thank you, God.*

"Abbie!"

A voice rang out as she stepped back into the shop, and she turned to see her new friend coming up the sidewalk. "Renee, hi. And hi, Max. I'm so glad to see you both. C'mon in."

"I'm so happy to see you." Renee exclaimed.

"Hi, Mrs. Grayson," Max said politely. He even made eye contact.

"Hi there, Max. Hey, those shirts you like are on sale over there." She winked at the boy and tried to hide her shock at his pleasant demeanor. Max thanked her and walked toward the rack.

Abbie turned to Renee. "Wow, what a change in Max. Things are going well, I guess?"

Renee smiled without the hint of sadness that was there before. "Yes, really well. He's such a good kid. And all your advice has helped so much."

Abbie's spirits soared. Could this day get any better? "Oh, I want you to meet Hannah. She's in the back stock room." They walked to the back where Hannah sorted donated clothing that had just come in.

"Hey, Hannah, I want you to meet someone. This is Renee, and over there, is her foster son, Max, who I was telling you about."

Hannah's eyes lit up. "I've heard a lot about you. It's so nice to meet you. And guess what? I think some of these new clothes are about Max's size. Do you think he'd want to come back here with me and take a look?"

"Oh, yes, I'm sure he would. I'll go ask him."

Max and Renee followed Hannah to the stockroom, and all was peaceful for the moment. Abbie went to the register and pulled up the sales log from yesterday when Wendy and Isabella worked. She whistled at the long list of items sold. Yesterday had been a great sales day. Their little shop was gaining ground, and people who shopped here told their friends.

The buzzing sound coming from her purse in the cabinet below caught her attention. She pulled out her cell phone. Five missed calls from Kyle. Her stomach dropped. *Please, God, don't let this be a setback in Sam's troubles.* She prayed as she dialed Kyle.

"Mom, I've been trying to get ahold of you." Kyle sounded breathless.

"I'm sorry, hon, we just got to the shop and—"

"Mom, Dad's in the hospital. You have to get there right away. It's his heart. Cassie and I are on our way back from Knoxville, but we'll be there soon. Please hurry."

The floor swayed beneath her, and she yelled for Hannah to come quick. "Your dad's in the hospital. We have to go now. Oh no, the shop, I, umm—"

"Mom, it's okay. Go. I'll lock up and call Wendy. I'll meet you there. Just go!"

Abbie flew out the door and sprinted to her car. *Please, God, let him be okay.* She prayed over and over through her tears the whole way to the hospital.

* * *

Sam had no idea how long he'd sat in his father's room. Finally, he walked out of the room in a daze. He stood in the hallway for a moment to get his bearings. Which way did he walk in from? Where had he parked? He couldn't remember. That'd been hours ago.

"Sam!" A familiar voice shouted from farther down the hallway. He turned toward the sound. It belonged to his brother. Kyle ran toward him.

"Oh Sam, we've been trying to contact you for hours."

Sam reached into his pockets. "Oh, I, uh, must have left my cell phone in the car when I got here. I was in such a hurry. But how did you know?"

Kyle tilted his head. "C'mon, I'll take you to his room."

"Kyle, no." Sam pointed to the room behind him. "He's gone. It's too late."

His brother shrugged and looked past Sam to the room behind him. "Who, Sam? Who's gone?"

"What?" Sam asked. Confusion clouded his thoughts. He must be more tired than he thought. "My father. Andy Quinn. He's dead."

His brother's eyes widened. "Andy Quinn is dead? What happened?"

"He was stabbed in prison." Sam said. "But ... you didn't know that?"

"No, Sam, I didn't." Kyle put his hand on Sam's shoulder. "I'm so sorry."

"Yeah, umm, thanks." He thought he'd be more upset, but the words the man had whispered gripped his mind and heart. Should he tell Kyle what he— "Oh no, if you didn't know about him, then why are you here?" Panic overtook all his other emotions.

"It's Dad. It's his heart. Come on." Kyle put his arm around Sam's shoulder, and they jogged down the hall.

fifty-five

"Oh, Sam." Abbie couldn't contain the tears when he walked into the room. She rushed to him and pulled him into an embrace. They'd been trying to get in touch with him for hours and couldn't imagine where he was.

"How's Dad?" Tears fell down his cheeks.

"Oh, honey, he's going to be fine. The doctor was in a moment ago. It wasn't a heart attack. He had a heart catheterization, and he'll be back up from the procedure soon. They said he has a minor blockage that doesn't require surgery. He'll have to go on cholesterol medicine and manage his stress better, but he's going to be fine."

Sam clung to her and sobbed. "I'm so sorry I wasn't here sooner. I can't tell you how relieved I am."

Hannah stood and went to Sam and hugged him too. "We were worried when we couldn't get ahold of you."

"I know, I was, um ..." He fumbled his words and turned his head toward Kyle.

"Do you want me to tell them?" Kyle asked.

"No, I can."

"Tell us what, hon?" Abbie's worry shifted from John to Sam

now. Had something else happened? This poor boy had been dealt blow after blow. "What is it?"

"While you all were here, I've been down the hall." Sam sucked in a deep breath and looked from Abbie to Hannah. "Andy was stabbed in prison this morning. I've been with him. I swear I didn't know about Dad, or I would've been in here with you. I guess I must've left my phone in the car when I got here."

"No. Oh, Sam, is he going to be okay?" A pang of guilt hit her for not feeling sorrier than she did about Andy Quinn, but she felt awful for Sam to have to go through this.

Sam stared at the floor and shook his head, then lifted his eyes to meet Abbie's. "He's dead."

Hannah gasped and was the first to hug Sam again.

Abbie hurt for him. She put her arms around Hannah and Sam. "I'm so sorry, sweetheart. No matter what's been said about the man, he was your birth father, and I'm so very sorry. We're here for you. You know that, right?" She framed his face with her hands.

Sam swallowed. "Yeah, I do. I'm happy John, my real dad, is going to be okay.

* * *

The relief of his dad being okay outweighed the sorrow over losing Andy. What Andy had told him was meant to be a confession. But it'd only proven no matter how much the man had changed, he'd never be good for Sam. He had lied until the very end.

If the man was truly saved, maybe they would have a different relationship in eternity. But now, he needed to focus on his real dad, the one who'd always protected him, given him a home and a family, and set him on the right path in every aspect of his life. John Grayson.

The rest of the family had gone to the cafeteria, but Sam

wanted to sit and wait for Dad to wake up. Finally, he stirred and opened his eyes.

"Sam," Dad said. "I'm glad you're here."

Tears blurred his vision, and he reached for his dad's hand. "I'm so sorry I wasn't here earlier, Dad."

"It's okay, kiddo. You're here now. That's what matters. And the doctor said I'm gonna be fine." Dad managed a smile, though he could barely hold his eyes open. But even in this hospital bed, groggy, he still looked strong.

"I'm so glad. I don't know what I'd do if you weren't here. I'm sorry about all the conflict I caused with Andy Quinn, and I'm sorry about the time we missed out on because of it."

"It's okay, son. And like I told you before, we won't stand in the way of a relationship with him. I was selfish and jealous. I see that clearer more than ever." Dad paused and swallowed hard. "Nothing like thinking you're going to die to put things in perspective."

Sam wondered if this was the time and place to tell him. Dad's color improved with each passing minute. *Thank you, Lord.* He'd feel bad if his dad was the only one who didn't know.

He cleared his throat. "Dad, the reason I wasn't here this morning is, well, I got a call Andy was in the hospital, and I rushed in and left my phone in the car. So, I didn't get any of the calls saying you were here and—"

"What? Andy's here? What happened?"

Sam realized he was squeezing his dad's hand. "He, uh, was stabbed in prison this morning. He didn't make it."

John's mouth fell open. His eyes widened, and his face turned a shade paler. "Oh, Sam, no."

"It's okay, don't worry about me." Sam was sorry he told him. His dad didn't look so good all of a sudden. "I probably shouldn't have told you until you got better."

"No, I'm glad you told me. I'm so sorry, son." John's tear-brimmed eyes met Sam's. "I know I've said a lot of bad things about him, but that doesn't diminish the fact he was your birth father. I'm terribly sorry. You know we'll help you through this."

Sam debated whether to tell him Andy Quinn's final words. No, not here. His dad had just had a heart procedure. This needed to wait until he was better. "I'm okay, really. I've realized you and mom are my true parents. And you never said anything about him that wasn't true. I know that now."

"Still, I shouldn't have acted like I did all these months. I made things worse than they had to be."

"Dad, you've always wanted what's best for me. But Andy, well, I'm going to be living the consequences of his actions for the rest of my life."

"What do you mean?"

"Daddy, you're awake!" Hannah squealed as the rest of the family returned from the cafeteria. They all hugged John and chatted happily. He would be released in the morning, and they expected him to make a full recovery. He'd be back to normal soon.

The whole family gushed over Dad. He thanked God for saving him and for this family. And he also prayed that Andy Quinn had truly been saved.

fifty-six

Sam stayed with Mom and Dad for a few days to help out since Dad got out of the hospital. Thankfully, he bounced back quickly. He was supposed to be taking it easy, and physically, he was. But he wasn't so good at working to keep his stress level down.

"The sunshine feels good," Dad said as the three of them ate salad and grilled chicken on the deck. "But I'm getting a little tired of salad."

"You know what the doctor said, John. You have to change your diet and manage your stress. I can help you control the diet part, but the stress part is something you're going to have to work on."

Sam laughed. Stress was part of his dad's everyday life as a basketball coach, especially with his competitive nature. "I don't get it though. You eat pretty healthy."

Mom gave Dad the side-eye. "Well, see, your dad here likes his fast food when he's away on recruiting trips. And pretty much anytime he's away from home. I see the debit card charges." Mom winked.

"I can't get anything past you, can I?"

"You just keep that in mind."

Sam loved being back here with them. How he regretted letting Andy Quinn come between them. He now realized how much he'd missed his family. And Lauren. He took a deep breath. She didn't know any of this had happened. One more relationship he'd messed up completely.

"I was thinking," John said. "Have you thought of any kind of service for Andy?"

His dad's words caught him by surprise. "Umm, he's being cremated. They asked me if I wanted the ashes. But I don't think I do."

The feelings he had for Andy had changed since his death. Or rather, since his final words, and his confession before that. For the past several months, he'd been glad to have a relationship with Andy Quinn, but it'd all been based on lies.

The man's final, dying words revealed the biggest lie of all. And proved once again the man's horrible actions and decisions would follow Sam for the rest of his life.

"I understand." John said. "Your mom and I were thinking, if you wanted to have his ashes buried somewhere, we could have a small service for him."

"It might give you the closure you need too," Mom added.

That hadn't even crossed his mind. This would give him a place to put the ashes. And a place to visit, should he ever want to do that. Right now, he couldn't imagine he ever would.

"I hadn't thought of anything like that. I didn't even know they would bury ashes, but yeah, that may be a good idea."

"We can help you get it all figured out and help you pay for it." John added.

"Oh, well, thanks for offering. But Kyle told me the prison would pay for his burial. But yeah, I think maybe I want to do this." Even with all the pain Andy had caused, it was the right thing to do. And if it gave him closure, that was a plus.

They talked through lunch, and Abbie offered to go with

Sam to talk to pastor Rob about doing a quick service for their family and whoever Sam wanted there.

He thanked God for this amazing family. They proved once again they'd do anything for him. Even after he'd treated them badly.

* * *

The last day of June was cooler than normal and rainy. Not hard rain, but light, steady rain. "Good for the flowers," Mom had said earlier.

But not a great day for a graveside service.

Pastor Rob stood next to the small hole where Sam's birth father's ashes would be buried. Next to the hole, a modest slab with Andy Quinn's name, date of birth, and date of death would eventually be installed. The man at the mortuary sales place had told Sam and his mom it would take several weeks. He had nodded along.

Since the day of the man's death, Sam still hadn't cried. In fact, he hardly felt anything. Instead, Andy Quinn's final words kept rolling around in his mind. Sam had yet to share those words with anyone, and he didn't exactly know why. Maybe he was still processing. Still trying to decide if his biological father's last words had meant to be a show of love to Sam, or a final slap in the face for all the man put him through during Sam's almost-twenty-four years. He leaned toward the latter.

"Are we ready to begin, Sam?"

Sam jerked his head up. "Yes, please." He gazed at this circle of nine people, including himself, huddled under umbrellas. His mom and dad were here, of course. His true parents, John and Abbie. He'd never forget that again. Kyle and Cassie were here. They were always there for him.

But he was most touched that his grandparents, Ed and Sarah, stood with him today. They certainly weren't expected to come. Sam was unsure whether they were even aware of Andy

283

Quinn's story. He doubted it, but they were here for him too. And sharing an umbrella with Sam was his sister, Hannah. They'd been through a lot together, and he was forever thankful for her.

If not for him being adopted into the Grayson family, not a single person would be here today. Probably not even himself.

Pastor Rob, holding his umbrella in one hand and his old, worn Bible in the other, talked about the promise of eternity. How Andy, having accepted Christ, would live a life in eternity he couldn't live on this earth. A good and honest life in the presence of God. And he'd one day be reunited with his family. Pastor Rob looked up at Sam.

Again, Sam felt nothing. He wished he did.

"Now, I'd like to read Psalm 23. The Lord is my shepherd, I shall not want ..."

Sam's eyes burned with tears, but they weren't for Andy.

Instead, he thought of almost losing the dad who *chose* to be a father to him, *chose* to love him. He lifted his head in time to meet Dad's gaze. He gave him a sad smile. No doubt, it was hard for his dad to be here. Andy Quinn had caused problems in Dad's life for a lot longer than he'd caused problems in his own. But he still chose to be here today.

"... Amen." Pastor Rob concluded.

Sam thanked him, then hugged each family member. *Thank you, God, for allowing me to be a part of this family.*

They turned to go to their cars. Someone stood by his car. He squinted. It was hard to tell with the distance and the umbrella, but ... *no way. Could it be?*

"Sam, is that who I think it is?" A huge smile crossed Hannah's face. "C'mon, I'll walk you with my umbrella."

They hurried to the car as Sam put his thoughts together. There was no question who stood by his car under a black-and-white checkered umbrella. He closed the distance between them.

"Lauren." Sam breathed out her name. "How did you know?"

She smiled through a tear. "Your favorite sister here might've had something to do with it." She tilted her head toward Hannah.

He didn't know what to say. He'd been agonizing over how he'd treated her. His one-time girlfriend, and best friend of many years. He was so wrong to treat her like he did. And here she was today. Here for him when he certainly didn't deserve it.

"Thanks for coming," he whispered.

Lauren bit her lower lip. "I wanted to be here for you, but I wasn't sure if you wanted me here."

"Hey." Hannah broke into the conversation and touched Sam's arm. "I'm going to get a ride with Mom and Dad so you two can chat. I'll meet you back at the house."

"Thanks, Hannah." Sam was thankful for the time with Lauren, as well as Hannah asking her to come here.

Hannah took her umbrella with her and ran to her parents' car, and Lauren moved closer to Sam and covered him with hers.

"Do you want to sit in my car and talk?"

Lauren gave a single nod, and they climbed into his vehicle.

He started the engine and turned the air conditioner on enough to get rid of the stuffy air. "Are you comfortable?"

Lauren nodded. She hadn't said anything since they got into the car.

He glanced at her. Her hair was straight today and fell below her shoulders. Her green eyes darted nervously. He hated he made her feel that way.

"I'm so sorry, Lauren. You have no idea how much I regret how I treated you. You didn't deserve that." He shook his head and gazed into her eyes.

She smiled, ever so slightly. "It's okay. You were going through a lot. I realize that. I wish you would've let me be there for you."

"I wish that too. I guess ... I don't know how to be in a relationship. I've never had a good one modeled for me until John and Abbie, and that's only been for the past few years, you know?"

"I know." She admitted. "But they're probably the godliest example of a relationship that you'll see."

"Kinda like your mom and dad."

She nodded. "Even if I didn't want to admit it. I've missed you Sam. I miss *us*."

"I miss us too." Sam exhaled. "But ..."

"You don't know if you want a relationship right now. I get it, and that's okay. I just want to be your friend again."

His heart skipped a few beats, and he turned to her. "Nothing would make me happier than if we could start as friends again. And see where it goes. What do you think?"

Lauren tossed her head back and laughed. "Yes. Best friends again?"

"Best friends."

* * *

Sam and Lauren walked into the Grayson family kitchen. Everyone pitched in to prepare lunch. Mom had told him they'd have lunch back at the house after the service, but he certainly didn't expect all this. Takeout from his favorite eatery, Newk's. There were sandwiches, salads, and soup, and Hannah had picked up the apple cider cake he loved from the farmer's market.

"Mom, you went to way too much trouble." Sam kissed her on the cheek.

"I did no such thing, but maybe Newk's did." She gave him a hug, then turned toward Lauren. "I'm so glad to see you." She hugged Lauren, too, and whispered something to her.

"What's all that about?" Sam joked.

Mom winked at Lauren. "Maybe just an answered prayer."

Dad and Kyle brought water and canned drinks from the spare fridge in the garage. Once the food, plates, and utensils were lined up the way Hannah wanted them, Dad bowed his head.

"Heavenly Father, words cannot express how happy and thankful we are to be together here today." John paused before continuing. "We pray for Your comfort and peace over Sam, and we thank You for his place in our family. His place as a son, a grandson, and a brother. Please don't ever let him forget how much he is loved." Another pause.

"We thank You for each and every member of our family, Lord, and we pray You will bless the food and the fellowship we have here together today. We pray for these things in Your Son's holy name. Amen."

His dad's words touched him deeply, and he managed to barely choke out an "Amen."

Everyone grabbed a plate and filed in line to get their food. They ate together at the giant dining room table that would easily fit a dozen people. Sam sat directly across from John and spoke to him quietly. "Thanks for the prayer. And for everything."

"We love you, kiddo."

"Did anyone think to invite Pastor Rob?" Grandma Sarah asked.

"I did." Mom blotted her mouth with a napkin. "He and Anna had someplace else to be, but they're stopping in for dessert shortly."

Sam wanted to discuss Andy's final words with his family and Lauren. But not with Rob and his wife here. His pulse quickened. Everyone was almost finished eating, so they'd probably be here for dessert soon. If he waited until they left, Hannah, Kyle, and Cassie might leave. He needed to tell them now, while his whole family was here. Who knew what their reactions would be?

Most of their plates were empty. Now would be as good a time as any. He didn't want to miss his opportunity.

"Umm, I'd like to talk to you before Pastor Rob and Anna arrive." He swiped at the sweat beads forming on his forehead. He hadn't expected to be this nervous.

"Sure, what is it, Sam?" Dad asked.

He cleared his throat and drew in a deep breath. "This is hard for me to talk about." Anxious faces around the table stared at him, and he focused his eyes on his empty plate instead. "Before Andy passed away, he told me something."

"I didn't realize he'd regained consciousness." Hannah said.

"Hannah," Abbie said in a sharp tone.

"It's okay, Mom. I didn't tell anyone, but he was awake long enough to tell me something he said I had to know."

The room grew quiet, and his pulse raced. He didn't want to hurt them, and he didn't want a repeat of his falling out with his family. But he needed their guidance. He certainly didn't trust his own since he'd messed everything up so badly before. He'd never been more confused.

Over the past few days, his emotions had been all over the place. He desperately needed his family's help.

"I need your help to sort things out, to decide what to do. If anything." Sam shrugged.

"What did he tell you, son?" John asked in a soft voice.

Sam paused while his life with this family flashed in front of him. The first day he showed up on their doorstep, he couldn't even look at them, but they showed him care and comfort. The next day, he couldn't remember their names, but they treated him with patience and concern. He kept his walls up and closed himself off, but they loved him anyway and showed him he was safe.

That first dinner with Kyle and Hannah. Kyle immediately disliked him, but that eventually evolved into the closeness they now shared.

He remembered being intimidated by his grandparents, but they welcomed him with open arms and always showed up for him.

His adoption day. The happiest day of his life.

Thank you, God, for the people in this room. The greatest gifts of my life. And he glanced at Lauren. *Lauren too, God. I don't deserve all the people you've surrounded me with.*

He cleared his throat. "He told me …"

As hard as this was, as inconceivable as this was, he just needed to say the words.

"My mother is alive."

The End

Jess stood at the kitchen sink washing the breakfast and lunch dishes as her little girl tugged at her pant leg. "Mommy, can I please play in the sandbox?"

Her precious, beautiful daughter. A precocious five-year-old for sure. Jess smiled to herself. It was so bittersweet to see her, this little girl, so loving and full of life. She was the spitting image of her big brother all those years ago.

"Yes, let's go play in the sandbox." Jess stooped to little Gracie's level and gave her a big smile. "Let's build a sandcastle to show Daddy when he gets home."

"Yay, Mommy!" Gracie exclaimed and ran to the back door.

Jess laughed and followed her out back to the sandbox and removed the lid. Her daughter jumped in with both feet, picked up a yellow plastic shovel, and moved the sand around.

How gracious was God to give her this second chance at being a mother? Her sweet baby, Grace. Her miracle girl. After her first pregnancy, she didn't think she could have another child, but God had the last laugh in the form of a surprise pregnancy at age thirty-seven. It was a good surprise for both her and Alex.

Her sweet husband. He adored both her and their daughter.

He worked hard so Jess could be a stay-at-home mom for Gracie. He had truly rescued her.

"Help me build the castle, Mommy." Grace shoved a digging implement into Jess's hand.

The mother and daughter moved and packed the sand, and slowly, it took the form of a castle. Something about Gracie in the sunshine, her blonde hair reflecting the sunlight. She looked so much like her older brother had at that age. The familiar pain floated through her stomach and her chest and almost made her wince. She should be used to the pain by now. Afterall, it had been twenty-four years, this month.

Gracie giggled and had sand in her hair already. Jess kept adding to the castle, but her mind was on him. How sad her life had been back then. A single, broke, drug addicted mother with no help and no plan.

She closed her eyes briefly to remember the sensation of hugging her little boy, but the memories were too hazy. She couldn't feel his hugs anymore. Watching her Gracie girl, so full of life, her heart was full. It saddened her to realize she'd never looked at her son that way. She'd been too broken at the time, too young.

And she'd certainly never made time to make a sandcastle with him.

acknowledgments

Dad, Nicole, Derek, Brandon, Vanessa, and Dana – your love and support means everything to me. My world, our world, changed forever in December, and without each of you I wouldn't be standing today. I love you all.

They say it takes a village, and in my case it has taken a village to see me through these past few months. And my villagers are the best: thank you Dana, Gina, Joy, Krista, Dava, Marshall, Kim R., Vicki, Mick, my amazing church family at FCC Borden, Ben and Porsha, my Tallahassee family, and my Scrivenings Press family. I hesitated to list names for fear of leaving someone out. Every single person who has been there for my kids and me, whether through text, visits, or all-important prayers, I love you and appreciate you all more than you'll ever know.

To my publisher, Linda Fulkerson, and my editors at Scrivenings Press—Thank you for believing in me and this series. You've made my dreams come true.

To Daisy and Winnie, my fur babies, thanks for your constant companionship, and for reminding me when it's time for you to eat.

And a huge THANK YOU to everyone who read *Just Another Home* and encouraged me with your kind words. You are the reason *Just Another Dream* was written.

Kimberly Banet left the corporate world after working in Human Resources for nearly two decades. She started a small craft business, and after a couple of years spent creating inspirational and seasonal crafts, she felt called to follow her dream of writing a Christian fiction novel.

It took three years of writing and re-writing, learning the craft by reading books, attending online conferences, and entering contests to learn from judges' critiques, for her dream to become a reality. Her debut novel in the Family Forever series, Just Another Home, was published in May 2024 and was an ACFW Genesis Award finalist that same year. The next book in the series, Just Another Dream, was published in May 2025.

Kimberly received her bachelor's degree from Indiana University where she majored in Business and Psychology. She and her late husband of more than thirty-six years, Jeff, raised two wonderful children: Nicole and Brandon. Today Kim shares her long-time home in southern Indiana with her dachshund, Daisy Mae and yorkie-poo, Winnie.

When not working, Kimberly's hobbies include reading, Bible journaling, crocheting blankets, making seasonal crafts, and spending time with family and good friends.

also by kimberly banet

Just Another Home

Book One of the Family Forever series

Sixteen-year-old Sam Keller has lived in foster homes and group homes most of his life and has long ago given up on the dream of a stable, forever family. Adults have always let him down, and so has God, and he has no use for either.

John and Abbie Grayson are a respected, successful couple in their fifties with two grown children. They live in their dream home in Franklin, Tenn., an idyllic suburb of Nashville, where John is a successful college basketball coach, and Abbie works part-time at their local church. But Abbie feels something is missing from her life and convinces John they should become foster parents.

Their worlds collide when Sam is placed in the Grayson home for a few days. Days turn into months, and Sam thrives with the Graysons and allows himself to dream of a forever family, while John and Abbie realize the teen has found his way into their hearts.

As the Graysons begin to investigate the possibility of adopting Sam, an evil agenda emerges, and a secret past is revealed. Nothing short of a miracle can save Sam from a harrowing ordeal and keep the Grayson family together.

Get your copy here:

https://scrivenings.link/justanotherhome

* * *

Stay up-to-date on your favorite books and authors with our free e-newsletters.

ScriveningsPress.com